Of Hoaxes and Homicide

Also by Anastasia Hastings

Of Manners and Murder

Of Hoaxes and Homicide

A Dear
Miss Hermione
Mystery

Anastasia Hastings

MINOTAUR BOOKS
NEW YORK

First published in the United States by Minotaur Books, an imprint of St. Martin's Publishing Group

OF HOAXES AND HOMICIDE. Copyright © 2024 by Connie Laux. All rights reserved. Printed in the United States of America. For information, address St. Martin's Publishing Group, 120 Broadway, New York, NY 10271.

Design by Meryl Sussman Levavi

ISBN 9781250848581

*Though I have acknowledged my wonderful
brainstorming group many times,
I don't think I've ever dedicated a book to them.
This one's for Shelley Costa, Serena B. Miller, and
Emilie Richards. Thank you for your ideas and your
insights. Our conversations and the time we spend
together is as precious to me as you three are!*

Of Hoaxes and Homicide

Dear Miss Hermione,

　　What is a mother to do?

　　Every minute of every day, I am consumed by worry. I am sleepless, filled with panic. I am desperate for help, and as you will understand when you are apprised of my problem, I cannot turn to anyone to provide it but you.

　　It pains me even to write these terrible words, but if you are to assist me, you must know the truth, and the whole of it.

　　My dear Miss Hermione, my daughter has run off.

　　You will notice, yes, you will surely notice for you are both wise and worldly, that I did not say my darling girl has disappeared, for you see, it is no mystery where she has gone. I have received a letter and I know where she now dwells.

　　Miss Hermione, my sweet and innocent daughter has gone off to join the Hermetic Order of the Children of Aed.

　　Surely you have heard of these self-styled Children, for the group and its leader travel the country preaching their blasphemous doctrine, promoting (how is it even possible they should want to speak of it in public?) their unsavory way of life. Even if you have not seen the notice of their gatherings in the newspapers, you have surely read—for who has not?—the lurid accounts of their activities in Count Orlando's stories. Yes, yes, in the tales, he calls them the Children of Ud, but that is obviously a thinly disguised ruse. A man of great talent, not to mention courage, Count Orlando has gleaned intimate knowledge of the Children. He knows how wanton they are.

　　Human sacrifices. Devil worship. Orgies! If I was not obliged *to put on a brave face for the sake of my family's reputation, I would swoon.*

My daughter has made a terrible mistake, and for her and the sake of our family's honor, I am keeping her absence a secret, but I do not know how much longer I can continue the subterfuge. Even her father does not know where she is, thinking she has gone off to visit relatives. Oh, how the lie torments me!

Miss Hermione, you must help. For the sake of this mother's wounded heart. For the cause of our family's good name. For my dear daughter's innocence.

Please, offer me some guidance. Counsel me. Oh, Miss Hermione, what am I to do?

A Brokenhearted Mother

Chapter 1

Sephora

London
November 4, 1885

It is a sad day, indeed, when even an orgy does not interest me.

Shrouded by an ennui the likes of which had not enveloped me since that wretched but memorable occasion when the newest of the autumn bonnets were not put up for sale at Madame Dupont's Millinery due to a sunken ship and its lost cargo of ostrich feathers, I cast aside the penny dreadful I'd been reading. Count Orlando's tales of darkness and depravity had always captivated me and made my heart flutter. In a very ladylike way, of course. Yet this one, the latest in a series of shocking stories about the Children of Ud, could neither hold my interest nor lighten my dismal mood.

I rested my head against the back of the chair where I languished. I laid one arm across my forehead. I sighed.

I confess, I am somewhat of an expert when it comes to this particular form of expression. As a proper lady, I was schooled by my late mama in the well-timed sigh. After long years of practice, I know how to employ the sound to convey longing and express yearning. I appreciate how, used efficiently and with just a modicum of emotion, it might hasten the end of a boring conversation or prolong a favored suitor's goodbyes. I had never, though, felt it communicate so thoroughly the fact that I was totally, completely, and utterly bored.

My exhalation of despair should certainly have plucked at the heartstrings of all who heard it. Which of course explained why Violet, in the chair opposite mine, a book open in her hands, never flinched. But then, I am convinced Violet doesn't have a heart.

Being more charitable than she, I gave her another chance to display some sign of sisterly devotion. I sighed yet again.

"Really, Sephora." She glanced up from her reading only long enough to shoot a look at me that spoke both her impatience and her disinterest. "If you're going to distract me with your dramatics, perhaps you should go into another room."

"And do what?" I sat up and flung out both my arms, the better to demonstrate the desolation that was my life. "How you can sit all day with your nose pressed in a book is beyond me, Violet, especially when you're reading . . ." I leaned nearer for a better look at the book in her hands. "*The Ideals of the Art of India.* It is no wonder you never get bored. You live and breathe tedium."

She closed the book and set it on her lap, and I knew from the way she pressed her lips together and lifted her chin that a lecture was forthcoming. "It is actually quite fascinating. It takes a special look at the paintings inside the caves at Sittanavasal. Surely you remember the place? I have always considered visiting it one of the highlights of our time in India."

Yes, I remembered the journey we'd made while Papa served with the Foreign Office, and doing so, I was forced to amend the thought that I'd never been as bored as I was that very day. There was, after all, Sittanavasal.

Rather than remind Violet of what she should have already known, I sprang from my chair and paced to the fireplace, empty and cold on so mild an afternoon. From there, I made my way to the windows that overlooked the brown and tattered remnants of our summer garden. All the roses trimmed. All the hollyhocks bent by wind. Little left but a smattering of baby's breath, but the tiny white flowers, too delicate to last much longer into the month, only served to remind me of the very long, very tedious days ahead until the social Season started again. It was all too cruel, and I spun and made my way back to the fireplace. There, I turned to face my older half sister.

"Reading hardly takes the place of living," I told her. "I mean, really living. You should know as much. There was, after all, the matter of the murder we dealt with last summer. Admit it, you felt truly alive then. You felt energized. Interviewing suspects. Searching for clues. Finally bringing the perpetrator to ground." Here, I was forced to swallow the sudden tight knot of emotion in my throat. But then, I had my reasons, for I'd been involved in the matter in the most heartbreaking way. I did not need to point this out to Violet, so instead, I said, "During the excitement, I know you felt your blood coursing through your veins in much the same way I did."

"Let me remind you, that excitement included you getting kidnapped. Who knows what might have happened had you not been rescued." I thought she might elaborate, and that surely what she added would have to do with my bad choices, my poor judgment, or my questionable taste in men. But whatever she was about to say, she sloughed it away with a twitch of her shoulders. "The incidents you speak of are over and done." As if to emphasize the point, she tapped the cover of her book with one finger. "As pleased as I am that justice was served, we need to get on with our lives. Our real lives. Those do not include . . ." Here she cast a glance at the thin publication that lay on the floor between us. "Really, Sephora, reading romantic novels is one thing, and I've always wondered how you can stomach such balderdash. But when you start into the likes of Count Orlando . . ." She did not need to comment further; her shiver took care of that.

As bored as I'd been with the Children of Ud just a short time before, I felt the need to defend my reading matter now. I scooped the eight-page dreadful from the floor and held it in front of me, a shield against her criticisms.

"It is heady stuff," I told her. "As you would know if only you'd read a number or two. This is number six of the series." I poked the periodical closer to her so that she was sure to notice the spine-tingling illustration on its cover, printed in lurid, luscious color. Dark-cloaked figures circling a leaping orange bonfire. A tall, commanding presence dressed all in black, lurking in the shadows, his skeletal fingers clutching the arms of a fair maiden. Her ruby lips were parted with terror, her sapphire eyes were wide, her white gown was diaphanous.

"There is such fear in her expression," I pointed out. "Just looking at the illustration, can't you feel the excitement of the scene? Aren't you eager to read every last word so that you, too, can become part of the story?"

"I'd much rather read about Sittanavasal, thank you very much." As if to prove this beyond any doubt, she opened her book again. "Why don't you . . ." Already reading, she waved a dismissive hand toward the parlor door. "Aren't there things you can do with Margaret? You and Margaret Thuringer, you go out every day together. Only—" Her gaze snapped from the book and met mine. "You haven't been out with Margaret. Not in ages. Have you two had a falling-out?"

I plunked onto the couch. "At least a falling-out would be interesting. I mean, if it was over a beau we both had our eyes on. Or the last of the Honiton lace at the dressmaker's." I know a pucker is not attractive, but I couldn't help myself. This was a subject worth puckering over. "Margaret is visiting relatives and has been gone for weeks, and without her, life is dreadfully dull."

"You have other friends, surely."

"None as amusing as Margaret." This time I didn't even try to control the depths of despair contained in my sigh. "Oh Violet, I am so bored!"

The wretched state of my being did not move her in the least. But then, Violet's character is so different from my own passionate nature. Just as her looks are so much a contrast of mine, strangers never guess we are sisters. Violet takes after our father's side of the family. She's tall and gangly, not petite and delicate like I am, and her brown hair isn't nearly as striking as my golden tresses. I do believe she might look far more fashionable if only she paid attention to the colors that are au courant and the styles that best enhance a woman's figure. Instead, as exemplified by that very morning where she was dressed in a gown the color of the autumn-brown leaves on the oak tree outside the window, she insisted on earthy colors and she never—it was hard to even imagine!—wore layers of petticoats or even a bustle.

Her personality, I am sorry to say, was as dull as her wardrobe. Violet is logical and thoughtful in all things. She is careful, her thoughts measured, her actions deliberate. Over the last months, I had often found myself wondering how she'd mustered the cleverness she must surely have needed to solve the mystery in which we'd found ourselves entangled over the summer. Were there depths to my half sister I had yet to discover? It seemed unlikely given we had known each other for the entire sixteen years of my existence. And yet, in the aforementioned affair, she had saved my honor as well as my life. For that alone, I must admit, I found myself thinking occasionally and much to my own surprise that I might actually admire Violet.

This was not one of those instances. Not when she showed me no sympathy at all, but simply turned back to her book.

"You'll think of something to do," she said. "Why don't you go see if Bunty needs help in the kitchen."

"The kitchen? Me?" It was all I needed to convince me Violet has no sense at all, not when it comes to an understanding of the proper use of a lady's time. I dragged myself from the couch and shuffled to the door. "I believe I will go to the shops on my own. Bunty will come along if I insist." Even as I said the words, I realized they contained none of the excitement they usually did for me. I gave her one last chance to prove she had a shred of compassion. "Perhaps you would like to accompany me instead?"

Violet didn't bother to look up from her reading. It was all the answer I needed.

Violet

I waited until Sephora shut the door behind her before I put down my book. Then I waited a full minute more. After all, I had my reputation to consider as well as my pride. I had to be certain she was well and truly gone before I let down my guard, threw back my head, and groaned.

Bored? Sephora was bored? She had no idea of the meaning of the word!

Bored had nothing to do with not having a friend to go out with to fritter away the day. Bored was all about the exhilaration of investigating a murder, uncovering a scheme that was both devious and heartless, using one's wits and tenacity to solve a crime and capture a fiend—and then after assuring the triumph of Justice, spending the next months trying to find a way back to the satisfaction of ordinary life.

Trying, and failing miserably.

The thought settled deep, and before I even realized it, I found myself echoing one of Sephora's mournful sighs. It was ridiculous, of course, to be so morose. All I needed to do was embrace the day with enthusiasm and curiosity as I had always done. A trip to the Victoria and Albert Museum to view the Chinese ceramics, perhaps. A visit to the library at the British Museum. A dive into the fascinating *The Ideals of the Art of India*.

I gave the book in question a dubious look and wondered if, when Sephora glanced at it, she'd even noticed that for as long as I'd sat there supposedly reading, I'd never made my way beyond page four.

This was not a salubrious way to live, so mired in dark thoughts, and I shook them off and reminded myself I had work to do. Thus impelled, if not encouraged, I pulled myself to my feet, exited the parlor, and crossed the hall to the library.

The house in St. John's Wood where Sephora and I were fortunate enough to reside belonged to our dear Aunt Adelia, our father's sister, who on the event of Papa's death in the Far East invited us to return to England to live with her. We had spent a year settling into our new life. Sephora with her friends, her fashion magazines, her questionable reading matter, and her frivolous spending. But then, Sephora's mother was an heiress and Sephora was an only child. She had an income that far outpaced mine and would come into a more-than-adequate fortune once she turned eighteen.

I did not hold this against her. I was the only child of Papa's first marriage to the daughter of missionaries, and having been raised by a sensible woman and doted on by a father who believed women should use their intellects, I cared little for the fripperies that occupied Sephora's hours. Since arriving in the country, I'd spent my time exploring the great metropolis, and I'd found museums and art galleries, libraries and lecture halls where I immersed myself in the heady culture of London.

That is, until five months earlier when Adelia suddenly and quite unexpectedly announced she was leaving for the Continent with her current paramour. I hardly begrudged her either the trip or the romantic liaison, but at her leaving, I did find myself in something of (as the great diarist Samuel Pepys put it) a pickle. Before Adelia set off, she confided a secret that left me not simply astonished but positively flabbergasted.

Adelia was Miss Hermione, the agony aunt who doled out advice in *A Woman's Place* magazine and was extolled from one end of the Empire to the other! As if that wasn't enough of a surprise, she proclaimed she had chosen me to take her place.

Adelia is not a woman to be argued with. Her formidable personality (not to mention that she never takes no for an answer) mingled with my desire to show my gratitude for all she'd done for Sephora and me. Since that day, I had dutifully answered the letters sent to Miss Hermione via the magazine. I had offered advice on everything from manners to marital spats, decorum to household decoration, and I knew there was a stack of just such letters waiting for me to attend.

I pulled the key from the chatelaine that hung from the belt at my waist and unlocked the door to the library where I worked. Though our indomitable housekeeper, Bunty, knew the truth of the letters and the face behind Miss Hermione's persona, according to Adelia's wishes, Sephora had been told nothing of the matter. Sephora was a devotee of both the column and the woman. And she was not one to keep a secret. No, Miss Hermione's true identity must remain hidden.

To that end, I closed the library door behind me and proceeded to my desk where earlier, I'd deposited a cache of letters. Adelia had devised an elaborate delivery route that assured the utmost secrecy and like clockwork, the letters arrived with each post. Some were pleading, some hopeful; some, like the one that had sent me on the trail of a killer just months before, predicted doom. Not so the ones I opened that morning.

A woman who signed herself Concerned about Crinolines wondered how she might stiffen a petticoat.

Another, whose atrocious spelling, watery ink, and the inexpensive foolscap she used told me she was young and in service, asked Miss Hermione to advise her on the best scent to wear to catch the attention of the fishmonger's boy who called at the kitchen door on Tuesdays. I did not wish to insult the fishmongers of our great nation, yet I was tempted to tell her he'd surely never catch her scent over what was his redolent own.

A third—a man by the look of his thick handwriting—wondered how he might clean up "just enough" to be presentable at the next lecture of the church mission society social given that he was not fond of bathing.

It was at this point I tossed the letters in the air and shrieked.

I might have known Bunty would not miss hearing so pitiful

a sound. When I answered the knock on the library door that came just minutes later, her lips were pinched, and she had a tea tray in her hands.

"Thought you might need a little bolstering." She stepped inside and I closed the door behind her. "Even before I heard you wailing like a banshee."

I bristled. "It was hardly a banshee wail. It was more—"

"Pathetic," she ventured.

"Pathetic," I concurred, and my shoulders drooped.

"Come over here." She led the way to the settee near the window and put the tray on a nearby table. "Tell me all about it."

"If only there was something to tell." I sank onto the settee. During my time as Miss Hermione, we'd established a comfortable routine, Bunty and I. She advised on household matters so that when Miss Hermione recommended recipes or offered guidance on the best way to clean stains and spills, there was some authority behind the advice. Bunty also handled correspondence to and from Adelia. I was grateful to have Bunty's assistance and her counsel. As she had been in Adelia's service for years and she was also intelligent and experienced, Bunty was the perfect confidante. Now, like always when we put our heads together, she handed me a cup of tea and poured one for herself.

My cup poised in my hand, the steam tickling my nose, I told her, "The letters Miss Hermione receives are trite and they are hackneyed. Reading the same sorts of things day after day makes me feel as if my intellect is stifled and my instincts are growing duller by the hour."

Examining me closely over the rim of her cup, she sipped. Her expression was as passionless as was expected of a silver-haired housekeeper. There was, however, a knowing gleam in her eyes. "You're not looking for another murder, are you?"

Almost against my will, my gaze traveled across the room to the filing cabinets lined against the wall. Adelia had established a rather slipshod system for cataloguing and storing her letters, one I'd refined and perfected over the last months, and each cabinet was marked according to subject matter: *Mothers-in-Law, Unfaithful Spouses, Manners, Morals.* At the end of the summer, I had added a new label to an empty cabinet: *Murder.*

"Of course, I don't wish anyone harm," I confessed. "But Bunty, just a hint of the excitement and exhilaration I felt as I investigated might help me feel alive again."

Her lips pinched just the slightest bit. "And here I thought Mr. Eli had taken care of that."

It was a cheeky thing for her to say, and so true, it struck at my heart. Eli Marsh was an American I'd encountered while investigating, a fine-looking and secretive fellow who was evasive when it came to answering questions about either his occupation or himself. He carried handcuffs and a pistol, both of which had proved useful in our endeavor to bring a murderer to ground. He was quick on his feet and courageous while at the same time being infernal, maddening, and the most attractive man I'd ever met.

It would do me no good to remember Eli or his kiss, the one that had thrilled me to my bones. And I, as I reminded myself, was hardly the type to pine.

"I haven't heard from him," I told Bunty. "Not since he appeared here after we'd wrapped up last summer's mystery then disappeared again just as quickly."

"Busy, no doubt," Bunty offered. "As men so often are."

If Eli was busy, then he was not as bored as I.

I frowned and shook away all thoughts of Eli as so unproductive and discouraging they would only sink me further into the mopes. "How did Adelia do it?" I wondered. "She is so mercurial, so intelligent. Yet she'd been writing as Miss Hermione for years and no doubt seeing the same sorts of letters I see. How did she manage?"

"Miss Adelia is not one to take life too seriously," Bunty told me. "Whereas you . . ." Another sip of tea gave her time to form her words. "Murder is a serious business. Adelia would not have been able to handle an investigation such as you did or to deal with the darkness you encountered. You were the perfect person to take on the task."

"And now I am left with nothing but empty hours and endless letters that make me feel as if I'm drowning in dullness."

She set down her cup and her gaze wandered to the letters that had fluttered to the floor when my patience snapped. "You have yet to examine all of the morning's post."

She was right, and though I had little hope any of the remaining letters would bring the intellectual stimulation I so badly needed, I plucked them from the floor, then sat back down so I might go through them.

"How much jewelry can a woman wear without looking gaudy?" I tossed the letter down on the settee next to me. "Is it fitting to serve the fish before the fowl?" This letter, too, I discarded. " 'Dear Miss Hermione, What is a mother to do?' " I grumbled. "Oh dear, Bunty, I'm afraid I am in for a question about engagement announcements. Wasn't it just a fortnight ago I answered a question about the proper way to announce a daughter's engagement?"

"And yet there may be something further to the letter," Bunty offered.

More to appease her than for any other reason, I kept reading.

"'Every minute of every day, I am consumed by worry. I am sleepless, filled with panic. I am desperate for help, and as you will understand when you are apprised of my problem, I cannot turn to anyone but you to provide it.

"'It pains me even to write these terrible words, but if you are to assist me, you must know the truth, and the whole of it.'"

I could not contain the groan that escaped me. "It might still be about an engagement," I groaned. "You know how fretful mothers can be when it comes to engagements. And yet . . ." My fingers played over the paper and suddenly and quite unexpectedly, a frisson of electricity tingled through my bloodstream.

"Thick paper. Expensive. This is from a woman who would not need to inquire about trifles. She's been brought up to know how to deal with every contingency. She's neat and intelligent. There are no misspellings, no ink smudges. She may be consumed with panic, as she says, but still, she is as steady as Gibraltar. She's surely been schooled in how to be a lady. She would know exactly what to do if her daughter was recently engaged. Plus, Bunty, did you catch the subtle reference?" I quickly reread the line where I'd left off. "'. . . you must know the truth, and the whole of it.' To me, that indicates there are others who have not been apprised of the whole of the situation. Ah, secrets! We may be on to something here, Bunty!" I settled back and kept reading.

"'My dear Miss Hermione, my daughter has run off.'" When Bunty sucked in a breath, I refused to be distracted, but kept on reading all the way to the line where a familiar name caught my attention, The Hermetic Order of the Children of Aed.

My head came up. "Bunty, isn't that the ridiculous cult Sephora reads about? Those sordid stories about human sacrifice and such? You mean there really is such a thing? It isn't a fiction?"

Bunty's shoulders quivered and spots of color rose in her cheeks. "Real, indeed! Count Orlando is not so much a writer of fiction as he is a journalist, and he's risked his own life to investigate these heathens. This poor mother! It is no wonder she's beside herself. The count's stories, they leave you breathless!"

"You, too, Bunty?" I might have been tempted to laugh but could not in the face of this new problem we'd been presented. Besides, Bunty didn't allow me the chance. She scooted to the edge of her seat and poked a finger toward the letter in my hand. "Keep reading. We must learn what's happened."

I did as instructed. At least until I could stand it no longer. "'Human sacrifices. Devil worship. Orgies!'" I plonked the letter onto my lap. "This is beyond the pale! Really, Bunty, this cannot be more than bunkum. Human sacrifices? Here in England?"

Bunty nodded and leaned nearer, her voice low with the weight of her words. "And worse, according to Orlando. It is wantonness itself."

"And I imagine the telling of it sells a good many copies of the publications," I mumbled, but as Bunty was poised, her breath caught and her expression eager, I went back to the letter and read all the way to where the distraught writer admitted to lying to her husband, to hiding the truth for the sake of the family honor.

"There's the stiff upper lip I talked about, Bunty. And here she closes, asking for Miss Hermione's help and declaring herself brokenhearted."

Bunty shook her head. "Of course she is brokenhearted. And that poor lamb of a daughter. Yet I cannot think what Miss Hermione can do about it. What might you tell her?"

I did not answer. But then, my brain was busy spinning over the spark of a memory. Something I'd paid little attention to. Something I'd disregarded as unimportant. Something—

I sprang from my seat. "Bunty, yesterday's newspaper. Where is it?"

She was rather slower to stand. "In the bin where I always put the newspapers when we're done with them."

"I must look through it." I hurried forward and opened the library door, stepping back to let her by, and while she was gone, I cleared off my desk. By the time Bunty returned, I had plenty of room to spread open the pages of the London *Times*.

A long article about a possible dock strike. A story about the Queen's scheduled return from Balmoral. An event of some grandeur hosted by the Prince and Princess of Wales at Sandringham.

I ignored the lot of it, and when I found what I was looking for, I called Bunty over.

"Here," I told her. "I thought the whole thing sounded familiar. The Children of Aed, the group this mother speaks of, they will be visiting London tomorrow."

As if she wasn't quite sure she believed me, Bunty took a pair of spectacles from the pocket of her trim white apron, put them on, and read over the information.

"In Finsbury Park?" She shivered. "I do not see how the authorities can allow it. Human sacrifices and naked virgins?"

"I doubt either will happen in Finsbury Park," I assured her. "Though I do admit, it would be interesting."

She flinched, and I put a hand on her shoulder. "You have nothing to worry about, Bunty. I do believe your Count Orlando may exaggerate reality for the sake of making a name for himself."

"That may be, but—"

"But there's only one way to find out."

She sucked in a breath and her face paled. "You're not going to—"

"A brokenhearted mother has asked for Miss Hermione's help. I cannot know what to tell her if I don't research the problem, and the only way to do that is to attend this lecture by . . ." I consulted the notice again for the details. "Master. Tomorrow afternoon at three o'clock sharp, I will be in Finsbury Park, meeting with the Children of Aed."

Chapter 2

November 5

"You're going out? Now?"

I will admit, I am used to having my comings and goings questioned by Sephora, so the fact that she challenged me as I set my hat upon my head and reached for my umbrella did not surprise me. The desperation in her voice, though, did. As did the fact that she stepped into my path, blocking me from the door.

"It's Bonfire Night." I wondered if she knew how much of a whine her words contained, and decided instantly that even if she did, Sephora would not care. If moaning and complaining could get her what she wanted, she wasn't above it, though what she wanted, exactly, I couldn't tell. "For months, Margaret and I have been planning to watch the parade outside the Lewisham Road station this evening. There will be bands and banners, and costumed riders. The homes and shops along the way will be illuminated, too."

"I trust you'll have a lovely time."

This was, apparently, not what Sephora wanted to hear. She didn't move a muscle.

I tried another tack. "I hope the rain holds off until after the festivities."

This did not please her, either. She folded her arms across the front of her dove-gray gown.

I have never been fond of her games, and this was more than I could countenance. I needed to be on my way. "Really, Sephora, I have no idea what you expect of me. You said you're going to the celebrations and I wished you well and—"

"And Margaret isn't here to go with, is she?" She stuck out her chin and glared up at me.

I'd forgotten. But then, I'd had more important things to worry about than Sephora's social life. I'd spent all of the day before and most of my time that day reading everything I could find about the Children of Aed. I now knew the group had been started some five years earlier and that its members lived at a sort of compound in the countryside outside of Nottingham. They were named after Aed, the Irish god of the underworld, whose name translates to *burn* or *kindle,* so he is also considered by some to be the god of fire. Such is the case for the Hermetic Order of the Children of Aed, who, according to what I'd read, believe themselves connected to the sacred fire of life that powers the universe.

It should be noted, that was the sum total of the factual reporting I could discover about the Children. My other reading—and I am much to be commended for soldiering through it—had consisted of numbers one, two, and three of the stories of the Children of Ud series by Count Orlando. The count, it seems, had perfected the art of writing prose more purple even than a plum. Each of his stories was embellished with melodrama, danger, and a good deal that was titillating. True or untrue? The count claimed every word was based on fact. I, certainly, could not tell. I was sure of only one thing—

damsels in distress, the threat of torture and sacrifice, and a dive into all things arcane and unwholesome meant the count's stories assured him a hefty income.

None of which would matter a whit if I failed to arrive at Finsbury Park in time for the lecture. With that in mind, I offered Sephora as kindly a smile as I was able to muster considering her mulish behavior. "I'm sure you won't have nearly as much fun at tonight's celebrations without Margaret as you would with her," I told her. "But you two can make other plans when she returns home. Now if you'll just kindly step out of my way—"

"Without Margaret"—she bit off the words from between her clenched teeth—"I cannot go at all. You would certainly frown upon me being out in the evening on my own."

She was right. I would disapprove, and not simply because Sephora would be without a companion. Sephora was not canny enough to safely maneuver through so public an event. Pickpockets. Drunkards. Unscrupulous men. Sephora could no more be trusted celebrating the demise of Guy Fawkes on her own than she could to navigate a frigate.

I stepped to get around her. She remained unmoving.

I grumbled my frustration. "I'm sorry you're going to miss the celebration," I told her, and I meant it. I knew how much Sephora enjoyed spectacle. "I'm sure you were looking forward to the fireworks. Perhaps next year?"

She latched on to my arm with both hands. "You've got to come with me and it's already after two. If you go out now, you'll be gone for who knows how long and you'll come back late. All the excitement will be over. I've been looking forward to this night for such a long time. You can't abandon me like this."

She did not need to bat her eyelashes to convince me

of her sincerity. As much as she liked to think of herself as a worldly woman, Sephora was a child in so many ways, and this was, after all, a special occasion. I could hardly blame her for being disappointed.

I didn't give quite so much away as I explained my reasoning, but still tried my best to find a compromise. "I am going to a lecture," I told her, and watched her roll her eyes. "It starts at three and I can't imagine it will take longer than an hour. I will be back before the parades begin. And yes, then I will go with you to Lewisham and we can watch the festivities together. We'll take Bunty along."

In place of the thanks I expected, she stuck out her lower lip. "If you come back in time. If you are not tired from whatever interminable lecture you're going to attend. Let me guess, it's about something incredibly boring. Chinese art, perhaps? Or is it Sanskrit grammar? Good heavens, Violet, if it is, you'll be half asleep from the dullness of it all before you ever get home."

I admit to being surprised she even knew there was grammar attached to Sanskrit, and it was that more than anything that put me in a benevolent mood. "If you must know," I told her, "I'm going to Finsbury Park to hear a lecture by the man who heads the Hermetic Order of the Children of Aed."

Her mouth fell open. "Master? He's here in London? Oh, Violet!" She danced from foot to foot, a display which allowed me to dart around her and nearer to the door. "You simply must let me come with you. I wouldn't miss it for anything in the world."

"It is sure to be dull."

"How can it be? Count Orlando says—"

"Count Orlando writes fiction."

"Based wholly and completely on fact. I know that much

to be true. He wrote a letter to his readers that was printed at the beginning of number five in the series. He knows of what he speaks. In his letter, he told how he researches, how he spies on the group at the risk of his own life and limb. Oh, there is bound to be ritual at this lecture, and chanting and . . ." Her words were lost in a whoosh of breath that signaled her excitement. "Do you think there will be sacrifices?"

I hoped my stony look spoke volumes. "In Finsbury Park?"

She wrinkled her nose. "Well, perhaps not, then. But chanting and rituals, surely. I hear there is one special prayer Master says in an ancient language and the words can mesmerize a crowd and make every person in it follow him to the home the Children have near Nottingham. It is mystical, surely. And oh, Violet, I would dearly like to see it."

I considered, but only for a moment, and in the end, I think it was the Sanskrit grammar comment that tipped the scales. "Get your hat and your coat," I told Sephora, and she squealed with excitement and raced up the stairs.

I had not realized Bunty was listening to all this until she stepped out of the parlor and glanced up the stairs. "Do you think it's wise for her to go along?" she asked.

I wondered the same thing, but not for long. "She did prove herself plucky when we faced down the murderer last summer," I admitted. "But I hardly think she'll need that sort of courage today. In fact, I think she will be bored to tears."

"Or she'll be beguiled. Just like what happened in those dreadfuls I gave you to read."

"Really, Bunty." I put on the hip-length capelet I'd chosen to wear with a dark, tailored skirt. Though it was already autumn, the weather was mild, the skies overcast. "You do not believe such nonsense as magical chants, do you?"

"Oh, you should. It's true." Sephora bucketed down the steps, her hat and coat already on, ready to defend her belief in the rubbish that was the Children of Ud. "I've read it myself. Master can make fire explode from his hands, and smoke rise from his bare fingers." She scampered to the door. "He has even been known to levitate."

"As any stage magician can do," I told her, but really, she wasn't listening. Sephora checked her reflection in a nearby mirror, adjusted her hat, and chose an umbrella from the eighteenth-century Qianlong porcelain stand near the doorway just as Bunty stepped forward and opened the door. When she stepped back to allow us outside, Bunty took the opportunity to wring her hands.

"Don't look that Master fellow in the eye," she warned. "Don't let him say his heathen magic words in your ear. He'll mesmerize you for certain."

Outside, I turned to offer her a smile. "You have nothing to worry about. We will be back, and we'll collect you and head out for the Bonfire Night celebrations. We are sensible young women." I glanced to where Sephora fairly skipped down the pavement in search of a cab. "Well, one of us is. But believe me, this talk of magical powers is nothing more than exaggeration, surely. I promise you, Bunty, no one is going to be beguiled."

♋

"Oh, Violet! I feel as if I'm walking on air." As if to demonstrate, Sephora bounced along, the movement sending the fog that pooled along the pathway in Finsbury Park into tiny eddies that whooshed and whirled around our ankles. Just as I'd hoped, the rain had held off, but the afternoon was gray and dull. Lowering clouds gathered and a sporadic breeze whipped the trees as well as our skirts. Sephora noticed none of this. Her color high, her eyes glimmering, she grinned. "This is the most exciting thing I've done in as long as I can remember."

I will admit to thinking it was not as exciting there in the park as it was crowded. It seemed we were not the only ones interested in the Children of Aed.

Hanging on tight to each other's hands, Sephora and I dodged between two hulking workmen. We sidestepped a young woman pushing a pram with a baby in it. We negotiated our way through a clutch of elderly ladies in dreary mourning carrying placards that proclaimed THE LORD HATES A SINNER and BLASPHEMERS WILL BURN.

"If we can get closer . . ." Sephora tugged me along and we squeezed between a man with a massive mustache and a woman in purple who was not happy about having to step out of the way to let us pass. "If we can stand near the front, we'll be able to see Master better. Won't it be marvelous?"

I would have been just as happy to stay back and simply listen to whatever it was this Master fellow had to say, but seeing as I couldn't let Sephora wander off by herself, I dutifully followed along. We squeezed, nudged, and bumped our way to a spot near the base of a broad oak where a table had been set, a pitcher of water and a glass ready on it. Obviously, this was where the lecture would take place. We could get no closer, though, for holding back the crowd by their mere presence was a ring of robed figures. Their backs were to the crowd, their hoods over their heads. There were fifteen of them and they stood unmoving, seemingly oblivious to the clamor all around us. Unlike in the illustration that accompanied the latest from Count Orlando, they were not clothed in black, but in a rainbow of cheerful colors. Some of the robes were yellow, others were blue. There was one figure draped in purple; a woman by the lithe shape of the figure beneath the gown. A few more wore green in a shade that reminded me of a spring meadow.

"They hardly look dangerous," I commented, but Sephora would have none of that sort of sensible talk.

"I told you it would be a marvel!" She clung to my arm and, because she is so much shorter than I am, stood on tiptoe to better see what was happening. "I think they will conduct a ritual. They are surely dressed for it. They are Master's devotees . . ." Sephora let the words trail away on the end of a breath of awe. "I wonder which of them is steeling herself, praying to be worthy enough to be sacrificed this afternoon."

"No one is going to be sacrificed," I told her in no uncertain terms. "Nor would you want them to be."

"Not really, I suppose." She lifted one shoulder and wrinkled her nose. "Though as Count Orlando tells it, the sacrificial ceremony is thrilling. There is . . ." She leaned nearer and lowered her voice. "Nakedness."

"Really, Sephora!" I could not contain the sharpness of my words. "We as a people are far more civilized and modern than to believe any of that sort of claptrap. Think your way through it and you'll see the truth of the thing. Do you really think this Master fellow has the power to make everyone here in the park watch a sacrifice and not try to intervene? To forget our consciences and our good sense?"

"You'll see, miss." A fellow next to me who smelled of tobacco and alcohol had obviously been listening in. He gave me a poke. "It's all very mystical-like. Except . . ." He grunted and turned to the equally malodorous man beside him. "Don't know, Fred, it ain't exactly like you promised. I don't see no naked virgins around here anywhere."

"Just you wait," his chum said. "I tell you, Jacky, all them

women there, they're as naked as robins under those there
robes. When that Master fellow gives the signal, they'll pull 'em
off and then you'll see. Oh, you'll see." At the very thought, he
grinned.

"And say what you like, but a'course there's gonna be a
sacrifice." On the other side of us, a woman with a round
face, her coat stained with candlewax, joined in the conversation. "What kind'a devilish ceremony would it be without a
blood sacrifice?"

"Didn't I tell you?" Sephora smiled. "I said it would be
exciting, didn't I?"

"It seems rather that too many people have read the same
ridiculous fiction you have," I told her. "I wouldn't be at all
surprised that when they find out the decadence they're expecting isn't going to happen—"

The rest of my words were lost in a gasp when I was banged
into by a thick fellow with ruddy cheeks. I might have gone
down in a heap if Sephora did not grab my arm to keep me on
my feet. I steadied myself, and once I did, I found myself with
my nose nearly pressed to the stickpin the man wore in his left
lapel. It was gold, and a lion if I was not mistaken, though as
the bauble was not fashioned with particular artistry, it was
a bit hard to tell. His clothes were of a better quality than
those of the rough workingmen around us, but they were not
those of a gentleman. And his manners left a great deal to be
desired, as he offered me neither assistance nor an apology.
In fact, I wondered if he noticed me at all. His fingers plucking nervously at the pockets of his jacket, his gaze was fixed
on the hooded figures at the front of the crowd. Still eyeing
them, he stalked off without a word.

I had just resettled myself when a man stepped from behind the oak tree and, as raucous as it had been before, the

crowd was instantly hushed. All around us, I heard gasps and whispers of wonder. The robed figures standing at the front of the assemblage bowed to the man. Clearly, this was Master.

He, too, was clad in a robe, but his was white, the color so much a contrast to the murkiness of the day, it was blinding. He was tall and his golden hair was brushed back from a face that looked as if it had been chiseled from stone by a skilled hand. His nose was long and straight. His chin was firm. His eyes were blue fire.

"He's beautiful," Sephora purred, and I could hardly argue. Whoever this Master was, whatever he believed or preached, he was the most striking man I'd ever set eyes on.

He glanced all around and had just said, "Good afternoon," when a voice cried out from the back of the crowd.

"Where are them virgins?"

"Yeah! We come to see women!" another called out.

The woman who stood on our left poked a fist in the air and yelled, "And sacrifices."

Master was fazed by none of this. A tiny smile playing over his lips, he clutched his hands at his waist, and started to speak—about the sacredness of trees.

To Sephora's everlasting credit, she gave the lecture exactly three minutes before she lost patience and huffed out a breath. "Trees? Violet, are you certain you brought me to the proper place? These people surely cannot be the Children of Ud."

"Aed," I corrected her. "And I do believe you are getting a taste of what the group is really about, not what your Count Orlando says in his stories."

"What's this then?" Jacky, too, had apparently had enough. He scratched a finger under his doughy nose. "The spirits of our ancestors livin' in trees?"

Master took all of this in stride. His voice as steady and

as calm as the look he aimed at the crowd, he nodded. "The roots of trees are doorways to the underworld," he said. "Their branches"—he raised his arms to his sides—"are a stairway to heaven."

"Rubbish!" someone called out, and the word was taken up throughout the crowd. "Rubbish. Rubbish. Rubbish." Each repetition of the chant gained volume and seethed with the frustration of people who had clearly come to see heathen sacrifices and not learn that oak trees embody courage and wisdom.

Through it all, Master simply waited. And when the chant grew louder, he waited longer. And when the disaffected finally capitulated and stomped off in all directions and the crowd thinned to less than half its original size, he told those of us who remained about the holiness of hawthorns and that hazels were the first creations on earth and thus hold the wisdom of the universe in their branches.

As we were not hemmed in on every side now, Sephora had more room to move. That allowed her to step back, shake her shoulders, and grumble. "And here I thought I was bored at home."

I will admit, I was less so. Not that I necessarily believed that hawthorns provide love and protection to those who honor them. I was, in fact, far more interested in Master's character. He was certainly a skilled speaker. Caught on his every word, his cloaked followers barely moved. There were those in the crowd, too, who seemed entranced. His philosophy had nothing to do with wickedness and there was certainly no mention of sacrifice. Instead, his message was all about living as one with nature.

I tipped my head, considering this, and I wondered if it was the man or the philosophy that appealed to one young girl so much that she abandoned her home and left her mother brokenhearted.

I might have considered the thought even longer if I didn't notice a movement at the edges of the crowd and turn to look that way. There I saw a man cloaked in all black. His back was to me, his collar was turned up, and his cloth cap was tugged low on his head. I couldn't see his face. I didn't need to. I instantly recognized his type. The clothing might be different, and the weather certainly was, but I had seen such men at the Chitpore Road bazaar in Calcutta and the Central Market of Hong Kong.

"Hold tight to your valuables," I told Sephora. "There is a pickpocket among us."

He slipped past the ladies holding their BLASPHEMERS WILL BURN placards (who were, it should be noted, clearly disappointed they had not encountered any wantonness at which to aim their righteous indignation). Slowly and steadily, the man made his way in our direction, nearer to the front of the crowd, closer to Master.

Another few steps and I might have been able to take better measure of him, but at that moment a gust of wind caught my hat and I was obliged to slap a hand to it and duck my head.

When I looked up again, the man was gone. It was at just this time that Master told us that he and his followers must hurry to the train station. He wished us all a pleasant afternoon and a lifetime of peace.

"That's it then?" I might have laughed if Sephora did not look so thoroughly disappointed.

I shifted my umbrella from my left hand to my right so that I might lay a hand on her shoulder. "Perhaps you'll find more entertainment at the bonfire celebrations tonight."

"That won't be hard." Her upper lip curled. "I cannot believe you made me come here with you, Violet. What a dreadful way to spend the afternoon. How can Master think people will leave their homes and devote their lives to talking to trees and living in the wild? My goodness, can you even imagine it?" Her objections continued nonstop as we waited for those around us to move so that we might be on our way. Just as we started off, the robed figures fell into a line, two abreast, and made their way toward where Master waited for them.

Whatever Sephora was nattering about, another blast of wind blew her words away, just as it whipped at the rainbow-colored robes of Master's followers.

That is when it happened. That is why Sephora didn't see it. She was so busy offering a commentary on the joys of life in London and how awful it must be to live in the country, she missed seeing the hood of one of the yellow-robed figures blow from her head.

I, though, saw quite clearly, and the moment I did, I realized I had lied to Bunty earlier in the day when I told her no one would be beguiled by the Children of Aed. Sephora and I were leaving the lecture with our free wills intact. But the robed figures, surely, had been beguiled. Enough to leave their homes and join Master. So much so that a certain Brokenhearted Mother was obliged to write to Miss Hermione to beg for help. And in that moment, looking at the girl with the upturned nose and the nut-brown hair, I knew exactly who that mother was, for even though she quickly grabbed at her hood to tug it back over her head and fell into place alongside the other acolytes, I recognized the girl in the yellow robe.

It was Margaret Thuringer.

Chapter 3

As quickly as I caught a glimpse of Margaret, she was gone, filing out of the park with the other devotees. I could not let her go so easily. Her mother had pleaded for Miss Hermione's help.

I grabbed Sephora's hand and started after the robed figures. "Come along."

She held back. "Whatever for? We're not going . . ." Her golden brows low over her eyes, she watched the group walk away, unaware that her best friend was among them—then, as if some horrific realization was suddenly upon her, her eyes shot open. "You're not going to join, are you? You've always been odd, Violet, with your books and your museums and your thinking all the time. But really, this is too much! Worshiping trees? Digging in the dirt?" The very thought made her groan. "You don't mean . . ." She gulped. "You don't mean to take me to Nottingham with you, do you?" she asked, true horror coloring her every word.

I had no time to deal with her histrionics, so I gave her another tug. "Of course not. Leaving the park this way is faster. We'll be home in no time at all and then we can get ready for the bonfire celebrations."

It was a lie, and had Sephora bothered to learn her way

around London as I had, she would have known it. But then, as she had proved the summer before when she fell in love with the wrong man, Sephora can be too trusting, so she took my comment at face value and started along with me. She kept up with the quick pace I set, her gaze on the troupe ahead of us in their rainbow-colored robes.

"Do you suppose they actually dress like that? I mean, each and every day?" She pulled a face. "I can't even imagine it. Not having a tea gown? Not having evening clothes? They all look alike, don't they? Except for the color of their robes, that is. How frightfully dull it would be to look the same as every other woman. Don't you agree, Violet? I say, Violet." She locked her knees and wrenched me to a stop. "Why are you hurrying so?"

I was, but I did not want to stop and explain, potentially losing sight of the group. A prospect that, it seemed, was becoming more and more of a possibility. No sooner had we left the park than a crowd gathered along our route. Men and women called out to the Children of Aed, falling in step behind us, darting to and fro into the group and out of it, laughing and doing lively dance steps. A squib flew from somewhere on our right and cracked in the air above Master's head. His chin high, his steps sure and even, he paid it no mind and simply nodded a greeting to the people who hemmed us in on every side. They in turn pointed and called out as had the people at the lecture, comments about sacrificial virgins and the evils of Satan worship. All of this peppered with inquiries about the time and place of the next orgy.

Had I been with a pluckier companion, I might not have felt the remorse that soured my stomach. Already, Sephora's cheeks were shot through with color and her eyes were wide with confusion and fear. I wanted to comfort her, to tell her that, as I always did when I went out into the great city, I had my pistol in my chatelaine. I didn't. She wouldn't hear me above the clamor. Instead, I gave her hand a squeeze and offered as much reassurance as I could with a quick smile.

Caught up in the tumult, we moved toward the station, fueled by the necessity of my singular mission. Margaret Thuringer's father was a banker. Her mother came from a family of Harley Street physicians. Margaret had attended a fine boarding school and though she did not show particular academic acumen there, it hardly mattered. Margaret's future was determined not by intelligence, but by her background and her breeding. Her family had every hope of a suitable marriage. Margaret was just as flighty as my sister, just as preoccupied with looks and fashion, just as innocent. How she had come to wear a yellow robe and follow Master was a puzzle, one I would like to unravel. But there was an even more important matter to attend to first, that of Mrs. Thuringer's broken heart, of her lies to her husband, of her sense of dread.

While these thoughts occupied me, we neared the station and I saw that some in the environs had already started their bonfire celebrations. A pile of kindling blazed in the middle of the street where we walked, and we were forced to snake our way around it. Three young boys, their voices tight with excitement, leaped over the flames while calling out the words of the nursery rhyme I remember learning even though I spent my childhood in the far-flung reaches of the Empire.

"Remember, remember, the fifth of November, the gunpowder treason and plot. I know of no reason why the gunpowder treason should ever be forgot."

The crowd roared its approval, the youngsters took a bow and joined our ranks, and we rounded a corner and came in sight of the railway station. On the pavement in front of it, another fire sizzled and snapped, the flames whipped by a sudden gust of wind. Ash shot into the air and dotted our cheeks and our clothing. The glow of the flames lit the tendrils of fog around us and reflected off the stone façade of the station, flashing at us in gold and orange and creating shadows that flickered along the building. They were hulking and twisted, much like the black-cloaked figures on the cover of Sephora's latest penny dreadful.

It took a moment for me to realize one of the shadows was no shadow at all. It was the pickpocket I'd seen in the park. His collar still obstructing any view of his face, he slipped along the front of the station and closed in on the last of the devotees in line, the figures in yellow.

I thought to warn Sephora of his presence, but before I had the chance, I was jostled by a familiar creature, the man with ruddy cheeks and the lion stickpin. This time, like the last, he paid me no mind. His fingers nervously plucking at his pockets, he, too, moved toward the station, just as a man in a blue robe stepped forward to hold the door open and one by one, Master's disciples went inside.

I fought my way nearer to them, wondering now which of the four figures in yellow was Margaret. If I could but step up to the side of the man at the door, I might see the acolytes' faces as they entered the building. Then I could catch Margaret's eye and take her aside for a quick word.

I dropped Sephora's hand so that I might elbow my way closer to the robed figures. The firelight shifted and trembled, giving the scene an otherworldly radiance. It reflected off the robes of the devotees who were now near enough to touch. All around me, people sang and laughed. Flames jumped, and instinctively, I glanced over my shoulder to catch sight of Sephora, eager to make sure she was safe.

It was then, when I took my eyes off the devotees, that it happened, and by the time I saw it, I was in no position to stop it. The man I presumed to be a pickpocket had pushed away from the façade of the station and slipped into the line of devotees. When I caught sight of him again, he had an arm around the waist of one of the yellow-robed figures. The woman was as surprised as I was, but only for a moment. The next second, she screamed and fought against him. The man, though, was far taller than she, and well-made. He lifted her off her feet and half dragged, half carried her away from the other stunned acolytes, farther into the shadows.

Was it Margaret? It didn't matter. Not when I saw the way the woman kicked and flailed. The man held on tight. Some of the other devotees, seeing the danger, shook away their surprise and called out for help, and they may have gotten it except those in the crowd assumed this was all part of the show. Finally, the type of theatrics and titillating excitement they had read about in Count Orlando's stories! They cheered and whistled. They yelled their encouragement to the ruffian, and they surged forward to block any of the Children from going to the woman's aid.

As quickly as the man moved, I knew help would not come. Not unless I, closest to the fray, was the one to provide it.

I had not a moment to lose and no desire to use my pistol in so crowded a place. I closed in on the heels of the abductor and his victim and considered my choices. The best one was at hand. The lout's back was to me, and I had the advantage of surprise. I gripped the handle of my umbrella and, using it as a club, I battered him over the head. He winced and cursed but kept right on. His hold on the woman tight, he lifted her further and headed for a dimly lit alley where he could safely disappear.

I had one last chance. I clutched my umbrella in both hands at its pointed end and swung the gold-filled and mother-of-pearl handle as if I were a cricket batsman, slamming it into the backs of the man's knees. He buckled and nearly hit the pavement, throwing out a hand to right himself and thumping my arm. Instinctively, I grabbed for him. It was not enough to stop him, but he knew his plan was thwarted. He thrust the woman in yellow at me and the last I saw of him before the two of us landed on the pavement in a heap was the man sprinting away and disappearing into the fog that wreathed the entrance to the alley.

It took me a minute to catch my breath, and another for me and the woman to untangle ourselves from each other. When we finally did, we sat on the pavement, side by side, spectators all around us, seemingly disappointed the excitement was over.

A woman with two chins and sagging jowls looked down at me. "You've gone and spoilt it," she spat.

"We was hoping for a little more fuss and bother." A man at her side rubbed his hands together.

"And 'cause of you," one young fellow hissed, "it's all over now."

My arms braced on my knees, I traded them glare for glare and was just as happy when they resigned themselves to the fact that the hubbub was over and one by one, shuffled away. Finally, I had a chance to examine the girl who sat next to me.

In the scuffle her hood had fallen away, and it was not Margaret Thuringer who looked back at me, but a girl with carroty hair and a face awash with freckles. Her hair, once a neat braid, was disheveled. Her yellow robe had a smudge of muck on it. The color in her cheeks had nothing to do with the firelight. The girl's breaths came deep and quick, her ginger

brows low over her eyes, her bottom lip caught in her top
teeth, and in a second, I knew she was not distressed. Nor was
she surprised by the assault. In fact, she seemed nothing if not
well and truly angry.

It was that more than anything which made me ask, "Who
was he?"

Rather than answer, the girl pulled herself to her feet and
glared down at me. A rather inappropriate response considering I had just saved her from being abducted. Without a word,
she pushed past what was left of the people around us and
through the skirts and legs of the crowd. I watched her join the
other devotees and march into the station. Gone. As was any
chance I had to find Margaret and speak to her.

The thought soured a mood already spoiled by the ingrati-
tude of the girl in yellow, so much so that when Sephora burst
through what was left of the crowd, tears staining her cheeks
and genuine worry in her eyes, there was little I could do but
grumble.

I suppose I might have stayed right there in the middle
of the road, despondent and discouraged, if a hand hadn't
reached down to take mine. I thought about not accepting the
assistance, but then I would be as churlish as the girl I'd saved,
so I twined my fingers with those of the man who'd come to
my aid and assisted as much as my quivering knees would allow when he pulled me to my feet. I found myself face-to-face
with Master.

His voice was as gentle as the look he gave me, as kindly as
the touch of his hand against mine. "Are you all right, miss?"
His intonation was that of public school, and this close, he
smelled of sandalwood, like the religious shrines in India.
Firelight played against his chiseled features, all planes and

angles, and added a spark to his blue eyes. "I am sorry it took me so long to come to your aid. I was inside the station with the others and didn't see what was happening until it was too late."

"What was happening?" I asked him.

It took a moment for him to comprehend what I was asking, and I knew exactly when he did because he dropped my hand. "That seems clear enough," he said, his serenity suddenly masked by the too-stiff civility of a gentleman. "That ruffian attacked one of our Novices. If it had not been for your quick action—"

"Who was he?" I asked him.

"I cannot possibly know."

"Then who is she?"

"She is called Luna." His gaze traveled briefly to the station before it landed again on me. "And yours?"

"Violet Manville," I told him, and it wasn't until I put out a hand to shake his that I realized my sleeve was torn, my arm was bloodied. I imagined the rest of me looked just as terrible. I dusted my skirts and then was obliged to ask, "Why did someone wish to spirit Luna away?"

He shook his head. "As you have seen, we are often the targets of unwanted attention. I doubt he targeted Luna specifically."

"I believe he did. And so does she. You may be wise to question her about it. This was far more serious than foolish people calling out to you while you spoke in the park."

"You were there?"

I held out a hand to Sephora and she took it and stepped to my side. "We were there," I said.

Master's eyes sparkled. "And the two of you followed us

here to the station. That's marvelous! You are interested, then, in the Children of Aed?"

More interested in why he'd evaded my question about Luna and the man who'd thought to snatch her, but unable to admit to that, I smiled. "Your philosophy is intriguing."

"It certainly is not!" It seemed Sephora had her limits, even when it came to a fine-looking man with a great deal of charisma. Her chin came up and she traded Master look for look. "If you ask me, it's ridiculous to expect people to live so. Out in the woods? Eating nuts and berries?"

His laugh was muffled by the fog that snaked around us. "We are hardly uncivilized. As you would see if you came to visit. We call those who wish to learn more of our philosophy Seekers, and we welcome you to spend time with us. You'll see we live quite comfortably and eat more than nuts and berries. We grow vegetables, raise chickens. The milk we use comes from our own cows, and the water we drink is directly from a well on the land where we live, one that has been sacred to the locals for more than a thousand years."

As her pout clearly showed, Sephora was not convinced, so Master turned to me. "I know, Miss Manville, that you are a kindred spirit," he told me. "Even if you had not stepped up to help Luna with not a thought for yourself or your own safety, I can see your integrity and strength shining in your aura. Perhaps you are a Seeker?"

"I am a scholar," I told him. "And thus, interested in various philosophies."

The shrill whistle of a train broke into our conversation, and Master moved toward the station. "I must go. But consider it, Miss Manville. We have a group of Seekers arriving soon. Join us. See how we live. Learn about our community and our beliefs."

I hesitated only long enough to glance toward the station and wonder. About Margaret. About Luna. About the man dressed all in black who was so determined to kidnap the girl.

"Yes," I said, and I ignored Sephora's gasp of horror. "I will do it."

He backstepped toward the station, his smile as bright as the light of the nearby bonfire. "I'm happy to hear it. Be here Sunday morning. Members of our company will meet you and accompany you north." He bowed from waist. "Good evening to you, Miss Manville. I look forward to seeing you on Sunday."

He was barely inside the station when Sephora exploded. "Are you mad? You can't go running off with these people."

"Can't I?"

"Not unless you wish to condemn yourself to eternal damnation. Were you not listening, Violet, when I told you about the rituals? About the—"

"Orgies. Yes." I dismissed her fears with the wave of one hand and stooped to pick up my umbrella from where it had fallen in my attack on the kidnapper. My breath caught when I saw it wasn't the only thing lying there. Was it an illusion? A pebble or a lost coin, made to look more than what it really was by a queer trick of the light?

My heart suddenly beating double time, I bent to retrieve the object and held it to the light. No pebble this, but a polished ebony cuff link. One I recognized instantly.

"Violet, are you listening to me?" Sephora tugged at my sleeve. "I'm trying to talk some sense into you. You cannot go haring off to who-knows-where simply to satisfy your curiosity about these Children. You need to listen to me. Are you paying any attention at all?"

I was not. But then, I could hardly be blamed, for I now

had more to think about than simply Margaret Thuringer's foolish choices. There was the matter of Luna, after all. And the mystery of why the owner of the cuff link, none other than Eli Marsh, had been intent on abducting her.

Chapter 4

November 8

I was consumed by the mysteries that swirled around the Children of Aed.

Margaret.

The unpleasant red-haired girl in the yellow robe.

Eli.

As important as were the other problems I must consider, I could barely pull my brain away from thoughts of him, and it was, perhaps, that above all else that set my nerves ajangle and made my mind race. What was he doing there outside the station? Why was he trying to carry off the girl? And if his intentions were honorable—could they be?—why hadn't he contacted me to explain himself?

I tried to console myself with the thought that he may not have known it was I who smashed him over the head with my umbrella, and now and again—a second here and a second there—it was enough to assuage my worries. Yet in all the times between, even those thoughts did little to soothe me. He knew. I was certain Eli knew, just as I sensed it was him from the moment I clapped eyes on him in Finsbury Park. My logical mind might not have been aware of the identity of the man

I thought was a pickpocket, but my instincts said otherwise. Else why would I have been drawn to watching him again and again, like iron to lodestone?

Even by the next Sunday—the day I was invited to meet the other Seekers at the Finsbury Park train station—my curiosity had not waned. In fact, it had grown by leaps and bounds—so much so that there was never any question about what I would do.

"You'll miss it when it arrives." Bunty knew what I would do, too. Otherwise she would not have given me this little reminder in an attempt to make me stay. Her back to the library door, her hands folded at her middle, she looked across the room to where I stood behind my desk, packing the last of the things I would take north with me. Her chin was high, her shoulders firm. In fact, she looked very much like a nurse-maid trying to tempt an unruly child with the promise of a sweet in exchange for good behavior. "Your package will be coming soon from America."

"And you will have it brought here to the library and it will be waiting for me when I return."

"Yes, but you were so eager to order that typewriting machine, and you'll be anxious to open it and learn to use it and you don't know when you might expect it and—"

"I have already received a letter from the Remington Company regarding its shipment." Said letter was on my desk and I lifted it briefly and waved it in the air by way of showing Bunty. I had the situation well in hand. "They assure me it will arrive by week's end, and yes, Bunty, I am quite anxious to learn to use the typewriting machine. In fact, I am told in this letter that I can visit the Remington representative here in London and at that office, they will gladly school me in use of the machine. I am looking forward to it. It is quite the most modern thing, don't you think?"

Her lips pinched. "A machine will never take the place of—"

"Good, old-fashioned handwriting." I laughed, interrupting her again. "Yes, I know, Bunty. You have mentioned that before. I, though, think the machine will save me a great deal of time and effort when it comes to writing Miss Hermione's letters. And Bunty, if it's good enough for Mark Twain . . ."

Bunty quite enjoyed Mr. Twain's stories. She could make no further argument. At least not in the name of my soon-to-be-delivered typewriting machine.

She sniffed. "Be that as it may, it isn't wise for you to do what you're thinking of doing." If I was not very much mistaken, the way she stood with her feet slightly apart told me she was acting as something of a human barricade. She thought to keep me from leaving! So determined a stance was surely not meant to be endearing, yet knowing Bunty was so concerned tangled warmth around my heart. "I told you earlier in the week, Miss Violet, those Children, they'll mesmerize you if you are not careful."

"Earlier in the week," I reminded her, "we did not realize the woman who wrote so desperate a plea to Miss Hermione was Lucille Thuringer, Margaret's mother." Yes, I left out any mention of Eli. I told myself it was so I did not muddy the waters of my investigation, and I would have liked to believe it. The truth, of course, was far uglier. I did not mention Eli because I didn't want to admit to Bunty—or to myself—that he had not been in contact with me to explain his actions outside the station. Because he did not feel he owed me an explanation. Because he did not care.

I cleared away a sudden tightness in my throat. "I must pursue this, Bunty. And admit it, you wouldn't be pleased with me if I did not. You know Margaret. She is sweet and naïve and as insubstantial as Sephora. Could you rest at night knowing she is living with the Children? Would you be happy with me if I didn't pursue this and find out what's really going on?"

Her chin trembled. "I suppose not, as I've barely been able to sleep these past nights as it is. And yet, maybe there is some logical reason a girl like Margaret would do such a thing."

I tucked my wooden lap desk into the carpetbag I would take with me to the station. I had already packed my clothing; my trunk was outside. "There is no logic to it. Margaret certainly does not use her brain to consider philosophy or the sacredness of hazel trees. So how is it a girl like that could have been talked into such a thing as running off to join a cult? And even more importantly, how could she go off on what might seem to her a rollicking adventure and not confide in her best friend?"

"She might have," Bunty suggested, but it was a weak argument at best. We both knew that if Sephora had any idea Margaret was among the yellow-robed acolytes in the park, she never would have been able to stand at my side and watch the proceedings there with such disinterest.

Ever since the previous Thursday when I took Bunty aside, far out of earshot of Sephora, and told her the news about Margaret, the two of us had been trying to make our way through the thing. We were no closer now to an answer than we were then.

"And then there's Luna, of course," I added, thinking out loud. "Who is she and why was she nearly carried off?"

"Another young woman whose family wants her back," Bunty suggested.

"That may be. But then, why did Master evade my questions about her?"

Bunty considered all this, and watching her work over her bottom lip with her top teeth, seeing the way her eyes narrowed with the effort of concentration, I felt nearly guilty for not telling her all of the story.

Eli Marsh was involved.

It was the one bit of news from the Bonfire Night's happenings I could not share. Not until I better understood it myself.

I let the thought settle, but only for so long before I kicked it from my consciousness. I was no yearning miss. And I had better things to keep my mind occupied than the flights of fancy it took whenever Eli popped into my head.

My mind made up, I closed my carpetbag and hoisted it in one hand. I rounded the desk and went to the door. "I will write as often as I can, Bunty," I told her. "And I will see you in exactly one week. By then I will have answers and with any luck, I will have Margaret, too."

At the station, I was greeted by two men in blue robes, Cygnus and Gwydion, who told me they would be in a second-class carriage and would see me again when we arrived at our destination. For my part, I secured a first-class compartment and I hoped to be the only one in it for the duration of the journey. I did not need conversation from other passengers. I did not need questions. I wasn't sure how my hours with the Children would be occupied, and I'd tucked letters addressed to Miss Hermione in my lap desk. The journey north would take a little more than three hours, and with any luck, I could finish my letters by then so as to free up my mind and my time.

I might have started into my work directly if I hadn't walked into the compartment and found a man already seated on the blue velvet bench. He smiled, nodded, and stuck out a hand.

"You may call me Phoenix."

Phoenix—an odd name, surely—was seventy if he was a day and he had a face that reminded me of a topographic map, all lines and wrinkles. He was short and slight; so gaunt, in fact, his bones showed from beneath the skin of his fingers.

"It's a fine day," he told me after he assisted me with my carpetbag, then again took his seat opposite from mine. "A good day to start a new life, don't you think?"

It was not something I'd considered when I left Parson's Lodge in St. John's Wood, so naturally I asked, "Are you starting a new life?"

"Indeed." He flattened his hands on his knees. "Though, truth be told, I started it more than a year ago. That was when I first came in contact with the Children of Aed."

"Ah." It was hardly a proper response, yet I could think of little else to say. To my mind, Phoenix did not look the type who would be in search of orgies. "You've heard Master speak?"

"Many times," he confided. "I still remember the first time I encountered him at Speakers' Corner in Hyde Park. It was kismet, surely, a moment in time I'd waited for all my life, though I didn't know it. I knew right then and there that I must give up what I'd been doing and follow Master."

"And what is it you had been doing?"

He grinned. "I was known as Granger Patterson then, and

I was a vicar. Spent my entire life caring for my flock, looking after my church and its grounds, going through the motions, as it were. Thus the name the Children have given me. I have risen, you see, from the ashes of my old life. All that time, I never knew it, but I was searching."

"You're a Seeker."

He laughed. "Not exactly. I have visited the compound before, you see. Spent months there last summer while I discerned if being one of the Children was my real vocation. And now when I return, I will be made a Novice and wear the yellow robe."

It was not that I didn't appreciate the excitement in his voice, the sincerity that rang through his words, yet I had seen enough in the last days to make me skeptical. "You are not expecting sacrifices, are you?"

Phoenix threw back his head and laughed at the same time he reached into the bag he'd set on the seat beside him and pulled out a familiar-looking publication. "You mean like in these silly stories? Do be assured, miss, it is not the fiction that interests me, but the facts."

"And what are those facts?"

His expression sobered. "That we are one with the Earth which gives us life. That we are connected, all of us. To each other and to the creatures around us, to the forests and the fields and the oceans. There is a great deal to be learned from meditation and service to a community. There is wisdom to be gained from silence. More wisdom than in what I learned in all the years I worried about how many candles I should order for the Christmas celebrations or how I might keep the choirmaster and the organist from going at each other's throats when they did not agree on the music for a Sunday service. Life is simpler with Master. Are you . . ." He looked over my sturdy cloak and my traveling boots. "Are you perhaps a Seeker?"

I could hardly lie to a man who was so genuine, but I could skirt the complete truth. "I have questions that need to be answered and I think I may find those answers with the Children."

"Yes. Yes." He was thrilled to find a fellow devotee. "Only, you are not expecting what you find in the count's stories, are you? For I tell you, miss, the Children are poorly represented by this Orlando fellow. Well . . ." He gave his shoulders a shake. "Except for when he writes about the ghost, of course."

For a few moments, I was too taken aback to reply, and Phoenix knew it. That would explain his nervous laugh.

"I know. I know." He held up one hand to stop what he was sure would be my statement of incredulity. "I thought it a fiction, too, when I first heard the story. Until I saw the specter with my own eyes there in the ruin of Alburn Abbey, where we pray and meditate."

At the same time his statement sent a shiver up my spine, my sensibleness warned me not to be taken in by such nonsense. "A ghost? And how does Master explain that?"

"He doesn't need to," Phoenix assured me. "If we are one with the universe, then so are we one with all its secrets. Oh yes, you'll see. The abbey, the old monks' quarters where we are housed, the forests that surround us . . . it is all magical. It is hardly a surprise there are spirits about."

"And this Count Orlando, he's written about this ghost?"

His sigh said it all. "He has. Though he's added weeping and wailing, and my goodness, in number four, he had the spirit strangle a Seeker. Such nonsense!" He looked at the penny dreadful and wrinkled his nose. "You've read them?"

"Not all," I told him.

"Then take a look at this one." He passed it to me. "It includes a letter from the count to his readers. In it, he talks about how he has risked his own safety to learn the truth about the Children. But then, my goodness, he doesn't speak one word of truth about them at all!"

I paged through the penny dreadful and found the letter he spoke of. It was accompanied by a photograph, not of the face of Count Orlando (who claimed that if the Children discovered his true identity, his life would be in danger) but simply of his hands where they were poised against a desk. There was a sheaf of papers in front of him, a quill (how terribly old-fashioned!) in one hand. There was little else that could identify him other than the ring he wore on the pinkie finger of his left hand. It looked to be gold and featured a larger diamond in the center flanked by two smaller stones.

"If only this count fellow would give the Children their due." I had been so distracted looking at the photograph, I wasn't following Phoenix's chattering, but if he noticed, he didn't care. He simply went right on. "Then he would learn that there's a great deal that goes on within the compound that is good. And he wouldn't besmirch the reputation of a man like Master. Imagine such libelous aspersions. I do believe if Master was not so gentle a creature, he might be moved to do violence against the man!"

"Do you suppose that has something to do with what happened at the station the other night?" I asked him.

"Happened? At the station?" Phoenix wrinkled his nose. "I cannot help you there, for I was not at the Finsbury Park oration. I had other business to attend to before I departed London forever. Something reprehensible happened?"

"Someone tried to abduct one of the Novices."

His mouth fell open. "And is the Novice . . ." He could barely speak the words. "Was the person hurt?"

The longer I waited to hear from Eli after the incident, the more I was sure that I would not. I certainly hoped Eli was hurt by my defense of the Novice, but this, of course, was not what Phoenix meant. "The Novice managed an escape. She boarded the train with the others."

He pressed a hand to his heart. "Thank goodness. It wasn't one of the young girls, was it? I would hate to see their spirits dulled by violence."

"She had red hair."

"Ah." He nodded. "That one."

"Who is she?"

"Her name is Luna. Before she came to us . . ." He lifted his shoulders and let them flop again. "I've heard her called Birdie, but I know nothing more about the girl. But then, that is the whole point, isn't it? We are all seeking a new life, and in that new life, we all find our new identities. Our old names, our pasts, none of it matters any longer."

"Yet she mattered to someone. So much so that he tried to carry her off."

He shook his head with disgust. "Such dangers are why we never travel alone. And I daresay if it wasn't for Count Orlando none of it would have happened. People either think we have lost our minds and our souls and they want to save us, or they are degenerates who believe Orlando's claptrap and they wish to involve our women in their depravity. Orlando should be taken before a judge, that is what I believe. He should be made to pay for his libel." Phoenix pressed his lips into a hard line and grumbled, "Or worse."

It was hardly what I expected from a retired clergyman who now believed in his oneness with the universe, but I had no chance to query him further on the Children. The train jolted to a start, and Phoenix put his head back. He was soon snoring softly.

I had no such luxury. I took out my desk and slipped comfortably into the persona of my nom de plume. As Miss Hermione I answered letters, offering sage bits of advice on the proper way to host a luncheon, the intricacies of wearing the proper gloves to the opera, and how much was too much sugar to include in a blancmange.

The tedium of it all was almost enough to make me grateful for the mental stimulation of considering Luna's near abduction and the Thuringers' quandary.

It did not, however, make me feel one bit better about Eli.

Dear Miss Hermione,

One teapot or two? It is such a dilemma. As I am hosting a tea for the ladies who sit with me on my church's Committee Against the Disorderly Poor, I must know the answer.

My cousin, Rose, insists on one so that all guests are served from the same pot. My neighbor, Mrs. Garnier, a lovely woman in spite of her being French, says two, so that assam and also bohea may be prepared and the guests decide which tea they would most like to drink.

Like all of your readers, I am convinced you surely know best, Miss Hermione, for your vast experience must certainly include attending and hosting many such events.

What say you? One pot or two?

A Concerned Hostess

Dear Concerned Hostess,

It seems to me it is not so important how many different teas you serve so long as those teas are of quality and are properly prepared. A weak assam surely has no appeal. A Ceylon that is too strong is, in its own way, just as unpleasant.

One pot or two? I will leave the decision to you, Concerned Hostess. For now, I think it might be best if you spend less time worrying about the tea you serve and more time considering that if you included those who you call the Disorderly Poor at your table, you might find them not so disorderly after all. And you, yourself, would surely not be as poor.

Miss Hermione

Chapter 5

We changed trains at Peterborough and again at Nottingham, and by the time we arrived at the market town of Burton upon Trent, a place known for its breweries, I was bone-tired. Aside from being jostled by the train, I had taken care of all of Miss Hermione's correspondence and the good Phoenix had woken and regaled me with more stories of the Children of Aed. Oh, how I longed for peace, quiet, and a long nap.

Our journey, though, was not yet over. There was a pony trap waiting for us at the station and while the two Adepts (those acolytes who wore blue, or so Phoenix explained) who'd come with us from London squeezed onto the seat at the front of it with the yellow-robed driver, Phoenix and I climbed into the back of the cart and sat as we had in the train, facing each other. We were joined there by two shabby girls whose constant giggling might have rattled my nerves if not for the fact that I was so stunned by the last of our traveling companions, the man from Finsbury Park, the rude fellow who wore the lion stickpin.

The girls sat next to Phoenix, and so, without greeting me or even meeting my eyes, the man took a seat at my side. I'd barely had time to think what he might be doing there when our trunks were loaded, the trap started forward, and Phoenix encouraged introductions.

"Joan." The girl with buck teeth and straw-colored hair poked a finger at herself and tittered while she was doing it. "And this 'ere," she added, turning that finger to the other girl, "is Kitty. Come from London, we did, so that we might . . ." Her face flushed scarlet. "That is, so that we might—"

"We'll be meetin' Master," Kitty chimed in. She chortled and her wide-open mouth revealed that two of her front teeth were missing. "Been readin' all about 'im because Joan here—"

"I do the readin'," Joan explained. "On account of how Kitty cannot. And oh!" She pressed both her hands to her ample bosom. "How Master does set a girl's heart a'racin' in them stories. So you see, we left service with old Mrs. Beechum—"

"She what smells like a horse's stall and does not give us a day away or enough to eat."

"And we come here. To be what Count Orlando calls . . ." Proud of herself for remembering word for word what was apparently a part of the stories, Joan sat tall and pronounced, "among the legions of Master's sex slaves."

Phoenix and I exchanged looks, but neither of us bothered to try to contradict this unfortunate ambition. It wouldn't have mattered if we had, as Joan's and Kitty's renewed giggles drowned any response.

"And what of you, sir?" Phoenix asked, turning from the girls to the man with the stickpin. "As we will be together at the compound, we must certainly get acquainted. Who do we have the pleasure of traveling with?"

The man grunted. "Pullman. Enoch Pullman."

"And Enoch . . ." Phoenix offered him a smile, and I wondered if it was second nature to a man of the cloth to be so kindly or if it might be, instead, an indication of how living with the Children had made Phoenix mindful and considerate. If so, it was a mark in their favor. "What brings you on this journey to seek the truth?"

"Truth. Aye." It was hardly an answer, but it was all Enoch said before he turned away, his gaze locked on the path we traveled.

So it went, with Phoenix trying his hardest to get us all to share our hopes for what life with the Children would be like, Joan and Kitty whooping and laughing, and Enoch Pullman being sullen. And I? As the trap took us farther from town, I will admit I wondered what I'd gotten myself into. The countryside here was not as foreboding as it was simply desolate. We saw no more than a handful of cottages scattered along our route, heard no sounds of cattle lowing or barking dogs. We saw no one at all except for one farmer leaning against a tree. He had a young boy at his side and the moment he clapped eyes on us, he shooed the child away. He took a long look at the Children at the front of the cart, another at the passengers in back, and spat on the ground before he turned his back on us.

In London, it had seemed that the Children were a source of amusement, the stories about them enticing those who came to gape at them with horror and titillation. Here, it was hostility I felt quivering in the air like the last of the leaves on the oak trees that trembled all around us in the autumn wind. The Children were not welcome here. They were not trusted. They were feared.

A shiver skittered up my back, but it was short-lived, for we rounded a bend and the path widened, and I was engrossed, taking it all in. A stone wall ran along one side of the path and there was an open field on the other side that sloped gradually so that finally, it seemed to meet the slate-colored sky. Just there, where the grassy field met the heavy November clouds, stood all that was left of Alburn Abbey.

I imagined that, like so many other monastic institutions, Alburn had been deserted since the Reformation. At the time, the church building would have been desanctified, its population of religious scattered or killed, its vast lands and the fortunes associated with them gobbled up by the Crown. But even then, subjected to the machinations of Henry VIII some three centuries before, Alburn was already old. Early Medieval, I thought, judging by what was left of the honey-colored stone columns that stood beneath the open sky thanks to the missing nave roof.

When the path looped, the ponies plodded uphill and we headed directly to all that was left of the front of the church. What must have once been a rose window was missing, as was most of the stone that had encircled it. The rest of what remained was hulking and ruinous and reminded me of what I'd seen of the bones of the dinosaurs. All framework, no flesh. When a wind blew and the clouds scuttled and the sun broke through, it bleached the weathered stone and made the arches that once contained stained-glass windows look like empty eye sockets. The whole of it was choked by ivy that scrambled up the walls while nettles and wild fennel poked through cracks and carpeted the ground. Ash, and beech, and wych elm trees jostled for position where once monks rang bells to call their fellows to prayer.

It was the most fearsome thing I'd ever seen.

And the most beautiful.

"You feel it, don't you?" Phoenix asked, watching me. "The sacredness of the place. It is why Master gathered his followers here. Why we remain."

"And then there's the ghost, too!" Joan squealed with delight. She turned in her seat, the better to peer at the ruin. "Will we see it, do you think?"

"You may," Phoenix told them. "Though you should know, it is not exactly as Count Orlando describes it."

"Skeleton fingers." Kitty wiggled and jiggled hers.

"Blood runnin' from its jaws." Overcome by the very thought, Joan fell back against her seat.

"And only Master can control the beast," Kitty announced. "Through his magic and what with his sacrifices and all. He is the only one who can keep it from devouring the innocent."

"Skeleton fingers. Gory jaws. Is that the spirit you saw?" I asked Phoenix.

He laughed. "It was less than that. And more. As insubstantial as the air, yet as real as you or I. Perhaps you will be lucky enough to catch a glimpse of it, Miss Manville."

At this point, I wasn't as interested in catching a glimpse of the ghost as I was in watching what was suddenly going on around us, for no sooner had the trap stopped than a dozen robed figures surrounded our cart. I did not see Margaret among those who took charge of our trunks and scurried off with them. Blue robes and yellow robes, Adepts and Novices, their hoods down in the freedom of their own community. They called their greetings to Phoenix, a member of the family returned, and gave the rest of us smiles and nods. One particularly burly fellow with a bristling mustache offered me a hand down, and after I safely landed, he assisted Joan and Kitty. He might have helped Enoch Pullman step down, too, but one look at Pullman, and the blue-robed man froze. His face went pale. His mouth dropped open. It took him no more than a second to recover, and when he did, he darted away and disappeared around the other side of the church.

Without a word, Pullman jumped from the cart and started off after him.

"Welcome!"

I had been watching the two men and wondering what their history might be when the voice that called a greeting interrupted. I whirled to find a tall woman in a purple robe standing just beneath the arched branches of an ancient elm. Her long hair was as dark as pitch, and she wore it in an odd fashion that was nonetheless flattering. It was combed away from her face, fastened with a band at the nape, all of it pulled over her right shoulder. Her eyes were amber, like a cat's. The smile she gave us fairly glowed through the gloomy afternoon.

"I am Celestia," she said, bowing slightly from the waist. "And I am happy you've arrived just in time for tea."

"Tea!" Kitty poked Joan with an elbow. "Not nothin' we ever got from old Mrs. Beechum."

Joan purred and said out of the side of her mouth, "Unless it ain't tea at all, but some mix of magical herbs."

Celestia heard and took the comments in stride. In fact, she laughed. "Our tea is only as magical as oolong can be," she said, "though come to think of it, there is nothing quite as enchanting as a cup of tea in the afternoon." She stepped back to allow us access to a stone walkway flanked with what was left of summer's foxglove.

Joan and Kitty skipped away. Phoenix followed, Children at his side, chatting about how good it was to see him again and how he had been sorely missed. I took another look around for Enoch Pullman and the Adept he'd followed, but wherever they'd gone, whatever was happening between them, I did not catch sight of them, so I dusted off my traveling cloak and brought up the rear. I did not get far before Celestia stepped into my path.

"You are the young lady who helped Luna when we were in London."

"Yes. Violet Manville."

Her smile was radiant, her face so smooth and serene, she reminded me of a Roman statue. "We are so grateful."

"And I am curious," I admitted. "Why would someone—"

My question was interrupted by the sonorous knell of a gong, and just like that, Celestia's smile settled, her expression became not so much stony as it did inscrutable. Beautiful. Unfathomable. Perhaps she had not heard my question about Luna. Perhaps she had, and like Master at the train station, she did not wish to answer it. She beckoned me to follow and, one graceful step after another, strode down the path that wound around the crumbling walls of Alburn Abbey.

We found ourselves in a broad stone courtyard surrounded by three long, low buildings. The last vestiges of summer—flowers with brown, papery leaves; herbs, still green—grew in beds all around. There was a table set in the middle of it all and on it, apples in a basket, slices of cheese arranged on a platter, dishes of watercress sandwiches, and a plate of biscuits of the kind I'd seen in Italy that were called biscotti and I knew were crispy and sweet. In the center of it all, two pots of tea and sturdy earthenware cups.

Two pots. I couldn't help but smile when I thought of Concerned Hostess.

"These were once the monks' quarters," Celestia said, gesturing toward the buildings. "One of the rooms will be yours while you're here. We'll help you get settled after tea."

We stood to the side as the acolytes finished with our trunks and welcomed us to the table, and Celestia poured tea while we filled our plates.

I easily recognized Margaret Thuringer where she stood at

the end of the table. As she handed a roughly woven serviette to each of us in turn, she chatted with a man in a blue robe. A cup of tea in one hand, a plate of sandwiches in the other, I closed on her.

"Violet?" On seeing me, Margaret's surprise was complete, her elation genuine. "What on earth are you doing here? Have you come with the new Seekers? Oh, Violet!" She was a short girl and she had to stand on tiptoe to plant a kiss on my cheek. "I always knew you to be a thinker. That explains how you found us. Why you've come. Oh, this is Albion." She looked toward the man at her side. He was young, tall, and he had a mop of curly brown hair and a long, pointed nose. "He is an Adept. Which means—"

"Someone who has advanced from being Seeker to Novice and then beyond." When I filled in the information, both Albion and Margaret smiled. In fact, I noticed they had not stopped smiling since I clapped eyes on them. I barely had time to register this and align it with what I knew of Margaret—sometimes cheerful, occasionally sullen, oftentimes demanding, just as Sephora always was—when she bent her head closer to mine.

"I am sorry to admit this," she said, her voice low, "but Sephora and I used to mock you for using your brain instead of depending on the advantages of your female charms to make your way through the world. But in my time here, I have transformed. I even have a new name. I am no longer Margaret. Now I am Hestia." She stepped back and threw out her arms and her voice echoed against the stone walls around us and sent a small flock of wood pigeons whirling from the highest corner of the church and into the afternoon sky.

"I have learned how very right you have always been," Margaret . . . er . . . Hestia proclaimed for all to hear, her voice sharp with conviction. "It is the mind that leads us, Violet, and the heart that takes up its cause. The mind that helps us discern our path toward the ultimate happiness we achieve when we give ourselves to Spirit and let ourselves be led by the fire that is Aed."

I can be excused for being tongue-tied for so long that I was forced to take a drink of tea to cover my awkwardness. The last time I saw Margaret (I could not help but think of her so) was on a rather dull and rainy day in September when she and Sephora ensconced themselves with pots of cocoa and plates of biscuits in the parlor where they pored over the latest issue of *Cassell's Family Magazine* and discussed its "What to Wear" column ad nauseum.

A Margaret with deep thoughts was not something I'd ever thought to encounter.

Another sip of tea gave me time to fashion my words. "I am glad you like it here, Margaret, but—"

She turned a kindly gaze on me, the type a teacher might use on a child who means well but simply does not have the mental acumen to work through a problem. "Hestia," she corrected me. "And to say I like it here?" She threw back her head and laughed, then she reached for Albion's hand to give it a squeeze. "It is like nowhere else on earth, dear Violet! As if Eden were contained in Fortnum and Mason. It is heaven on earth."

My mouth went dry. I drank more tea. "That may be true, uh, Hestia, but your mother—"

I didn't expect her to laugh at the mention of the life she'd turned her back on. "She's a dear, isn't she?"

"She is worried about you."

"Well, she has no need. As you can see, I am quite fine. As you will be, as well, Violet, once you learn the way of Aed."

"That may be, but—"

"Mother will come to understand my decision to join the Children. Once I return to London to visit. Once she . . ." The giggle that escaped her reminded me of the Margaret of old. "Once she meets Albion, she'll know I am well and safe."

"Then you and Albion are . . ." I looked from one of them to the other.

"We are nothing, miss," he told me. He was a serious lad with a long face and pink cheeks. "We are but an Adept and a Novice who have learned to flourish in the fires of Aed. Though I will say . . ." His cheeks grew pinker. "Our status may well change this afternoon when Master announces the handfastings."

"Albion and I are hoping . . ." Hestia nearly swooned. "That is, we know Master will make the right decision when it comes to deciding who will be joined to who."

"Whom," I corrected her, and I hoped I would be excused for being pedantic. A sort of buzzing had started in my ears, and between that and a sudden bout of light-headedness, I found it hard to focus. I shook my head in an effort to clear it. "Master decides who you will marry?"

"As it should be." Hestia nodded and kept right on nodding. "First, each female Novice will present her dowry to Aed and then—"

"Wait! Are you saying . . . ? Do you mean . . . ?" I could not get my brain to work through the problem. I knew only that something didn't sound right. It was one thing to think of all these happy people living in the countryside, sharing their lives and their work. But to know there was money involved?

My dear, late papa had always told me I had far too suspicious of a mind. He was a wise man. The back of my neck prickled. My stomach knotted. I had never imagined those who joined the Children might pay for the privilege of being accepted into the fold. Was it, in fact, why "Hestia" was here, because Master knew she was a child of wealth and privilege? And where would her fortune go once she married this lad with the unruly hair?

Before I had a chance to inquire, Master strode into the courtyard and a hush as deep as the ages that enveloped Alburn settled over the assemblage.

"My dear friends!" Master bestowed a smile all around. Somehow, I wasn't surprised when everyone smiled back. "Celestia, you have once again outdone yourself by way of welcoming our Seekers." He held out a hand and she stepped forward and took it. "And all of you dear newcomers . . ." One by one, he picked us out in the crowd. Joan and Kitty, who squealed with delight. Phoenix, whom he looked on with genuine fondness. Not Pullman. For Enoch Pullman had not joined us for tea. Master's gaze lighted on me, and he tipped his head in acknowledgment.

"We have important work to do here today," Celestia told him. "Novices and Adepts, promised to each other. The handfastings will take place at the full moon. Novices, step forward."

When "Hestia" made a move, I stopped her, one hand on her arm. "You don't need to do this," I told her. "Not now. Come back to London with me. Go home and consult with your parents. Hear their advice. Learn from their wisdom."

Her only response was a smile. She pulled away from me and walked to Master's side. She was joined there by another girl who emerged from one of the monks' cells carrying a small parcel wrapped in fabric. Luna, who had come to the Children called Birdie and whose near abduction was clouded in secrecy.

"Novices," Master's voice rang against the ancient stones, "what have you brought to honor Aed?"

Hestia reached into the pocket of her robe and removed three objects—a silver fountain pen, a pearl bracelet, a gold pocket watch—and damn me, but again, my suspicions got the best of me. These were small things that might be overlooked in a home as fine as the Thuringers'. Things Hestia might have pinched back when she was simply Margaret and learned it would cost her a dowry to be accepted by the Children.

She gave the gifts to Master, who handed them off to Celestia.

It was then Luna's turn. She unwrapped the contents of the packet she carried and I saw a flash of brilliant green and a sparkle like the sun off the waters of the Indian Ocean. Emeralds and diamonds set in gold. A bracelet that was more than simply exquisite, it must certainly have been worth a good deal.

"Luna is a girl of some wealth, Papa," I whispered. "Tell me now I am too suspicious."

Oh, how I wished Papa were there to answer and offer me advice! Instead, I could do nothing more than stand there, powerless, watching the rest of the proceedings through a sort of haze brought on by a combination of travel weariness and the shock of all I'd just learned.

"Adepts," Master called out.

Albion stepped to the center of the courtyard at the same time the man with the bristling mustache, the one who'd helped me from the pony trap, emerged from somewhere near the church.

"We all know," Master said, "how sacred this occasion is."

"Ooh!" I heard Joan purr her excitement. "A sacred occasion. You know what that means, Kitty, my girl. There is sure to be an orgy."

If Master heard the comment, he did not acknowledge it. Instead, he held out a hand to Luna and she took it. "Today you will be promised to the man you will spend the rest of your life with," he told her. "The two of you will be helpmates, cherishing and caring for each other. Albion, step up to Luna's side and take her hand."

Suddenly, Hestia was no longer smiling. Her mouth fell open. Her jaw went slack. At her side, Albion stood rigid. His nose twitched. I could not help but feel sorry for them, and I was about to step forward to say just that when Albion shook himself to awareness. He would object, surely. But he did not. He did as he was told, approaching Luna with what I can only call apprehension, taking her hand, tipping his head to acknowledge those who applauded and called out their blessings, avoiding meeting Hestia's eyes.

He, then, did not see what I did. The way Hestia sucked in a ragged breath. The tears that started and that she brushed away with one finger. The smile—forced and stiff and as sharp as a blade—that she aimed at Luna and Albion, and at Master, too.

I do not believe I had ever seen mettle in the girl I knew as Margaret. Yet in that one moment, in her new persona, I watched her lift her chin. I saw her bottom lip tremble and the way she drew in a breath to control the reaction. She glanced at the man in blue with the bushy mustache before she looked again toward Master. "Does that mean . . ." Her voice broke, and Hestia swallowed hard. "I will be handfasted to Lucien?"

"Sage," Celestia corrected her. "He is Sage now, remember."

"And yes," Master said, "from this day on, you, Hestia and Sage, are promised to each other."

I could stand silent no longer. "You can't—" The words burst from me and I stepped forward, and when I did, the world around me tipped. The light fizzed. The November breeze snaked its way beneath my cloak and caused me to shiver. "I know this young lady." The words were heavy in my mouth. "She is young and inexperienced, and you cannot expect her to—"

"You are very wrong." Hestia lifted her chin and went to stand at Sage's side. She took up his hand and when she looked my way, her eyes were like stones. "I can and I will," she said. "We must all do what Master desires."

Chapter 6

"What do you think, eh?"

I was so deeply shocked by all that had just happened, so genuinely worried about Hestia, as I supposed I must now truly think of her, I had not realized that when the promise ceremony was over, Sage immediately left her side. He'd gone to the tea table and though there were only a dozen biscotti on the serving platter, and at least that many of us gathered around, he scooped up two of the biscuits. As he waited for me to answer, he crunched into one.

I did my best to force my brain away from the confusion that swirled in it, told myself I was weary from the journey, that I needed to rest, elsewise I would be able to make sense of all that had just occurred. My shock did not, however, stop me from saying, "If you are talking about the barbarity I just witnessed, sir, I think it was both cruel and archaic."

For a man who had just been part of said proceedings, he did not seem particularly distressed by my assessment. He continued chewing and crumbs dotted his mustache and rained down on his blue robe. Sage was a short, stout man, and older than his intended by at least two decades. His robe was snug over his round belly and his fingers were as thick as sausages. He obviously savored food, and his red and bulbous nose told me he was not averse to drink, either. The Thuring-ers would be horrified.

He grinned. "I was talking about the biscotti," he told me. "Although perhaps you think biscotti are cruel and archaic?"

It was a poor attempt at humor, and he expected me to laugh, but I found it impossible. My stomach knotted. I passed a hand over my eyes. "You have just been promised to Hestia, and all you can think about are biscuits?"

"Not just any biscuits." He had only one left, and he waved it at me by way of demonstration before he bit it in two. "Chocolate biscotti. They are a rare treat around here and everyone knows they are my favorite. Ah, how they cause me to reminisce. I once made the acquaintance of a pastry chef back in London, you see. The man was from Italy, and he introduced me to these little delights. I was so taken by them, I remember returning to my rooms and telling Mrs. Nibling, that is, my landlady, she should keep them in the larder at all times."

I was weary of the discussion of Italian biscuits. I could not make my mind or my words return to it. Instead, I looked around for Hestia, but saw her nowhere in the courtyard.

"Can you believe it, she refused! Mrs. Nibling, that is," Sage went on. As if it were interesting. As if it mattered. "And I'll tell you, miss, I thought about moving my rooms that very day. I would have done it, too, if Mrs. Nibling didn't have the most inexpensive rooms there are to let in Vauxhall."

"Is this how it's always done?" I asked, my mind on every-thing but biscotti. "The Novices and Adepts are pledged to each other? The Novices pay for the privilege?"

"Interesting, eh?" He gave me a broad wink I was unable to interpret. "When you stay, if you stay, you'll be expected to do the same thing."

"And do the men pay, too?" I wondered.

"In our own way, though it is not tied to the ceremony you saw today. I, for instance, made a generous donation to the Children upon receiving my blue robe. All the others have done it, too. Think those two realize it?" He glanced over to where Joan and Kitty heaped food on their plates. "The Children of Aed like nothing better than men of means and young ladies who will make willing wives. A healthy inheritance makes them even more appealing. Take for instance Albion and Luna there . . ." He poked his chin toward where a smiling Luna talked to Celestia. Albion was at her side, his expression blank, his shoulders rigid. "When they're finally married and then eventually Luna comes into whatever inheritance she might have . . . well, then the money will all go to the coffers of the Children. From what I've heard, that's the way it's always been done. If they have nothing valuable to present to the Children of Aed, those who come as Seekers are unceremoniously dismissed."

"You make it sound like a business transaction," I commented.

As if he had to think about it, Sage pursed his lips. "We must all pay for the privilege of living in the glow of the fire of Aed."

If I didn't know better, I would have read an undertone of mockery in his words. Yet he wore the blue robe. He'd just been promised to Hestia. He was one of the Children. "And the money?"

"Goes toward the sustainment of the place. There are only so many of their own apples the Children can grow to eat, only so many eggs their hens can lay. Now and again, they need to travel to town and purchase foodstuffs and sundries. Celestia handles it all. Cold and efficient, that's our Celestia."

"And Master?"

"Seems not to care a whit about the dowries or the payments," Sage said. "Is he acting?"

"A question I thought to ask you."

"Perhaps you'd rather ask him yourself." And with that, Sage went back to the table, appropriated two more biscotti, and walked away. I was so busy watching him, I didn't realize Master had approached until I heard his voice behind me.

"You are here on an auspicious day."

I spun to face him. "Is that what you call it?" My cup was nearly empty and I finished my tea. "I thought it rather tawdry. Are you trying to live up to the reputation you've earned from Count Orlando?"

He bristled. "Does it seem so to you?"

"It seems to me that girls who are not old enough to know their own minds—"

"Are married off every day in this country, and we both know the results can be terrible. Here, we take a great deal of time to decide who will be handfasted. We pray. We meditate on it. Aed inspires us so that by the time we announce our decision, we are sure our disciples will be loved and cherished by those they are pledged to. But . . ." He offered a smile. "I hardly wish to argue with you, Miss Manville. I thought you might allow me to guide you through the grounds. Then, perhaps, you'll have a better understanding of the Children and all we do here."

I fell into step beside him. "Your quarters are there," he said, pointing to the buildings Celestia had already singled out. There was a stone path between two of the buildings and we started down it and stepped out to a panorama that took my breath away. Here was the rest of what had once been the imposing monastic complex, most of it tumbled into ruins, stone buildings with crumbling walls, the remains of workshops and barns. Beyond it all was an orchard and to the right of that, gardens that were neatly tended, a shed with sheep and cows roaming nearby. There, the rise where Alburn stood sloped to rolling fields, and at the bottom of them was a forest. A glistening river twisted through the trees. On the far side of the trees, the country opened up again to rolling hills. Silhouetted against the slate sky was a castle, its turrets poking into the sky like a dragon's teeth.

"Each of us has a job within our community, just as the monks once did," Master explained. "Some work with the livestock, others tend to the gardens. We have an Adept who is skilled with herbs and serves as our healer, and another who has a fine voice so that on some evenings, he entertains us with his songs and on others, he reads to us. For now, you may spend your time as you wish. Wander and see how things are done. Visit the workshop where we spin wool and weave it. Help those in the kitchen bake bread. If you decide to return as a Novice—" Here, he gave me a smile. "—and we hope you will, you will be queried as to what most interests you and your work will be assigned."

"And what work does Hestia do?" I wondered.

"I saw you talking with her. You're acquainted?"

"Our paths have crossed in London."

"Hestia assists in the garden. She's been a great help bringing in the newest crop of carrots and she's even gone to Burton upon Trent to sell them on market day."

The picture that popped into my mind was nothing less than comic, yet I wasn't tempted to laugh. Margaret digging in the dirt? Selling vegetables out of a stall? Sephora would be appalled.

"We try to live as self-sufficiently as we are able," Master went on to say. "There's very little we need to purchase."

"Yet you take riches from young women."

His smile was thin. "It is their offering to Aed."

"Yes, of course." Did he notice the ice in my reply? It was hard to say, for at that moment the sun broke from behind the clouds and I could not clearly make out Master's expression. His face was a mask of light so bright, it caused my eyes to ache. I turned from him and concentrated on the horizon, that distant forest, the castle. Just as I looked that way, I saw a flash outside the castle walls, a single, sizzling ball of light that erupted in an instant and was gone again just as quickly.

Surprised by the phenomenon, I flinched, but if Master saw the singular light, he did not mention it. He simply turned and led the way to the church. "This is the center of our community," he said, gesturing toward the weathered stone walls. "Just as it was for the monks all those hundreds of years ago. What would they think, do you imagine, if they knew the Children of Aed had a home here now?"

"They would not be pleased. Perhaps that is why the ghost roams here?"

He was a couple steps ahead of me, and he cast a look over his shoulder. "You, too, read Count Orlando?"

"I listen to what others have said."

"If there is a ghost . . ." He shrugged and kept on walking. "We are one with the universe here, and the ghost is welcome to share our space."

And what a space it was! We stepped through what was once a doorway and found ourselves in the cavernous ruin, open to the sky and flanked by pillars that were taller than five men and shrouded in vines. Much of the church was choked with nettles and wild grasses. Where the altar once stood there were now hawthorns, the last of their red berries like dots of blood upon their branches, and blackthorn heavy with sloes, and of course, hazels, nuts scattered on the ground around them.

At the place where the nave once met the crossing, there was a single candle burning in a holder, a circular space cleared, large enough so that all the Children could gather around the fire, shoulder to shoulder.

"This is where we commune with Aed," Master told me. "As he is the god of fire, he speaks to us through his light. When we have decisions to make, he offers his advice through a shooting star, or the flash of a glowworm. We hear his voice in the twinkle of winter moonlight and the warmth of summer sunshine. In the light above." He pointed toward the clouds that scuttled above our heads. "And the light within." He pressed a hand to his heart. "This is the sacred place where he speaks to us. Do you mind if I pray?"

In fact, I was grateful for it. While Master bowed his head, I was able to close my eyes and try to gather my thoughts. It would have been easier if my ears didn't ring and my head didn't spin as if I'd had one too many glasses of champagne. The world wobbled beneath my feet and, hoping to steady myself, I opened my eyes and looked to where the altar once stood. I was just in time to see a figure appear there as if out of thin air. The image was blurred, the colors of it—yellow and red and blue—and the vegetation that grew around us in wild abundance met and melted, like a poor watercolor. The sun played hide-and-seek with the clouds, and shadows danced across the figure. It faded and grew smaller, then larger again. The sun retreated. The light grew dim. The figure vanished.

A second later, I saw it again near where I imagined the choir once stood, and I rubbed my eyes with my fists, exasperated by the maddening way my vision was distorted and my head spun so that I could not be sure what I was really looking at. My heart raced, and when I moved to start toward the figure, my legs felt as if they were weighted with lead. My boot caught on a tree root and I pitched forward and would have gone down if the sound of surprise that escaped me hadn't roused Master from his meditation and caused him to dart forward to grasp my arm and keep me on my feet.

"I do believe I have taken advantage of your kind nature, Miss Manville," he told me. "You must surely be exhausted from your travels. I should have let you rest before I insisted we explore. My apologies." He wound his arm through mine. "Let me accompany you to your quarters. You have time to relax before we gather for dinner."

With no choice, I allowed him to lead me out of the church, looking as we went for any sign of the figure I was sure I'd seen. There was no one.

"Yes," I told Master. Exhaustion overtook me and made me feel as if I were wading through deep water. I fear my words slurred when I told him, "I do believe I am quite tired."

✑

I, a thinking and rational person, do not believe in ghosts. Ergo, it was not a ghost I saw there in the church. It was a living, breathing person. It had to be. Yet the way the figure appeared out of nowhere and disappeared again just as quickly perplexed me.

I might have rested when I was finally settled in my small but comfortable room if the mystery didn't continue to whirl through my brain. Even so plagued, I was grateful for two hours of relaxation. With the paraffin lamp on the table near my bed turned low, my eyes did not strain so much as they did in the church under the dome of sky with its jumble of sun and clouds. My stomach settled. My head cleared. I felt ready, finally, to formulate a plan.

I knew I could not force Hestia to accompany me back to London. That would surely be too cruel. And yet, I had an obligation to Lucille Thuringer. After all, she was the one who set me upon the course that found me living with the Children. All I could do, I decided, was talk to Hestia again, gauge her true feelings, and determine if she was safe and happy. And if she was? Then perhaps she would spell out her reasonings for all she'd done in a letter to her mother, and I could deliver the letter to Lucille. It did not feel like nearly enough, but it was all I could do.

By the time the gong sounded to summon us to dinner, my mind was made up. I might not be satisfied to return to London alone. But that was not my decision to make.

It was a simple meal of roasted chicken, carrots, and potatoes, and though the food was on the table when I arrived in the narrow room the Children called the refectory, instead of eating, the Children were seated, talking and sipping cider.

"Master will say the invocation to Aed before and after dinner." Phoenix sat beside me, and he explained. "We cannot start until we pray."

As my mother, the child of missionaries, believed in grace before meals, and my father was often late to table because he had government work to finish, I had long ago gotten used to both waiting and praying. I didn't mind either, and the waiting gave me time to study those gathered around.

Enoch Pullman sat at the very end of the long table, and though the Children seated nearby did their best to make conversation, he answered with no more than a nod or a grunt.

Hestia, too, sat far away, but I could see her eyes were

swollen and red, poor thing. I had not seen her so wounded since the day she arrived at our front door in tears; her finest straw hat had blown off in the wind and was trampled by a horse, and she was inconsolable. Watching her with her head down, I couldn't help but wonder if her heart was broken because she had not been pledged to Albion. Or if it was more so a result of being promised to Sage, who, I noted, had yet to join us at table. The day's events might well turn the tide when it came to Hestia's decision to return to London. For Lucille's sake, I could only hope.

Albion sat next to Luna, his gaze darting now and then to Hestia. His stony countenance was a stark contrast to Luna's merry laughter and cheerful chatter.

The rest of the Children were a pleasant lot. Phoenix was to one side of me, an elderly woman named Veda was on the other, and together, they regaled me with stories, and made it clear they hoped I would someday wear the yellow robe.

Celestia did not join in the general camaraderie. She sat next to the empty chair at the head of the table, her hands on her lap, her expression blank, and after minutes of waiting with our food getting cold, she said something to the man closest to her. He nodded and rose to leave, but he hadn't made it far when voices boomed outside the door. They vibrated through the air like thunder.

Conversation stopped. Everyone held their breath. Like me, they all bent their heads to listen.

". . . will not abide . . ." The voice was a man's; that bit of the sentence was all I could catch.

". . . cannot stop me."

The reply was followed by a choking sound as if one man or the other had to struggle mightily to control his temper.

The next second, a "Bah!" ricocheted through the air and a moment after that, Master stormed into the room.

This was not the Master of the gentle smile, the kindly word. His cheeks were flushed. His jaw was clenched. His breaths came hard and fast. He broke his stride just inside the doorway, and as if he'd just woken from a deep and troubled sleep, he shook his head and looked around. He'd forgotten we were there. He knew we'd heard.

A muscle twitched at the corner of his mouth, and he and Celestia exchanged looks so telling, I could not help but wonder what silent message passed between them. Whatever it was, whatever had just occurred outside, Master didn't waste time either explaining the incident or being embarrassed by it. He raised his chin and strode the rest of the way into the room, his white robe flapping around him, and though he did his best to control his irritation, every tensed muscle and stiff movement told me he hadn't forgotten his anger. He wouldn't. His rigid shoulders said as much, as did his hands, clenched into fists at his sides.

He stopped at the head of the table and stood for a while, hauling in deep breath after deep breath. Finally, he let a breath out slowly and bowed his head.

"Aed, god of the underworld and of the fire of life," Master's voice trembled over the words, "we ask your blessings upon this food. We are grateful for your light which helps us to grow and for your fire within us that surely nourishes us, as does this food."

"Amen." Next to me, Phoenix mumbled the word, then blushed. "Habit," he whispered to me, and he passed the chicken.

Just like Phoenix, the other Children shook away their

shock. Hesitant conversations began, and by the time our plates were full, the room was once again alive with talk and the additional clank of cutlery. All the while, I kept an eye on Hestia, but once the meal was finished and the last of the cider in our cups was gone, she rose to help with the clearing and disappeared into the kitchen without even a glance my way. I had hoped to take her aside and talk to her privately, but I knew I would not have the opportunity that night.

Hestia might be able to avoid me, but there were other questions that needed to be answered. When Luna rose from the table and walked outside, I excused myself and followed, hanging back to see which room she entered. Hers was the room beside the path that led back to the orchard and fields. There was a rhododendron growing outside it, hugging the wall, taller than me. I knocked on her door, but didn't wait for her to answer.

When I stepped inside, she was seated on the bed, and she barely spared me a look. "I suppose you're here because I never thanked you for what you did at the train station and you feel slighted. You expect some sort of gift of appreciation from me."

"That would seem a poor reason to travel all the way here from London," I told her. Though she didn't invite me to take the room's only chair, I sat down. "Why did you come here?" I asked her.

The way she pouted reminded me so much of Sephora's peevish looks that for a moment, a stab of homesickness hit between my heart and my stomach. I cast it aside. This was but a reconnaissance on my part. I would see Sephora and Bunty soon enough.

"What business is it of yours?" she wanted to know. "We all come to Aed for our own reasons. His fire leads us."

It was so much like what Master had said to me in the church, I had no doubt she was repeating by rote. "You're quite young," I commented.

She shot me a look as fiery as the color of her flaming hair. "Are you saying I shouldn't devote my life to Aed?"

"I am saying that the young need time to learn their own minds. If you stay here, you'll be married to Albion. Is that what you want? To spend your life with a man who has been chosen for you by others?"

Her top lip curled, she looked beyond me, and whatever she pictured in her mind, it was not pleasant. "Life would be no different on the outside." Her gaze snapped to mine. "Women are but chattel, married off to the highest bidder."

"And your family is wealthy."

It wasn't a question, so I wasn't surprised when she didn't answer. Instead, she simply smiled. "At least here, I am in Master's presence."

"But someone wants you back. Someone tried to abduct you." I pictured Eli as I'd seen him that night, cloaked in black, moving like a shadow through the night. "Did you know the man?"

Her smile fled. "Should I know such a ruffian?"

Should I? I ignored the sting that came with the question and told her instead, "Once you are married to Albion, it may be too late to go back to your former life."

Her look was pure disdain. "Going back to my former life is exactly what I do not wish to do. I have no need for the people on the outside. None of them."

"If you have a genuine devotion to Aed . . . well, I cannot say I understand, I can only believe that you feel you're doing the right thing. But if you have made this decision for any other reason . . ."

Luna leapt to her feet. "We rise very early here," she said, her voice dripping the kind of patrician condescension that made the back of my neck prickle. "You may leave."

There was no use arguing. Not with a girl as pigheaded as Luna. I knew it; still, at the door, I could not resist one last attempt. "You know Hestia and Albion are in love, don't you?" I asked her.

"Good night" was her only reply.

I knew better than to let the comments of a mere girl sting, yet I was still seething when I stepped outside. It was dark, and the air was cool. I stood quietly for a few minutes, relishing the touch of it against my hot cheeks, and it was in those moments I realized how fully I had slipped into the role Aunt Adelia had created for me; I wondered what Miss Hermione would say to Luna.

Dear Pigheaded Girl,

By traveling to the back of beyond and pledging yourself to a society that worships a god so long dead, no one remembers his name, you have certainly gone to a great deal of trouble to prove a point. What that point is I cannot imagine. Are you angry with your dear parents? Distraught at the loss of a beau? Do you wish to show him you don't need him as much as he doesn't need you, that you can go off on your own, make your own decisions, create a new life for yourself? Do you really think, silly girl, that hiding behind a robe will change your world?

I am told Aed is the god of fire and light and I can guarantee this, you will surely see the light. I only hope that when you do, it is not too late to salvage your life.

In the meantime, you might take some time and learn from the Children of Aed. Graciousness and civility will serve you well, whether you wear a robe or not.

Pleased with the letter I'd written in my head, I chuckled. My own room was on the other side of the courtyard and I'd already started that way when I heard a rustling behind me. Not the wind, surely, for the breeze had quieted. Not one of the Children; I was alone.

Curious, I turned. I had just raised my hand to knock on Luna's door and ask if all was well with her when an imposing figure stepped out from the rhododendron. An arm went around my waist and a hand clamped over my mouth. A voice spoke close to my ear: "You're not going to thump me with your umbrella again, are you?"

Chapter 7

I might have taken a moment to savor the feel of Eli's arm around me, to relish the touch of his hand to my lips, to recognize that both our breaths pulsated to the same, rough rhythm—if I wasn't so completely overwhelmed by the anger that shot through me.

I ripped myself from his grasp and spun to face him, my fists on my hips. "What are you doing here?" I demanded.

"What are *you* doing here?" he countered.

I was not about to give him the satisfaction of an answer. Instead, I looked him up and down, assessing his dark clothes, his boots sturdy enough for tramping through countryside, his knitted cap, of the type seamen wear, pulled low on his head. "Lurking in the shadows. Dressed as a thief might be. You've come for Luna. Just as you did at the Finsbury Park station."

Perhaps it was the moonlight that added a twinkle to his eyes. "Would you have taken so mighty a swing at just any ruffian? Or did you strike with more vigor because you knew it was me? And how did you know, anyway?"

"Oh, I knew," I told him. "There are not many who would have the cheek to attempt something so outrageous in so public a place. Besides, when it was all over and I pulled myself from the pavement where you left me, I found your cuff link."

"It's one of my favorites. Do you still have it? I would very much like it returned."

I glared at him. "I should have swung harder."

Perhaps he agreed with me. It would explain the momentary look of repentance that crossed his face. But then, in the milky moonlight, I may have been making more of the expression than I should. "You weren't hurt, were you?" he asked.

"Were you?"

"If you must know, the backs of my knees are still bruised."

"And yet, you managed to run away quite quickly."

"Which allowed me to be here with you tonight."

"You are not here with me. And you are not here because of me. You are here for Luna. Why?"

Eli was an American and as bold as I'd heard people of that nationality can be. He had the brass to offer a smile as scorching as my anger. "Stop asking questions long enough to give me a chance to tell you how pleased I was to bump into you on Bonfire Night."

"Pleased?" When I realized my voice ricocheted through the courtyard, I lowered it to a rough whisper. "You have an odd way of showing it."

I will say this much for him, he spared me any awkwardness. He didn't ask for clarification, so I didn't need to admit how wounded I was to realize he'd been in London and hadn't contacted me. "I've been rather busy," he said, and really, he should have known that is hardly an explanation any woman finds acceptable when it comes to such matters. "It took a good deal of tracking to find the girl in the first place. It occupied me for weeks. Then after the debacle at the train station, I left town immediately. I've been in a charming little inn in Burton upon Trent ever since."

"Waiting for the right time to try your hand again at an abduction."

His curt nod was all the confirmation I needed.

"Why?" I wanted to know.

"Because I'm being paid very well to do it."

"Why?"

"Because . . ." Something about the way he shifted his shoulders told me he was going to acquiesce sooner or later and explain himself. This in itself might have been quite satisfying if the smile he gave me at the same time didn't reveal the dimple in his left cheek. In the months since I'd last seen him, I had dreamt of that dimple, I am sorry to say. Just as I'd dreamt of the taste of his kiss. "What do you know about her?"

It was just as well his question shook me from my musings. "Luna? She is ill-mannered. She thinks herself better than the rest of humanity, and is so dazzled by Master and so eager to stay in his presence that she has paid for the privilege with jewels and is willing even to be married to one of the Adepts."

"Is it a swindle, do you think?"

"Master? The Children?" It wasn't the first time I'd considered it, but I let the thought settle before I said, "They take offerings from those who wish to commit to their way of life, and certainly, there can be nothing to their claims of being led by messages from Aed."

And yet . . .

Like it or not, my mind traveled back to the mysterious figure I'd seen in the church. "No," I told Eli, and reminded myself. "There can be nothing mystical here. It is Master's charm that captures the hearts and minds of his followers."

"You think he's charming, eh?" Even in the dark, it was impossible to miss the way Eli's eyes sparked with mischief. "More charming than any other fellow you know?"

My lips thinned. "Far more charming than any other man I know. Especially one who has been dancing around my questions. Why are you here for Luna?"

He measured me with a look. "Do you know her real name?"

"I've heard her called Birdie."

"Yes, a nickname for Elizabeth. Elizabeth Victoria Alberta Fitzgibbons."

If this was somehow supposed to trigger an awareness in me, it didn't work. I am sure my blank expression told Eli as much, because he sighed.

"You should take to reading the Society pages. I'm sure that would please your sister, and then you'd know exactly what was happening in the world outside your head. Elizabeth had her coming-out just last spring. She was presented to your queen. She is the only daughter of the Duke of Avonton."

"And, of course, her father is not pleased that she's run off and is living here. He wants her back."

"He is not the only one. She is promised to Wilhelm Heinrich von Bausch, the only son of the Grand Duke of Kranichfeld. The wedding is to take place at the start of the new year."

"She as much as told me so." I felt an unexpected stab of pity. "She said here or in the outside world, her husband would not be of her choosing."

Eli's dark brows rose nearly to where his cap was pulled down on his forehead. "Do I detect some sympathy for the girl?"

"It does seem a cruel thing to send her to another country, to marry her to a man she probably has never met."

"She'll have a comfortable life. More than comfortable. Luxurious, I should think. And she will have the satisfaction of knowing she's pleased her powerful papa and the personage named Victoria who is his godmother."

"And you are being paid handsomely to make sure it happens."

"As I said, the girl is promised, and international incidents can get ugly. Which doesn't explain—"

Across the courtyard, a door popped open, throwing a rectangle of light into the night, and against the brightness, I made out a figure dressed in dark clothing. A man, I thought, by the size of him, and not wearing a robe. His steps were unsteady in the dark. Eli took my arm and pulled me further into the shadows. Our breaths suspended, we watched the man draw nearer and—seeing he was coming our way—Eli slipped into the shelter of the rhododendron. He hauled me in after him. There, hidden by the foliage of the massive bush, we waited, my body pressed to Eli's, his arm around my waist.

The man passed. We did not move.

Eli's voice growled in my ear. "You haven't explained yourself."

I lifted my chin, the better to whisper back. "Do I need to?"

"First Finsbury Park, now here. Have you decided to join the Children?"

"Did my aunt Adelia pay you last summer to keep an eye on me?"

"You ask more questions than you answer."

"You answer only the questions you want to answer."

"Your aunt is a considerate woman and her personality is, shall we say, formidable."

"Which you would not know if you were not acquainted with her. She is the one you were going to consult on the Continent when last I saw you."

"She has a genuine concern for you and a touching fondness. She believes you to be intelligent, resourceful, and capable of solving any problem put before you. She admires you. But then, you've probably never whacked her with an umbrella."

"And tell me, was Adelia so concerned for my well-being when I investigated last summer that she found you marking time in London, simply waiting for her to beg you to spy on me?"

He shrugged. False modesty. "Word of my talents has gotten around in certain circles."

"And at the time, your talents included dogging my tracks. Now, you have moved on to the kidnapping of young girls."

He smiled. "Those talents and others."

I had no doubt of it, but had not the luxury of letting the fantasies that popped into my head distract me. Though I could not keep my heart from racing or Eli from noticing it. We were pressed together there behind the rhododendron and so, I was sure, his heart was beating just as frantically as mine.

I did my best to pretend indifference. "Why haven't you returned to America?"

"Do you want me to leave?"

"No." My quick, fierce reply surprised him as much as it did me. His arm tightened around me. He bent his head closer.

"Why are you here, Violet Manville?"

I could not have resisted the question if I tried. Not when his voice was as smooth as a sip of fine whisky. Like that liquid, it made my blood buzz.

"Because Hestia . . . er, Margaret Thuringer is here," I told him. "Like Luna, she has thrown in her lot with the

Children. Margaret is a friend of Sephora's and of course, her mother is concerned."

"And you've come to talk some sense into her."

"That is not as easy a thing as I thought it would be."

"Ah!" His chuckle vibrated through his chest and into mine. "This Margaret, too, is bedazzled by your charming Master."

"He is not my Master."

"But he can be charming."

"He doesn't irritate me."

"And I do."

"Nor does he surprise me in dark places."

"An altogether unimaginative fellow. If I had my way, Miss Manville, I would surprise you in dark places regularly, and in astonishing and quite inventive ways."

"I have no doubt of it." Was that my voice, tight with anticipation? At that point, I hardly cared if he noticed. A door snapped open somewhere nearby and a person cloaked in yellow hurried by, heading in the direction of the church. I stepped even closer to Eli. His other arm went around me.

I cannot say if I kissed him or if he kissed me. I can report (with no small level of satisfaction) that the kiss was every bit as delicious and stimulating as the one we'd shared some months before. I tipped my head back. He deepened the kiss. I pressed myself to him. He tightened his hold on me.

How long we stood there, our hearts beating one against the other, our breaths coming hard and fast, I did not know. I knew only that it was not long enough. But then, it was difficult to concentrate on romantic matters when the stillness of the night was shattered by a bloodcurdling scream.

We leapt apart.

"Is that your doing?" I asked him.

"It is not. I swear. Though I will admit . . ." The screams

kept up, and all around the courtyard, doors flew open and Children (some still in robes, others already clad in their nightclothes) raced outside, all of them rushing to the church. "It's a damn fine distraction."

As soon as the last of them were past us, Eli slid from behind the rhododendron. He snatched up my hand. "Come with me," he said. "Now. Tonight."

I looked down to where our fingers were twined. I glanced over my shoulder toward the church and listened to the hubbub and the continued shattering sounds of a woman's high-pitched scream.

"I cannot. I must talk to Margaret. And I must see what's happening in the church. Go." I gave him a quick, hard kiss. "Get Luna and get away from here while they're busy and won't notice."

He spared not a second but went right to Luna's door. I didn't wait to see him go inside. I didn't have to. As Eli said, word of his talents had made its way around certain circles. I knew he would do what he had to do.

As would I.

❧

By the time I arrived at the church, the Children were clustered around the circle where Master had prayed that afternoon. From the back of the crowd, there was little I could see aside from the glow of the candle lit there, and I pushed forward, my steps punctuated by the continued screams of a woman I could not yet see and the gasps of horror of those gathered around. Master and Celestia stood at the front of the crowd, and I squeezed between them. It was only then that I saw Hestia there at the center of the circle. Tears streamed down her cheeks. Her hands shook and her body swayed. She let out one last shriek that dissolved into tiny, choking sounds, like the desperate cry of an animal, and she sank to her knees next to where Sage lay, lifeless, dressed not in his blue robe, but in traveling clothes.

His face was contorted in a frightening mask. His mouth gaped, his mustache bristled. In an expression of agony, his lips were pulled taut. They were a vivid shade of blue. His eyes bulged and his hands were twisted into claws. His fingernails, too, were blue.

A flash of remembrance crashed into me. I had seen such a terrible death before and had spent years masking the memory.

"What happened?" I asked nonetheless, convinced I must be mistaken, that the shock of all I saw must have jumbled my mind and distorted my memories. Certain that what I remembered could not have happened here in Alburn. I glanced around the circle of stunned Children. "Can anyone tell me what happened?"

Not one of them could pull away from their shock to answer, and with nowhere else to turn, I closed in on Hestia. I moved slowly so as not to frighten her, and when I was near enough, I laid a hand on her shoulder. "Are you injured?"

Somehow my voice penetrated her terror. As if she was not sure how to answer my question, she looked down at her trembling hands before she looked up at me. "I . . . I was here and . . ."

"Here? In this sacred place?" Celestia wore nightclothes, a thigh-length linen sheath, the color as creamy as her skin. Her dark hair was neatly arranged as I'd seen it before, gathered at the nape and cascading over one shoulder. Her feet were bare. I forgave her the acid in her voice. Such an upset can make anyone behave out of character. "What is a Novice doing here at night without a more senior member of our company?"

Master shushed her with a touch of his hand to her arm. "It hardly matters."

"It most certainly does." She yanked her arm from his grasp and aimed a look at Hestia that made the young girl recoil. "What were you doing here?" Celestia demanded.

"I . . ." Hestia's breaths were erratic and her words staggered with them. Her gaze searched the crowd. Albion stood not far away, and his presence gave her courage. "We had planned to meet," she said. "Me and . . ." Though she tried not to, she could not keep from being drawn to look at Sage again. A strangled gasp escaped her. "Sage said as we were to be handfasted, we should be better acquainted, and so we set a time. He was here when I arrived."

I remembered seeing a man leave one of the cells before I saw a yellow-robed figure glide by where Eli and I stood concealed.

"And when you got here," I asked Hestia, "how did Sage act?"

She shook her head, aligning her thoughts. She ran her tongue over her lips. "He appeared in some distress. His hands were clasped to his abdomen and he reeled like a drunkard. I knew something was wrong and I had just determined to run to find help when he fell to the ground in agony and convulsed."

It was as I feared. I left Hestia's side so that I could speak to Master in a hushed voice. "Sage has been poisoned," I said.

He flinched as if I'd slapped him. "That cannot be. How would you know—"

I cast a look around the circle, a reminder to him that this was not the place to discuss the details, and Master understood.

"Yes." He was wearing his white robe and he ran his hands down the side of it as if the motion might center him and remind him he had a duty to his followers. He raised his chin.

"I will need three of you to stay with Sage for now to guard his body and offer prayers," he said, and without hesitation, three of the Children stepped forward. He then turned to the others. "There is nothing we can do here this night. The rest of you may return to your rooms. Spend time in prayer and meditation. Think of Sage and what you can of his contribution to our community. In the morning, we will join in prayers for his passing to the Otherworld. Until then, rest easy, Children. You are safe and blessed under the watchful eye of Aed."

The Children dispersed, some of them crying softly, others talking quietly as they returned to their rooms.

"And Hestia?" I asked Master when they were gone.

He motioned to Celestia, who had not left with the others. "We will take her to her quarters."

They did not specifically say I might come along, but they did not object, either, and we soon had Hestia back in her room. I settled her on her bed and pulled a rough woolen blanket around her shoulders. Celestia and Master stood near the door, waiting for my explanation.

"My father's work with the Foreign Office meant I spent many years in India," I told them. "There, my father had dealings with those of the caste called Uppara, the people who collect salt."

"But certainly salt cannot kill a man," Master said.

I shook my head. "It was not the salt we eat. It was saltpeter, used in the manufacture of gunpowder and called by chemists potassium nitrate. I once saw a woman . . ." The memory choked me and my words caught in my throat. "She was quite young. Her family wished her to marry a certain man, but she was in love with another. She collected some of the saltpeter and put it in her tea. It is salty and odorless, I am told." I shivered. "It causes a most fearful death."

"Poison?" Celestia's voice was breathless. She did not wait for me to answer before she turned her gaze on Hestia. "You poisoned Sage? Why?"

"No!" Hestia threw aside the blanket and sprang from her bed. "I did not. I swear to you, Master . . ." She looked his way for support. "I did nothing more than exactly what I told you. I went to the church and he was already there and he was already ill and I didn't know what to do so I thought to get help and I . . ." Her bottom lip trembled and her tears started again, and when she looked my way, there was desperation in her eyes. "I didn't know what to do."

"There is nothing you could have done," I told her. "He must have already ingested the poison. He would have died quite quickly no matter if you went for help or not."

"But how?" Master's question hung in the air, and I knew we were no longer talking about what caused Sage's death, but who might be responsible for it.

I shrugged. "He must have consumed the saltpeter fifteen or thirty minutes before Hestia found him."

Master's face was stone. "Not in our dinner food, then."

It was not something I'd considered, and the thought made my blood run cold. "After dinner. He must have eaten something after dinner. And someone . . ." The thought was too terrible to put into words.

"She's the one who arranged to meet him." Celestia swung out her arm to point a finger at Hestia. "She is the one who was upset when Master announced she would not be marrying Albion. She wanted to be rid of Sage."

I stepped forward, the better to confront her. "We have no proof, and Hestia says she did nothing wrong."

"Do we have any proof of that?" Celestia asked.

It was my turn to swing out an arm to indicate Hestia. "I know this girl. She is sweet and unsophisticated. If she didn't want to marry Sage, she could simply have walked away."

"From the light of Master's presence?" Clearly, in Celestia's eyes I had no brains, or I would have understood. "Did you intend to leave?" she asked Hestia.

Hestia shook her head.

"Did you kill Sage?" I asked the girl.

She shook her head again.

"Well, someone did." Celestia folded her arms across her chest and strode across the room. "And certainly Hestia is the most logical choice."

"Unless someone else had a reason to want Sage dead," I suggested.

Master and Celestia exchanged looks. "I think not," Master said. "He was but another of Aed's Children."

"If someone has this poison, then we must find it." Celestia started toward the door. "We must search all the rooms."

Master stepped in front of the door. "And show such distrust for the Children?"

"Go ahead." Hestia's voice cracked. "Begin with mine, if you wish. Top to bottom. You help them, Violet. Tear the place apart. That will prove I had nothing to do with what happened."

Celestia did not wait for Master's approval. There was a shelf on the wall and she immediately went over to it and removed a few books, a hairbrush, a small bottle of scent.

"You search her trunk," she ordered me.

"I will not," I insisted. "Hestia had nothing to do with the foul deed."

"Yes. You must." Hestia darted forward and, clutching my arm, she hauled me to where there was a trunk at the foot of her bed. "Do it," she said, her eyes bright with indignation. "Show them how wrong they are. Show them I am not a monster, Violet."

I did as she requested, opening the trunk and carefully removing its contents layer by layer. Nightclothes. The green gown Hestia must have worn when she came to live with the Children. Pen and ink and paper for writing. Undergarments. It wasn't until I had dug through it all that I found something wrapped in fabric and nestled at the bottom of the trunk. Before I took it out, I looked Hestia's way. Her eyes were wide with confusion, and before I could decide what to do, both Celestia and Master came to stand beside me, and I had no choice but to pluck the parcel from the trunk.

I unwrapped the fabric and found a bottle, a white powder contained inside.

"That is not mine," Hestia insisted.

I wanted to believe her, but it was too late for such games. I took the glass stopper from the bottle and took a sniff.

"Odorless," I said. I tipped the tiniest bit of powder onto my finger and touched it to my tongue. "It is cool and slightly salty," I told them, and my gaze shifted to Hestia, my words colored with disbelief and horror. "Margaret, where on earth did you get saltpeter?"

Chapter 8

November 9

I knew in that instant I could not leave the Children. I could not abandon Hestia, not when the proof of her guilt was right there before our eyes. Master and Celestia confiscated the bottle of potassium nitrate and stationed two of the Children outside the door to make sure Hestia didn't try to abscond. They sent me to my room, and because I knew there was nothing else I could do then and there, I took to my bed, where I tossed and turned all night, plagued by all I had seen and all I knew.

The most obvious reason for my doubt in Hestia's guilt was that no matter what she called herself, the girl I knew as Margaret Thuringer was simply not intelligent enough to engineer a murder. Poisoning by its very nature demands careful attention to detail in its planning and a dreadful cold-heartedness in its execution. The murderer must devise the plot and carry it out knowing full well the victim will suffer through hellish agony. The Margaret I knew could no more formulate such a scheme than I could imagine her reading anything more substantial than Count Orlando's silly stories. As for her being coldhearted, I once saw her cry her eyes out when an injured butterfly landed on her shoulder in our garden and promptly expired.

Besides: Why on earth would she poison a man and stay to watch his death throes—alerting all to his death with her own screams? For that matter, why would she so forcefully have demanded we search her room? In my opinion, the truth of the matter was simple to deduce. Someone—the true murderer—had placed the bottle of saltpeter in Hestia's trunk to make her look the guilty party. And that, oh, that took an especially wicked villain! In the instant when I realized it, I knew my errand to take Hestia home to her mother had transformed into another mission altogether. Now I must find the real malefactor so I could prove the girl's innocence and save her from the hangman's noose.

To that end, the next morning just as the sun rose, I dressed and started out my door, intending to go to Hestia's room so that I might speak to her and learn more fully what had happened there in the candlelit church. I never got that far. The gathering gong sounded and all around the courtyard, doors popped open and the Children in their robes streamed outside, their expressions solemn.

"We're meeting in the church," Phoenix told me when he walked by. "There is talk of a forgiveness ceremony. Aed will speak to us and tell us what we must do."

The sun could not penetrate the heavy pall of clouds above us, and on entering the church and seeing Master standing at the spot I'd come to think of as the prayer circle, I was struck by the luster of his robe. That morning, though, he also had a stole draped around his neck, of the type priests wear. It was black and thin, and hung nearly to his knees, and it was embroidered in gold with arcane symbols. He stood at the exact spot where only hours before Sage had breathed his last, and Master's face was a stony mask. He held a wooden rod in his left hand. He neither spoke nor moved until the Children were gathered. Then, Master looked all around.

"Where is Luna?" he asked no one in particular.

Probably in Nottingham by now, and on her way home to her family, I answered in my head, but didn't dare say a word.

The woman named Veda whom I'd sat next to at dinner the night before spoke up. "Not in her room, Master. And there is no sign of her on the grounds."

A quick tip of his head was the only thing that revealed Master's confusion. "Gone?"

"Her belongings are still here," Veda told him.

"And her intended?" Master caught Albion's eye and, satisfied the couple hadn't made off together, he bowed his head. "We will pray for her safe return," he said, and the Children followed his lead.

They were still standing so with heads bowed—and I was still looking from one of them to the other, wondering which of them had a good enough motive and a cold enough heart to kill—when Celestia appeared in the doorway, a golden goblet in one hand, a quivering, weeping Hestia at her side.

On seeing them, Master's voice rang against the ancient stones and rose to the gray clouds that threatened rain above our heads. "Who comes into the presence of Aed?"

"We do," Celestia answered at the same time she took Hestia by the hand and marched her into the church. They stopped an arm's length from Master.

"Why have you come?" he asked.

Hestia's bottom lip trembled. She swayed and blubbered.

Celestia would have none of it. She gave the girl's arm a yank. "You must speak for yourself," she told Hestia. "It is no good otherwise."

Hestia nodded, but it took her a few long moments to find her voice. "I have come . . ." Her voice broke. She tried again. "I have come to ask Aed's forgiveness," she said, her answer no more than a whisper. "And to beg the forgiveness of the Children, for I have disappointed them with my actions."

"What have you done?" Master asked her.

Hestia's chin quivered. Her entire body trembled, and I felt the waves of despair and sadness that radiated from her. As much as I hated to see her suffer, I also worried what she was about to say. About why she was going to say it. She was here to ask forgiveness. For what?

My stomach bunched, and indifferent to the rules of this particular ritual, I stepped toward her.

She gave me a look so fierce, it froze me in place. Then she pulled back her shoulders and raised her voice so that it echoed in the abandoned nooks and crannies of the church. "I took the life of another of the Children."

"No!" This time I did not hesitate; I hurried to Hestia's side. "You can't do this. You don't mean it. Listen to me, Margaret, you cannot admit to something you did not do, and I know you did not kill Sage. Why would you say such a thing?"

"Because I did it." Her words tore through my flimsy appeal. "I took Sage's life." Her gaze fell on Master. "And because of that, I ask you, Master, and all of you assembled here, please forgive me. I beg Aed . . ." She fell to her knees. "I beg Aed to absolve me from this most horrible sin so that I might stay here with his Children and once again feel the warmth of the fire of his love."

Master touched one end of his black stole to her head. "Then it is done."

Just as easy as that?

A million questions hurtled through my head. Was Aed's forgiveness bestowed so quickly? And did it mean . . . could it mean exactly what Hestia had said, that she would be allowed to stay with the Children, that the authorities would not be brought in, that she would not hang for her crime?

I struggled to make sense of the thing at the same time I tried to determine if I was horrified by this miscarriage of justice, or relieved for Hestia's sake. Before I could decide, Master lifted the rod he held and touched it to first Hestia's right shoulder, then her left.

"You have Aed's blessing," he said.

From where I stood at Hestia's side, I had a unique perspective on the ceremony. I glanced to my right and watched Celestia lift the goblet in both her hands. She whispered a prayer over it before she handed it to Master. He passed his hand over the cup and spoke words in a language I could neither recognize nor understand, then held the goblet out as an offering to Hestia.

"You have Aed's nourishment," he told Hestia.

Hestia took the cup, her hands trembling so, I reached out to help her hold the cup without spilling it. I never had the chance. Just as she raised the goblet to her lips, flame flashed from the cup, then just as quickly went out again.

Hestia screamed and dropped the goblet, and all around, the Children gasped and stepped back and away from her. Like I did, Master stood transfixed with surprise. It was Celestia who stepped forward and retrieved the cup. She poured what was left of the wine that had been in it on the ground.

Our eyes met over the bloodred puddle, but only for a moment before Celestia swung her gaze to Master, her expression stone. "Aed speaks to us in signs of fire," she said. "This is surely a sign."

The Children murmured and bowed their heads in assent, but Master was not so quick to acquiesce. "Aed is a most forgiving god," he said, and suddenly, there was none of the ring of certainty I had heard before in his voice. He had been so willing to forgive Hestia, so eager to take her back into the fold. And now upon seeing this sign of fire, he was uncertain, questioning. When he looked at the girl, her eyes still bulging and her mouth still agape at what had happened, her nose red at the tip from where it was singed by the flash of fire, his own eyes shone with tears. "I cannot think that a god as kindly and forgiving as Aed would not accept Hestia's repentance."

"And yet we all saw it," Celestia said. "Aed has sent us a sign. He cannot forgive the taking of a human life. He is speaking to us, telling us we must call in the authorities."

Master would not so easily yield. He handed the rod he'd been holding to Celestia and approached Hestia, lifting her to her feet and going to stand behind her. Clearly upset, he chafed his hands together before he set them atop her head and prayed. "We ask Aed who leads us through this life with the fire of his presence to—" Master's words dissolved in a gasp that was echoed all around the prayer circle when smoke rose from his fingers.

Aed had spoken again. He was not pleased.

November 11

It was all settled quite quickly at the inquest there in the Hounds and Hares pub in Burton upon Trent. The coroner and jury members viewed the body of the man I knew as Sage who, we learned, was Lucien Tidwell, late of London. As witnesses to the finding of the body, various of the Children were questioned. I was asked to testify to the fact that I had found the bottle of potassium nitrate among Hestia's belongings. I tried to explain I didn't believe it could have possibly belonged to her, but the coroner would have none of it.

It took little time for the verdict to be rendered.

Homicide.

At the word, my heart clutched, and I stood helpless and distressed as Margaret was committed for trial and led off to a jail cell.

I did not, though, fail in my determination. Before I left Burton upon Trent to return to the compound with the Children, I wrote and posted two letters, one to Margaret's parents assuring them I was doing all I could to help their daughter, and another to Bunty. She was, after all, doughty and intelligent. She could find the information I so badly needed if I was going to make sense of everything that had happened and save Margaret besides.

It was a long, difficult day, and by the time we returned to Alburn Abbey, it was late in the afternoon and there was tea waiting for us. It was at that moment, just as the Children gathered in the courtyard and the tea was poured, that the sun broke through the clouds.

Aed was finally pleased.

Sephora

My eyes were filled with tears. My throat clutched so that it hurt to breathe. No matter how hard I tried, I found it impossible to read, for each time I began, I got no further than a paragraph or two before the words blurred in front of my eyes. Still, like the heroine in the latest from Count Orlando (she died a terrible death, but I thought instead on the earlier passages where she exhibited incredible bravery along with admirable panache), I was determined, resolute. Though my fingers trembled, I clutched the day's newspaper and did my best to read what was printed there under the sensational headline—*Foul Murder at Scandalous Cult*. The words swum. They made no sense.

Margaret brought before an inquest this very day? Accused of murder? My head ached from thinking about it, my heart slammed my ribs. It was bewildering, surely, and yet even that was not nearly as puzzling as the fact that at the time of this tragedy, Margaret was in company of the Children of Aed.

"It isn't possible." I did not so much speak the words as I squeaked them, for I had cried so long and so hard, my voice was gone, my nose was stuffy. "She could not have done it, that is certain."

"Miss Margaret? Done a murder?" Across the room from me, Bunty shook her head. "It does seem an unlikely thing."

"That is not at all what I'm talking about." Frustrated by the circumstances as much as I was by my own inability to make sense of them, I cast aside the newspaper. "She would not have gone off, Bunty. Certainly not to live with the Children of Aed. Not without telling me."

"And yet it seems that is exactly what she did. And told you she was visiting relatives." The news of Margaret's present predicament had arrived via a note from Mrs. Thuringer the evening before, and Bunty had been upset ever since. Not as upset as I was, of course, being Margaret's best of all friends, yet when Bunty brought the afternoon's post into the parlor where I sat weeping, she was pale. I had been schooled in proper household management by my dear, late mother. I knew there must be a fixed line drawn between upstairs and downstairs. Yet I could not help but think that Violet treated Bunty as she would an equal and, as much as it sometimes puzzled me, I decided in this instance, it was not only allowable, but wise. Bunty was old, after all. And without Violet in the house, I was not inclined toward dealing with an elderly woman with the vapors. I had insisted Bunty sit with me, and she had been only too happy to do so. While I heroically did my best to read news of the sensational murder, she had gone through the post and opened a letter and was reading it. Now, she set the letter on her lap. Face down, I noticed. I could not see a word of it.

"If you must know," she said, "that is why Miss Violet went off to stay with those terrible Children in the first place."

"She knew Margaret was there?" I found my voice again and it rang against the decorative plasterwork on the high ceiling. I was shocked by the perfidy of my own sister and a strong protest was called for. "Violet knew? And she did not tell me?"

"She did not want to upset you."

"And yet I might have been able to help," I insisted.

I am not sure Bunty completely believed this, for we exchanged look for look and she did not waver. "Well, I might have at least been able to talk to Margaret," I admitted with a huff. "To remind her that London is the center of the world and that she has no business haring off to parts unknown and leaving me behind so that she might listen to odd people talk about odd things." The very memory of all we'd seen and heard in Finsbury Park made me shiver and I shook my shoulders to be rid of it. "Sacred trees? Really, Bunty, there must be more to the story."

"Just as there must be more to the idea that Miss Margaret murdered someone, don't you think?"

"Yes." My golden brows drew low over my eyes. But then, I often found the effort of thinking to be difficult. I can't imagine why; it always seems so easy a thing for Violet. "They say Margaret has killed this Tidwell fellow, and I cannot believe it for one moment. Murder is, after all, in very poor taste."

"And it's immoral and illegal besides." Bunty glanced down at the letter in her lap. "You've never heard Miss Margaret talk of this Tidwell fellow?"

"Never," I assured her. "I would certainly remember. It says here . . ." I glanced the way of the newspaper. "He was old, Bunty. Forty-five. And he lived in Vauxhall. Margaret would never associate with such a person."

"He might have worked for her father."

Bunty should have known better. "All the more reason Margaret would have had nothing to do with him."

"He might have been on staff over at the Thuringers' house."

"Mrs. Thuringer has high standards. She employs only servants who are French. And they all live in. Certainly none of them are from Vauxhall. Margaret could not have known this man."

"And yet they both ended up in the back of beyond with the Children, and the authorities believe Miss Margaret had something to do with killing him."

"Yes." Worry closed in on me. Panic followed close behind. I drummed my fingers on the arm of my chair. "What are we going to do about it?"

Bunty pulled herself to her feet. "We can pray and hope for the best."

"That's as may be . . ." I rose, too, because I wanted to remind her that Violet was not the only woman in the Manville family with pluck, and standing, it seemed, emphasized the point. "Violet would not simply pray. She would act."

"I'm sure she is doing as much where she is."

"Then I should go there, too," I insisted. "After all, Margaret is in terrible trouble."

"No." It was as simple as that. At least to Bunty. "Miss Violet says—"

I darted forward, the better to try and get a look at the letter in Bunty's hand. "Says? Is that letter from her? She is right there in the center of the mystery. What does she say?"

"She says you must stay home and mind your own business."

Even a young woman of breeding is allowed a harrumph of annoyance now and again, and this was one of those moments. "And what are you going to do?" I demanded of Bunty.

"Me? I'm going to see if the veal pie you're having for dinner is done cooking. And then I'm going to serve you dinner, Miss Sephora. And then you're going to stay right here where you are and spend the evening reading and relaxing, and I'm going to . . ." Her hesitation here lasted no more than a heartbeat. "My friend, Alice, is ill, and I'll be off visiting her for a bit," she said, and she avoided meeting my eyes when she did. "I will be out."

Somehow, I managed to stand there and not react to this preposterous statement, though it wasn't easy. But then, as I have pointed out, I am not the only Manville with bravado. I waited until Bunty exited the room before I pointed a finger at the door she closed behind her and let go an "Aha!" of satisfaction. A mystery. A letter from Violet. Now, Bunty going off to visit a friend whom I'd never known her to mention before. It could mean only one thing. Violet had set Bunty a task, and that task had to do with the murder.

In spite of the shocking details that emerged from Violet's investigation the summer before, of the way my wounded heart felt like it might never recover from the horrible truth of it all, I could not help remembering the other sensation I felt as Violet and I faced down a killer.

Exhilaration.

Margaret's dilemma was certainly dire, and every inch of me ached on her behalf, but I saw suddenly the benefit of the problem. The ennui I'd been feeling slipped away and a shiver of excitement raced through me. Violet was investigating again. And Bunty was involved. They could not so easily keep me from joining in the chase.

I sat down, scribbled a message, and, being sure Bunty was nowhere to observe me, went out the front door with it. There were frequently urchins in the area looking for work, and I found one such lad and promised him a shilling if he would deliver my missive quickly to the one person I was sure would assist me.

Chapter 9

Due to a set of circumstances every bit as thrilling as any in a novel, I had found myself the summer before in a ramshackle neighborhood facing down a foul-smelling ruffian. I was, I must admit with no small amount of pride, as courageous under the circumstances as a lady of breeding can possibly be, but I am, after all, merely a woman and so, no match for a hulking villain. How lucky I was, then, that James Barnstable happened on the scene. James, a constable, provided timely assistance, and I was grateful. He joined in, too, some days later, when Violet discovered I'd been kidnapped and raced to the countryside to find me. As a public servant and a man whose family had no claim to gentility, he was, of course, not a gentleman. Yet I had seen how gallant James could be, and how brave. I could also not help but notice (for a young lady is schooled in such things) that when he looked my way, James inevitably smiled and a color rose in his cheeks that was much the same shade as his carroty hair. He was smitten, and as he was not of my station, I should have been offended.

I was not.

I found this astonishing, and I often wondered what it might mean. How was it possible that instead of the outrage I should experience, his attentions made me feel . . .

Even as I waited in the parlor, seemingly doing nothing
more than reading the latest from Count Orlando but really
keeping an eye on Bunty, I experienced a frisson of excitement. I tamped it down. As impossible as it would have
been for me to imagine before the aforementioned adventure of last summer, I had more important things to think
about this evening than the admiration of an attractive young
man.

Thus resolved, I waited as patiently as was possible and
was relieved when finally, Bunty left the house. The moment
she was outside, I peeped ever so surreptitiously around the
lace curtains in the parlor window and watched her hail a cab
and take off down the street in it. Then I wasted not a moment's time. My hat was at hand, as were my gloves. Seizing
them, I hurried from the house and looked up and down the
street. James was there, just as I knew he would be, waiting
for me in another hansom. With his assistance, I hopped in
beside him, and a minute later, we were in pursuit of Bunty
on her mysterious mission.

James and I exchanged greetings and, as usual, I watched
color flood his visage. "When are you going to tell me," he
asked, "what exactly we're doing?"

Incredibly proud of myself for being so cagey as to catch
Bunty unawares, I tugged on my gloves at the same time I
peered at the road in front of us so as to keep an eye on the
hansom she was in. "We're following that cab."

"Yes, of course." I imagined he sounded as patient when
he dealt with the common populace, and at the same time I
admired him for the skill, I wondered he didn't know not to
patronize his betters. "But why are we following that cab?"
he wanted to know.

"As I told you in my message—"

"You didn't. You said to wait and meet you and to be ready at any moment. But you did not explain why."

"And yet you came." It was something of a revelation, though at that moment, I could not begin to understand what it meant or why at the thought, warmth encircled my heart. Yet I understood I could not be distracted by it. I must keep my mind on the task at hand. To that end, I felt a diversion was in order, for the sake of both the blush in James's cheeks and my own errant thoughts. It was the perfect moment to present him with the gift I'd brought him, and I took the piece of cold veal pie wrapped in a tea towel from my reticule. He gladly started in on it with gusto.

While he enjoyed the pie, I set my hat upon my head. It was French, a postilion with a high crown, the right side of the brim cocked at a jaunty angle. The color was cocoa, and it matched the gown I wore beneath my mantle. I wondered if James noticed, as I had when I readied myself for the evening's adventure, that the rich autumnal color brought out the golden highlights in my fair hair.

He was, I think, too hungry to consider matters of fashion.

"You must have worked hard all day," I said. "And you are certainly hungry. And tired, too, I would wager."

James nodded. He had just taken another bite and he knew better than to talk with his mouth full. At least the lower classes are taught that much.

Another epiphany washed over me. "And still, you are willing to help me."

He stopped chewing and one corner of his mouth lifted in a smile. "You said it was important."

"It is." I turned in my seat, the better to see him when I delivered the news. "My friend, Margaret Thuringer, has been brought before an inquest. She is accused of murder.

Violet is on the scene, and I do believe she has asked Bunty for help in the investigation designed to prove Margaret's innocence."

James took another bite and nodded. He was still in his blue uniform but no longer wearing the blue-and-white-striped band on his left forearm that showed him to be on duty. "You wish to learn what Bunty knows."

"I doubt she knows anything. Not as of yet. But I do believe Violet has tasked her with gathering information, and I chafe at the fact that they do not believe me to be intelligent enough to assist. I must help. Margaret is my dearest friend. Yet how can I be of assistance if I don't have all the facts? It is so typical of Violet to want to keep me from the excitement. Well . . ." I sat up straight, my spine as inflexible as my determination. "I must discover what Bunty knows and what she is going to tell Violet—and since Bunty is not willing to share her plan with me, I have no choice but to follow her."

He had just popped the last bite of the pie into his mouth, but James neither chewed nor swallowed. He stared at me for a long moment, and did not move again until the hansom clattered into and out of a rut in the road. Then he swallowed and pounded his chest with his fist. "You are surprisingly resourceful, Miss Sephora," he told me. "And so steadfast in the name of your friendship with Margaret. Please forgive me if I am being too forward, but I cannot help but admire your mettle."

What young lady wouldn't puff with self-satisfaction at such a compliment? Still, I did not lose sight of the serious nature of our undertaking. "Margaret cannot be guilty," I told James. "I am sure of it. And we must prove it."

"And Bunty?" he asked.

"Bunty has not been forthcoming. That's why we must

take matters into our own hands. That way, we can help Margaret as well as Bunty. Bunty is, after all, quite old, isn't she? It isn't wise for her to be out in the city alone. While we learn what she learns, we can also watch her and assure her safety."

"I am honored to help you do it," James told me, and bowed as much from his waist as he was able to there in the cab.

I turned away before he could see the color that must surely accompany the heat I felt shoot into my cheeks. And so, occupied with thoughts of what Bunty was up to and what might be happening to Violet and why sitting next to James had the odd effect of making me feel as unsettled as if my stomach was filled with butterflies, we continued our journey past Regent's Park and through Mayfair. The swirl of London was all around us, making me think again how odd it was that Margaret would leave all the wonders of the city to pursue a simple and simply boring life with the Children. Yet as gloomy as the thought was, I was glad for it when Hyde Park came into view to our right. Then my heart clutched. My breath caught. This was the very place where I'd had trysts with the man I thought I loved, the man I thought loved me, and I felt both the weight of longing and the sting of regret. I had been a fool for love in every way.

Could James have known the misery that pricked at my heart? I could not say. I only know he chose that very moment to divert my dark thoughts with conversation. "We are not far from the Queen's home at Buckingham Palace," he said.

"Yes." I leaned forward for a better look, but the palace was far from sight. "And from Piccadilly, too."

Even at that time of the evening, the road as we approached Piccadilly became more densely crowded. Horses and carriages pressed around us. Fine equipage shared the way with shabby growlers. We slowed nearly to a halt and, as eager as I was to move forward and discover what secret plan Violet and Bunty had devised, I knew I had no cause to worry. I still had eyes on Bunty's hansom; it inched through traffic much as we did.

Watching it, I thought of the way Violet always theorized in such situations and how, like her, I must draw conclusions from the evidence before me. "Bunty must be going to meet someone of importance," I said. "There are many fine residences nearby. How might someone there help Margaret, do you think?"

James shrugged. "We cannot know."

And we did not, not until we untangled ourselves from the traffic much as the hansom in front of us did, and we followed it farther south and toward the river.

"I do believe we are headed to Vauxhall," James surmised.

I had anticipated a more elegant destination. I wrinkled my nose and plopped back against the seat. "I do not frequent places south of the river."

And yet it seemed he was correct. Our cab clattered over Vauxhall Bridge, and far below, I saw the Thames, twisting and muddy, moving to the sea.

"The old Vauxhall Pleasure Gardens." On the far side of the bridge, James pointed to our left at the place where the gardens once stood. Bunty's cab did not stop even there. It continued on, and so did we. Here, the road was not as wide as it had been north of the river, the buildings were not so impressive. In fact, when our cab turned as Bunty's did, when it made its way down twisted streets, we found ourselves in a portion of town that was as far from the wonders of Mayfair and Piccadilly as the Earth was from the moon.

I'd been told that Vauxhall had once been fashionable.

Obviously, those days were long ago. Now, the area was a mix of workmen's homes and industry. Factories belched smoke. Chimneys spewed ash. The residences looked not as poor, I thought, as they were simply nondescript. We passed any number of them before Bunty's hansom stopped before a brick building that stood on the corner where one street intersected another. Bunty alighted and went to the front door and I leaned forward, eager to watch and see what might happen. When James ordered our cabman to drive on, I tugged at his sleeve.

"We cannot keep driving. We need to see what Bunty is going to do, who she is going to meet," I said.

He did not argue this point, merely instructed our driver to take us around the corner and stop there.

He hopped out of the hansom. "I suppose there is no use telling you to stay here and wait," he said, at the same time he offered me a hand down.

Side by side, we inched toward the corner of the building, and then I understood exactly what James had in mind. From here, we couldn't be seen. But we could hear Bunty quite clearly.

"I'm looking for a Mrs. Nibling," Bunty said.

"And you have found her." The voice of the other woman was curt, her words making it clear she did not take kindly to being bothered.

"It's about Mr. Lucien Tidwell," Bunty told her.

"Tidwell," I whispered to James. "That is the man Margaret is said to have killed."

Mrs. Nibling sniffed. "Gone and got himself murdered. You must know that. Everyone in London does. The newspapers fairly scream the stories about Mr. Tidwell and them heathen Children." Her voice faded. She must have stepped back into the house. "There is nothing I can tell you about what happened to him."

"No. I don't believe you can." Was that Bunty speaking? I was sure of it, yet she sounded so different. Her voice contained a note of sweetness the likes of which I'd never heard her use before. It wasn't as if she was pleading. I knew Bunty well enough to know that would never happen. It was more as if she knew Mrs. Nibling might be caught and reeled in, like a fish on a hook, if only she used the right bait. "But I do believe you can tell me something of the man. After all, Mr. Tidwell, he's let rooms from you for some time, hasn't he? Near on three years."

"It's been four that he's lived here, and now he's gone, I will lose that much of my income."

There was a long silence and I dared not peek around the building to see what was happening, yet I could imagine it. Mrs. Nibling had made it clear her funds had been affected by Lucien Tidwell's death. It was time for Bunty to do something about it.

Apparently, she did, for a second later, I heard the satisfying clink of coin against coin as Mrs. Nibling weighed the money Bunty gave her in one hand.

She was content. She went on. "Mr. Tidwell and me, we were not friends."

"Of course not! A respectable woman such as yourself? And a man like Tidwell?" Bunty added the tiniest huff to her statement, enough to let Mrs. Nibling know the very idea was impossible, and it occurred to me to wonder how Bunty might know anything at all about either Mrs. Nibling or Tidwell. She was not acquainted with this Mrs. Nibling. And she certainly did not know Tidwell. The answer was obvious, and so unexpected, it took my breath away.

"She's lying! Bunty is pretending to know more than she really does in the hopes of eliciting information from this woman."

With the wave of one hand, James hushed me and again, we bent our heads to listen.

"Yet you must have known his habits," Bunty said. "I cannot think a woman as shrewd and intelligent as you, yourself, clearly are, Mrs. Nibling, would not. You know this Tidwell was employed, where?"

"Never asked." Mrs. Nibling tsked. "Never cared. All that mattered was that he paid for his rooms on time. And that he kept them tidy. Not that I would know." The acid in her voice told me she gave her shoulders a shake to emphasize her point. "Never let me in. Always said he could do all the tidying up that needed to be done. Imagine, a man wantin' to do his own cleaning! And now, can I find his keys? I cannot, and will have to suffer the burden of paying a locksmith to come and open the door."

"Perhaps by cleaning himself, Mr. Tidwell thought to save you time and effort," Bunty suggested, her words honeyed.

Mrs. Nibling grumbled her reluctant agreement. "It did allow me to have some time out now and again. Every Friday evening there is a social at St. Peter's. Now that you've paid up for the rest of the month, I won't need to clean up so soon, I will still be able to get out. I suppose for that, I'm grateful to Mr. Tidwell, God rest his soul."

"It's a fine thing to go out and about, especially when you're engaged in God's work," Bunty told her. "And Mr. Tidwell, how did he spend his free hours?"

"At the Crown and Garter more than he was here," Mrs. Nibling grumbled. "Man never met a pint of ale or a glass of gin he refused."

"That seems odd, don't you think?" I asked the question of James, sure to keep my voice to a whisper. "A man who loves drink would not easily give it up, would he? Not even for the sake of the Children."

Again, James waved a hand to quiet me, and it was just as well or we wouldn't have heard Bunty give Mrs. Nibling her thanks or the instructions she gave to her driver when she returned to her cab.

"The Crown and Garter," Bunty ordered, and after hers started on its way, James and I hurried back to our hansom and fell into place behind her.

"Bunty at a pub!" The very thought was impossible, and my voice betrayed both my disbelief and my indignation. "She wouldn't dare go inside. Not without a man to accompany her."

"I would think not," James agreed. "All the more to our good. If she is forced to speak with someone outside, we have a better chance of overhearing her."

That, alas, was not meant to be. No sooner had Bunty alighted from her cab in front of a stone building with a faded sign above its door than—yes, it was nearly impossible for me to believe, but I saw it with my own eyes—she strode inside.

James and I exchanged looks of incredulity, but we knew we had no time to waste. We hopped from the cab and considered our options—walking inside was not one of them since James's uniform was sure to attract attention. James looked around, told me to wait, then stepped into an alleyway alongside the building, and I was left there on the pavement feeling overdressed for the neighborhood and utterly conspicuous. I waited for him to emerge and when he did not, I saw no choice but to go in search of him. I was just in time to see him slip into the pub through a side door. I followed close behind.

"You cannot—"

"You cannot expect me to stand outside by myself." I could not abide a lecture, so, like he did, I looked around the narrow room packed with crates where we found ourselves. "What is our plan?"

"My plan . . ." James glanced toward the open doorway that led into the main room of the pub. "I thought perhaps I might be able to see Bunty from here, to at least make note of who she might be talking to."

"Then you best move quickly." I shooed him along the narrow pathway. "We don't want to miss anything."

He sidled through the wooden crates on either side of us, and I followed along, and when we arrived in the doorway, we held back. I could not see much. The back side of the bar, a beefy man in an apron tending it who must surely have been the pubkeeper. A crowd of shabbily dressed working-men. And one lone woman—Bunty—her chin high and her shoulders steady as she addressed the pubkeeper.

I strained to pick up her voice and could not, though I could hear the man's gruff replies.

". . . ain't able to say ceptin' sometimes Tidwell, he'd be in here beggin' me to give him a drink on trust and other times, there he was with a pocketful of coins, buyin' a pint for every bloke in the place."

Bunty must have asked how this was possible.

"Like I told you, I canna' say. Always seemed a tad odd to me, the man and his habits. But I can't tell you any more about him. Saw him in here once with—" The man swallowed whatever else he might have said.

Bunty would have none of it. She stepped closer to the bar and reached into her purse. She set a guinea on the bar in front of her.

The pubkeeper's nose twitched. "His name is Daggart," he said, clearly weighing the wisdom of giving out the information against the coin in front of him. "You'll find him over at the Royal Belfort, no doubt, but he's not a man you'll be wanting to deal with."

Bunty, it seemed, did not recognize the note of warning in his voice. She tipped her head by way of thanks and left the pub.

"The Royal Belfort," James told our cabman when we were back inside our hansom. "And you'd better go quick."

I latched on to his sleeve. "You're worried. About Bunty." When he hesitated to answer, I knew exactly what it meant and my mouth went dry. "We have reason to worry."

James's expression was pained. "The Royal Belfort calls itself a music hall, but there's more that goes on there than singing and dancing. Gambling, I've heard, and women who—" He turned ten shades of red. "Well, there's other things besides that happens there, and it's not a place your sweet housekeeper should be visiting. And then there's Daggart." His expression hardened to stone. "The man has a reputation."

My heartbeat sped to double time. "A ruffian?"

"Not quite. He has others do his dirty work at the crossroads. Daggart himself stays above the fray. I've heard tell he's behind half the crime in London. And as ruthless as the devil himself."

My hold on James's left sleeve tightened, and with his right hand, he gave my hand a squeeze. Should I have been thinking of Bunty in that moment? It wasn't easy. My conscience pricked and I pulled my hand to my side. It was better that than taking the chance that James would feel the way my heartbeat fluttered.

When it comes to such situations, a young lady must know

how to divert any awkwardness by directing the conversation back to the obvious, and I did just that. "We must hurry," I said.

"We'll be there soon enough," he said. "The Royal Belfort isn't far from the site of the old pleasure gardens. Don't worry, Miss Sephora. I will take care of Bunty and I will see to your safety as well. I promise my protection."

A safeguard! A promise! It was like something out of a romantic novel, and at the same time my heart swooped, my breath caught. The Royal Belfort came into view.

Though I had never myself attended a performance at a music hall (for they are designed for the lower classes), I had somehow pictured something more imposing than the Royal Belfort. Before me stood a stone building topped with a squat tower. There was a pub to one side of the front door, and a building to the other side that housed a butcher's shop. The character of those who milled out on the pavement was, to say the least, dubious. Men who were so drunk they could barely keep on their feet. Women in clothing that, in spite of the brisk autumn evening, was pulled down to reveal bare shoulders or up to expose their (dare I even mention it?) ankles.

James took one look at the lot of them and turned to me. "I cannot leave you here in the cab alone."

I took one look at the lot of them, swallowed hard, and lifted my chin. "I would not wait if you told me to. Bunty's going inside that terrible place. Look." Together, we watched her stride to the front door just as a young boy in tatty clothes popped out of the shadows to open it for her. "I am coming with you, James." I clapped my hand into his. "We must save Bunty!"

Brave words, but I hardly felt courageous when we made our way through the throng in front of the Royal Belfort. Men who reeked of alcohol bumped into me and did not offer their apologies. Women called out to James, smiling and winking, and one of them had the supreme affrontery to skim a hand along his shoulders. She was not even wearing gloves!

He ignored it all, and I did my best to follow his lead. The moment the same young boy opened the door for us, a wave of raucous music and laughter washed over us. From my vantage point, I watched a man and woman, their arms around each other's shoulders, stagger by. I saw another woman, her skirts hiked above her knees, hop on a chair and start into a lively dance. There were two men engaged in fisticuffs over in the corner.

And there was Bunty up ahead, sailing through the disorderly crowd looking like Her Majesty herself, all the while heading toward the stage at the far end of the room and the man who waited there.

He was dressed all in black, an enormous brute with a black beard, and he stood with his arms folded across his massive chest. He had a cigar pinched between his teeth as he scanned the crowd, his small dark eyes missing nothing.

"Daggart," James said, and led me through the pressing crowd. Inch by inch, we closed in on Bunty until we were close enough to see Daggart's gaze land on her. His left eyebrow lifted. When Bunty was within three feet of him, Daggart yanked the cigar out of his mouth and threw it on the floor. Two feet and he let out what sounded like the trumpet of a bull elephant. One foot, and he threw out his arms and folded Bunty into an enormous hug.

"Well, if it ain't Red Maggie," Daggart cried out. "Where you been, my darlin'? It's good to see you again!"

Chapter 10

Violet

November 12

Dismal mornings were made for funerals.

It was a cheerless thought, yet knowing I had but little time before I had to attend the ceremony for Lucien Tidwell, the man known to the Children as Sage, I could hardly keep it from my mind. In darkness, I rose and dressed, and though I waited for at least a hint of light to relieve the murkiness, it did not, and I knew I had not the leisure to wait. Over the years, I had learned the advantages of carrying my dark lantern when I traveled, and I removed it from my trunk and lit the flame, but kept the slide closed on the lens so as to hide its light. What I was about to do was best done undetected.

Thus ready, I ever so quietly opened my door and stepped out to the courtyard and into the fog that was gathered in doorways and hollows. It slithered across the ground and filled the air with wisps that guttered like ghosts, so thick I could barely make out the abbey ruins.

There was no one about and I was grateful. Muffled noises came from the church and I knew that just as I'd hoped they would be, the Children were preparing for the funeral. At the same time I breathed a sigh of relief, I reminded myself not to be complacent. The ceremony would begin soon, and I was expected to be present. I had to move quickly. I closed my door behind me, but I had yet to move toward the cell across the courtyard where I knew Lucien had stayed when the door there opened. I shrank back into the shadows and prayed my dark cloak and the fog were enough to conceal me, watching and waiting to see who would emerge.

It was not one of the Children, but Enoch Pullman, and at the same moment I wondered what the man with the stickpin was doing in Lucien's quarters, I remembered the day we arrived at the compound (it felt so long ago!) and how on clapping eyes on Lucien, Enoch had gone after him. They were acquainted, surely, and I knew I must find a chance to speak to Enoch as I watched him slink through the darkness toward his own room and disappear inside.

I wasted not another moment, but swiftly crossed the courtyard, the sounds of my footfalls muted by the fog. Once safely inside Lucien's room, I opened the slide on my lantern and directed my light all around. Like my room, this one was small and spare. The blankets were pulled up on the bed. The table was bare, as was the shelf on the wall. It seemed an odd thing, for even when I thought to stay with the Children only a week, I had set out my personal items in the name of comfort and efficiency, just as Margaret had done in her room. Yet Lucien had been an acolyte for some time; he was an Adept and wore the blue robe. Why he had yet to settle in was something of a mystery; at least, that is, until my light landed on the carpetbag that sat against the wall, its sides bulging.

Was Lucien readying himself to leave?

Or in the four days since his death, had someone packed his things knowing he would no longer need them?

Curious, I set my lantern on the floor and examined the

bag. As I thought, it was packed. But not carefully. Lucien's clothing was not folded but stuffed into the bag as if with haste. His personal items—a comb, a buttonhook with a bone handle, hair pomade—were in disarray. It did not take much prowess in the area of investigation to make a deduction based on the evidence. Someone had been there before me. Had Enoch Pullman made the mess? Or had someone else been there even before Enoch? Someone who had no fear of being discovered and so, no need to be tidy?

These questions did not keep me from rooting through the bag. After all, I did not know what Enoch—or anyone else—may have been looking for, or what he—or someone else—may have found. I, on the other hand, was searching for anything that might give me a clue as to who killed Lucien, and why.

The bag revealed nothing, but I refused to so easily give up. Careful now with my lantern—for the longer it burned, the hotter the brass casing became—I peered into corners and looked under blankets. It was not until I got down on my knees to examine the floor more closely that I discovered— rather painfully!—what I might have otherwise missed.

There was a sprinkling of what felt like tiny pebbles on the floor near the bed and they poked my knees. I shifted uncomfortably and aimed my lantern at the floor for a better look. Not stones. Crumbs!

"Chocolate biscotti," I breathed, holding one such crumb between thumb and forefinger. Not a surprise, I supposed, as Lucien had not been shy about taking more than his share of the biscuits at tea. I followed their trail. It ended at the bed, but in the name of being thorough, I directed my light under the bed. There I saw a folded piece of paper that had obviously fallen, slipped away, and been forgotten.

I retrieved the paper and read the writing there.

I've pinched a few of your favorites from the kitchen. I
knew you would enjoy them.

The note was not signed. Of course it was not, and the
full meaning of the fact slammed into me with all the force of
a winter gale. I knew who had written the note—the person
who knew how Lucien coveted the biscuits and so, left them
as a special extravagance. It was the same person, I had no
doubt, who had laced the biscotti with potassium nitrate then
waited and listened for Lucien's screams of agony, the killer
who had tucked the bottle of saltpeter in Margaret's trunk to
implicate her in the murder.

Knowing its importance and grateful I was the one who
found it, I slid the note into my pocket, prepared to stand. At
least until a flash of color caught my eye. It seemed the note
was not the only thing that had fallen, forgotten, to the floor.
My light revealed a bit of paper in the farthest corner under the
bed, and I laid myself out, stomach to floor, and stretched until
I pinched it in two fingers. I pulled the paper into the light.

It was a scrap of what looked to be the bottom left corner of a larger piece. The paper was cheap. The colors were
garish. A ribbon of red. A dash of blue. A blotch of yellow.
An advertising poster, if I was not mistaken, though from the
fragment, I could tell nothing more. Except . . .

Caught in a memory, I pulled myself up to sit on the floor,
my back propped against the bed, and held the paper closer
to the light. Red. Blue. Yellow. In front of the lens of my lantern, the colors mingled and merged. Just as those same colors had at the church the first day I arrived at the compound
and saw the ghostly figure near the altar and felt a wave of
dizziness wash over me.

I felt no such light-headedness now, and for this, I was

grateful, for I had clarity enough to pocket the scrap. Further investigation would have to wait. The gathering gong sounded. I would look suspicious, indeed, if I was late in joining the Children at the church.

I closed the slide on my lantern and slipped from the room and back to my own, where I snuffed my light, straightened my skirts, patted my hair into place. Shoulders squared, I opened my door, confident anyone I happened to meet would see me coming from my own quarters, and my clandestine adventure would remain my secret alone.

The first person I encountered was none other than Enoch Pullman, who was just walking by and unable to avoid me. He grunted a greeting.

I was in a rather more positive frame of mind. Our meeting was fortuitous, and I intended to make the most of it. "I hope you're well, Mr. Pullman. I see you've already been out and about this morning."

"How did you—" He froze and looked at me in wonder, and because I was not looking to accuse him of anything, at least not yet, I gave him a knowing smile.

"The cuffs of your trousers are damp," I told him, pointing. "You've been out walking?"

"Walking? Yes, yes. That's exactly what I've been doing." He shook away his discomfort and again fell into step beside me, and together, we followed the Adepts in front of us. In the fog, it looked as if their feet did not touch the ground, as if they floated to the church. "It has been difficult for me to sleep with the thought that a man has died here."

"A man you knew."

"I?" He winced. "How could I know anyone here? I am newly arrived, just as you are."

"And yet the day we arrived, you saw Mr. Tidwell and set out to intercept him."

"I never did."

I ignored him, going on. "And as you do not seem especially pleased to be with the Children, I must wonder why you bothered to come here as a Seeker at all. The answer is quite obvious. You are not here for the spiritual benefits of the place. And you are certainly not interested in deepening your acquaintance with any of the Children. Otherwise, you would be more congenial. You are here because Lucien Tidwell was here. And now, Lucien Tidwell is dead. You must concur, it is all quite curious. Especially considering I saw you walk out of his room not long ago."

His face flushed, he stopped only long enough to curl his hands into fists. "I never did."

"What were you looking for? And why?"

Enoch's mouth opened and closed. His breaths came in rough gasps. "New here, got lost, thought it was my own room," he finally grumbled, and, head down, he hurried to the church.

There was nothing to be gained from going after him. I would find another opportunity to question Enoch. Now, I heard the drawn-out, sonorous note of the gong again. It was time for me to lift my thoughts to things more otherworldly.

Inside the roofless church, under the dome of lowering clouds, the Children were gathered not at the prayer circle, but around a platform on tall posts that had been constructed at the farthest end of the nave. Lucien's body lay on it. All around him was piled straw and tinder, and when I neared, I saw that tucked here and there among the kindling were what looked to be his personal items—a pocket watch, a book, a shirt (neatly folded this time), his boots. I briefly wondered if these things were, perhaps, what the someone who'd gone through Lucien's room was gathering, but quickly realized they were not. A person sent to collect grave goods would be more respectful, I was sure. I realized something else, as well. Lucien was to be immolated.

I knew such ceremonies were important to cultures all around the world, but even when we were in India, as a woman, I had never been allowed to witness one. Still, Papa had always been eager that I learn local lore and customs, and when he attended such events, he openly shared his stories. I remembered once how he'd returned home from the funeral of a man who had such means that all the wood surrounding his body was sandalwood, and how the sensual, earthy smell of it lingered in the air for days after and how its smoke hung over the town like a gauzy blue veil.

"Sage's body serves him no purpose now." Master had come to stand beside me while I studied the pyre, and from the gentleness of his tone, I knew he thought me upset by the idea of the cremation.

When I turned to him, I tipped my head to tell him I fully understood. "Fire is the quickest way to release Sage's soul."

His smile was soft; he was pleased I understood. "And it is a symbol of Aed's presence. A gift to those who follow him. It is a sign of his—" Master's voice caught, his words dissolved in a gasp of reverence; just at that moment, sun split the clouds and flowed through the skeleton pillars to shine on us.

He pulled in a breath of pure wonder. "Aed tells us it is time to begin," he said, and he moved to the pyre. I followed along, stepping up beside Phoenix where he stood with Joan and Kitty, who held on to each other, sobbing. There, I watched Master position himself near Lucien's head and Celestia come forward with a flaming torch. She handed the torch to Master and he walked around the pyre chanting, firing the twigs and straw, watching them catch.

"Lordy! They're gonna burn the man." Joan's knees buckled and Kitty hitched an arm around her shoulders to keep her upright.

"Ain't fittin'," Kitty said between her tears. "Not to give a man a decent Christian burial, it just ain't fittin'."

"And yet it is done all over the world," I told the girls quietly. "If you do not wish to watch . . ." I gently piloted them farther from the pyre and deposited them at the base of one of the massive columns. "Stay here as long as you are comfortable," I told them.

Kitty shook her head so hard, her hair escaped its pins and tumbled around her shoulders. "Not here in this church. Not in this place, neither. Me and Joan, we're headed back to London, don't you know. As soon as we are able."

With that, the two of them started wailing, and as I could offer little more support, I returned to watch the ceremony alongside the Children. By now, twigs snapped and hissed, and smoke puffed off the pyre. It didn't take long for the white shroud that draped Lucien to spark with flame, and I will admit, once it did, like Kitty and Joan, I could watch no more. My eyes closed, I bowed my head. Praying? Let the Children think so. I was thinking rather that Lucien's was a life cut too short, and that the someone who killed him was no doubt standing nearby.

I cannot say how long the thought occupied me, I only know I was so taken with it, I heard nothing more for some time other than the crackle of the flames and Master's deep baritone. His chant was so much like those of the monks who must once have sung within the walls of Alburn, I wondered their ghosts did not rise up to join in. My breaths rose and fell to the tempo of the chant. My mind drifted.

That is, until a rough voice rang out. "So, this is what it's all come down to, eh?" and all of us, Seekers and Children, Celestia, and Master himself, gasped and spun toward the apse where once there was an altar.

There stood a man of perhaps sixty years. He was tall and broad; his hair was silver. His smile, when he bestowed it one to the other of us, was not as friendly as it was rapacious. The gleam in his eye was as sharp as a honed sword. Still, it was not his looks that transfixed me so much as it was what he was wearing. Sturdy knee-high boots with rough trousers and a blue jumper that was thick and woolly enough to keep out the morning chill. Yes, that much made sense. But all of it was topped by a metal breastplate of the kind a medieval knight might have worn and decorated as a knight's would have been, with metal rivets and a raised pattern just above his heart, the letters entwined, a *D* and a *C*.

The man spat on the ground and Master frowned. Either the man did not notice, or he did not care. He marched directly through the prayer circle, his steps plodding and uneven. Whoever he was, he was roaring drunk, and when he closed the distance between us and stopped, toe-to-toe with Master, I automatically moved closer to where Kitty and Joan stood trembling.

"This is it, then?" the man repeated, peering over Master's shoulder to the pyre. I did not have to look where he was looking to know that by now, Lucien's hair must surely be alight; a sulfurous odor drifted from the flames. "All the praying and all your working in the fields and all the—" He let go a resounding belch before he let his gaze wander the crowd.

"All of you have given up your lives. And this is what it's come down to? A burning body in a place of decay. The likes of you aren't worried? None of you? You should be. There's been a murder in your midst."

"The guilty party is apprehended." Celestia stepped up to Master's side, and how she remained so calm beneath the anger that flared in the man's eyes, I could not say. Stately and serene, she looked him up and down. "There is no danger here for the Children."

"The Children!" The man laughed. His eyes were a blue as hazy as the morning, and they raked the crowd. "The fools, you mean. Hiding here and playing games, as if this were some kind of real religion. Like this old ruin was a real church. And you . . ." His gaze landed again on Master and stayed there. "It's pathetic. And this new violence only serves to prove it. It's time to send these people home. To end this charade."

It was impossible to say how Master, too, managed to remain calm beneath the waves of anger that rolled from the man, yet he simply exchanged look for look with him, his expression as peaceful as that of Lucien, undisturbed in his eternal sleep.

"We are not leaving," Master said.

The man exploded. "Get your head out of the air, boy! Can't you see? Murder is a scandalous thing. These people you have enticed here with your pointless stories and your inane promises, they have no stomach to be associated with such things. They will leave you now. Eh?" He cast a look all around, waiting to see which of the Children would make the first move. The man lurched toward Phoenix and Albion, who recoiled in the face of him.

"Fools!" The man turned his fury on the others of us who stood there, stunned. "This stain will never wash away. Don't you understand? It is murder." He screamed the word, the echoes of it choked by the fog and the smoke that curled off the pyre. "It is time to walk away from this nonsense. To protect yourselves and your reputations. Leave. Leave now!"

No one did.

I might have known what would happen next, for when men of that ilk see no one is listening to them, they divert their anger to those who are weakest. I should have been prepared. Yet I, too, was so taken aback by the man's sudden appearance, by his peculiar clothing and his shameless behavior, I did not realize what was happening until the man's malicious look landed on Joan and Kitty. Clutching each other, they fell back even as the man in armor stepped toward them.

"Stupid, stupid girls. Go home! There is nothing here for you. No romance. No adventure." He wiggled his fingers in their faces. "No ghosts or ghoulies. Only this empty nonsense and this man"—he swung his arm out and back toward Master—"who says he is your leader though he does not know the meaning of the words *loyalty* and *leadership*. A man who worships a god who does not exist, who never existed. Does he protect you, eh?" He growled and sprung at them and at that, I had had enough.

I stepped between the sobbing girls and this oddly dressed bullyboy. "It seems you would be wise to take your own advice, sir, and leave," I told him. "Your behavior is unconscionable. You cannot interrupt a sacred ceremony and then intimidate those who are most upset by it. Yours are the actions of a blackguard."

"A blackguard!" When he laughed, the odor of whisky washed over me like a wave. "Is that what I am?" He shot a look over his shoulder at Master. "Am I?"

Because Master did not speak, I knew I had to. "You

are certainly no gentleman," I told him, and when he swung around again to pin me with a look, I refused to be intimidated. I lifted my chin. "You are nothing more than a drunkard in a silly costume. And you have no business here."

"No? Business?" He pulled himself up to his full height, considerably more than mine. "I do, indeed, have business here, young woman, and you'd be wise to remember it." He snorted and raised a hand as if to strike me.

Still, I refused to move. I would not give him the satisfaction of cowering, and as it turned out, I had no need. Another man had entered the church. He was as tall as Master, as fine-looking and as golden-haired, though his face was so lean, his cheekbones protruded.

He appeared suddenly behind the drunken man and in a movement both swift and forceful, he clapped a hand on the ragged knight's shoulder, spun him around, and shoved him some distance from me. The older man was having none of it. He lashed out, cuffing the newcomer, knocking him back. My protector was not as fragile as he looked. He stayed on his feet this time, seizing both arms of the man in armor, giving him a shake.

"Father! You must stop. Now!" Another shake and the drunkard's head snapped, his tongue lolled. "Nothing here is our concern, and we have no right to disturb these people in their prayers."

The enraged man growled. "Disturb? Prayers?"

"We are leaving now," the younger man insisted, and, one arm firmly around his shoulders and his free hand gripping his arm, he dragged his father from the church. From outside we heard the jingle of harness and tack and the snap of a carriage door closing. Only after the sounds of hoofbeats faded away did the younger man step again into the church. Master bowed, once toward the pyre in honor of Lucien and once toward us to excuse himself, then went to speak with him.

Their voices were so muffled, it was impossible to make out what they said, yet for some minutes we all stood there, straining to hear, waiting to see what might happen. It was Celestia who finally stepped forward.

"Phoenix, Veda, stay here and pray for Sage," she instructed. "The rest of you Children . . ." Her gaze traveled over us, gentle and comforting. "We have prepared a funeral meal. Let us go to the refectory and remember Sage with stories."

Led by Celestia, we filed from the church, leaving not the way we'd come in—the way that would have taken us close to where Master and the other man talked—but between and around the pillars closest to the pyre. She waited outside until we had all exited, then as I was the last to leave the church, she stepped up beside me.

"I daresay, such commotion is not what you expected when you came to us as a Seeker," she said.

"I cannot say what I expected."

She raised her arms and dropped them to her sides, and now that we were away from the pyre and the air was not so heavy with the coppery odor of blood and the sweet and musky undertones of burning flesh, she managed a laugh that contained no amusement. "Not murder, surely. Nor some drunken churl who—"

"Who is he?" I asked.

She shook her head, not to clear it, I didn't think, but to banish all thoughts of the man. "He lives nearby. A man of no importance."

"And the armor?"

"As you saw, he is a madman."

This did little to reassure me. "He would like the Children to leave this place."

"He has no right."

"Yet it seems he isn't above trying to frighten you away. His behavior today proved as much."

She stopped, the better to turn to me. "You think—"

"That he may have had something to do with Lucien's death in the name of driving the Children away? I think human behavior is unpredictable, and anything is possible. But why does he want you gone?"

"I do believe you will agree with me, there is no use trying to assign reason to a lunatic. Perhaps he finds us threatening."

"Yet no one threatened him."

"Frightening, then. We might terrify him as we do so many others. There are those who believe we gather to worship the devil."

"If the man in armor believed that, he wouldn't have tried to upset you with mention of a mere murder. Surely, the devil is far more fearsome than a mortal death."

She dashed away the very thought with the quick movement of one fine-boned hand. "As I said, he is a madman."

"One who may have had a reason to want to disrupt your lives here and thought a murder might accomplish his goal."

"Are you saying he might have engineered it?" She shook her head, and that thick plait of hair over her right shoulder twitched. "That cannot be. He must surely know the truth, as does everyone else, for I'm sure it is all they're talking about in Burton upon Trent and beyond. The authorities have the killer in custody."

"Margaret?" My pointed look should have been enough to remind her who we were talking about. "You cannot think a girl like that—"

"Who wished to be handfasted to someone else and did not like the choice we made for her."

"You knew she was in love with Albion, and yet you made the choice to promise her to Sage." It was not the first time the thought occurred to me, but the first opportunity I'd had to challenge Celestia with what it might mean. "It is as if you were trying to make Margaret unhappy."

By all rights, Celestia should have decried my insolence, but as she had during the incident with the man in armor, she did not bristle. But then, I could not help but notice that she did not dispute my assumption, either.

"You do not believe the girl killed Sage because she had feelings for Albion and did not wish to be handfasted to Sage. Very well." She ran her hands along her purple robe. Perhaps she was straightening it. Or she thought to whisk away the smell of fire and death that hung in the air. "Perhaps you should consider that she might have had some other reason to want Sage dead." With that, she turned to walk to the refectory, leaving me there to think about what she'd said.

Did Margaret have another motive for wanting Lucien dead?

I had yet to discover one, but I was certainly determined. I would get to the bottom of the mystery, to the note from the person who delivered the biscotti, and the motives of the man in armor, and what Enoch was searching for in the dark hours of the morning. I would learn Lucien's secrets, for I knew that in doing so, I would also learn who wanted him dead and why. There was no better time to begin my search for answers than that very moment.

Chapter 11

Once in the refectory, I took the seat beside Albion. I am not sure he noticed. His head in his hands, he stared down at the plate of sliced apples in front of him and the empty teacup next to it.

"Have you tried to see her?" I asked him.

He didn't bother to look up. He didn't have to. His voice was clogged; I knew he'd been crying. "She must be frantic all alone and in a cell. Hestia's spirit should be free to fly!"

I was tempted to mention the only place the Margaret I knew had ever thought to fly was to a milliner's or a dressmaker's for the newest fashions, but I did not. A Novice set a cup of tea in front of me and, eager to wash away the chill of the morning, the image of Lucien's burning body, and the lingering memory of the nasty man in the armor, I sipped gratefully. "Hestia is not guilty, and we must do something about it," I told Albion.

His head came up and he looked at me, his eyes red, but a tiny smile of hope tickling his lips. "What are you saying?"

"That I am going to prove Margaret had nothing to do with killing Lucien."

He apparently did not understand, and I wondered how Margaret might have fallen in love with a man with so little imagination. I explained, my voice low enough so that it was not overheard by the Children who sat nearby, "I'm going to find the true killer."

Albion swallowed so hard his Adam's apple bobbed, and again, a smile played around his lips. "That will assure Hestia's freedom, won't it?"

I nodded.

"How will you begin?"

"That is easy enough." Since he wasn't eating the apple on his plate and I was hungry, I reached for a slice and took a bite. Simply talking through my plan brightened my spirits; I found myself smiling, too. "I will begin in the most logical place. With you."

"Me?" He was not as outraged by the suggestion as he was confused by it.

"You are in love with Hestia."

His watery smile turned into a full-fledged grin.

"But she was promised to Sage."

"And Sage is dead and Luna is gone," he said as the truth of the matter made his smile bloom. "Don't you see what it means? If Hestia were to return, Master would have to promise us to each other."

"Only if we can assure Hestia's return."

"Yes. Certainly." He popped a slice of apple into his mouth and, watching him, I finished my tea and smiled at the sight of his sudden, youthful eagerness.

"We must begin by lining up the facts. Tell me, Albion, where were you in the hours before Sage died?"

He had been about to eat another slice of apple and he stopped, the fruit poised at his lips. "Are you accusing me?"

"I'm searching for answers."

"But you surely don't think—"

"I don't know what to think." If only he knew how true my words were, for the moment I spoke them, my head began to whirl and my vision blurred much as it had the first day I arrived at the compound. "What I mean, of course," I said, gripping the table to steady myself, "is that none of us knows what to think. And if we are going to find answers, we must have all the information. Therefore, I need to know where you were in the hours before Sage's death."

Albion's brow furrowed. "At the time he ingested the poison?"

As of yet, I was the only one who knew about the biscotti and the mysterious note, so I merely nodded.

"I was . . ." A Novice came by to refill our cups, and while Albion waited to speak, I couldn't help but think of the recent letter to Miss Hermione.

Two teapots.

I looked toward the serving table. There were two pots there. Just as there had been the day I arrived. As I watched, Celestia poured a cup for herself from a green pot. She refilled the pot the Novice was bringing around to the rest of us from a blue pot.

"I was in Burton upon Trent."

Albion's words jarred me from where my mind had wandered. "I'd gone to fetch the late post."

"That evening? After dinner?"

"Immediately after. It isn't far into town and I'm allowed to ride Belle." I assumed Belle was a horse and let him go on. "She's a swift little beauty and I was there and back in no time."

"And after?"

"I helped cool her and bed her down."

"Can anyone verify that?"

"Phoenix, surely. He works in the stable yard. He will tell

you he sent me off on Belle directly after dinner and saw me return just as the commotion started in the church. I would not lie to you about such a thing. I want to help all I can. To prove Hestia's innocence."

"Then tell me what you know of Lu . . . er . . . Sage."

His shrug spoke volumes. "He arrived here soon after I did and he seemed a sincere enough chap. Only . . ." Albion frowned.

"Only?"

"I am just remembering," he said. "Soon after Sage joined us, he took me aside one day and asked about sacrifices. Human sacrifices. You know, the way some of the ignorant do when they approach us."

"Perhaps he was simply one of the ignorant."

"I don't believe so. Those who come because they've heard the foolish stories find out soon enough that they are not true and leave directly."

"Yet Sage did not. Not even when he saw what life with the Children was really like."

Albion nodded and drank his tea. "He stayed. And I never wished to cause problems for him, but . . ." He leaned in close. "There was a time when he should have been mucking the stables, and I found him in the orchard, sound asleep beneath an apple tree. Another time, we were meant to learn a new meditation to lead us closer into the arms of Aed, and as I was just about to step into the room after finishing my chores, I know he slipped out once everyone's eyes were closed. He was a part of us, certainly."

"But he was not."

I thought back to something Lucien had said to me at tea the day he died: "There are only so many of their own apples the Children can grow to eat, only so many eggs their hens can lay. Now and again, they need to travel to town and purchase foodstuffs and sundries."

"He thought of the Children as *they*," I mumbled, as much to myself as to Albion. "And as himself apart from the Children." It was a pity I could not begin to unscramble what it meant. My head suddenly buzzed. Albion's face blurred in front of my eyes. Across the room, Celestia spoke with others of the Children and, though it had certainly not looked that way in the church, now her purple robe seemed to be lit from within by a violet flame.

"That makes no sense." Albion's voice was muffled in my ears. "Sage was an Adept. He'd been here long enough to learn our ways, to be accepted into our community."

"Yes." I drummed my fingers against the table. Or at least I tried. The drumbeats echoed too loudly in my head and I stood, eager to get back to my room. My knees shook and I paused to steady myself.

"What else can I tell you?" Albion asked. "How else might I help dear Hestia? We will be going to Burton upon Trent tomorrow to sell our produce. Perhaps there's something I can do then to assist?"

Was he smiling when he asked the questions?

Did I answer him?

I cannot say, for I knew I had to escape the refectory and the voices all around that reverberated in my ears. I needed air. And rest. No sooner did I get back to my room than I fell into a deep sleep. My dreams were filled with a kaleidoscope of colors—a swirling blend of yellow, blue, and red.

Dear Miss Hermione,

It is a shame, that's what it is. The way people look at a girl all suspicious, and tell falsehoods, and spread lies. Bickering over this and that in the household, claiming things what they have no right to, making off with two good wooden spoons when no one was looking.

All because a wife done gone and inherited her dead husband's property, lawful-like.

Yes, I am younger than what was my Chester. He was a creaky old man even when I started working there at the Bull and Button, the pub what he owned, and he needed a woman to look after him and tend his every need. Is it my fault I am prettier than some what tried to catch his eye? That I am the one he chose to marry? Believe you me, Miss Hermione, as Chester's wife, I earned every penny what I inherited from the old man. And them that want to come after it now—his children and his brothers, and even the vicar what claims Chester wanted his money to go to the church rebuilding— now they are spreading lies so as to try and keep me from what is rightful mine.

What should I do? For the pack of them is saying I had my eye on Chester's money all along, and I am sore worried. They are spreading the rumor that I killed Chester.

A Worried Wife

❧

Dear Worried Wife,
    Did you?

November 13

The letter addressed to Miss Hermione from Worried Wife was among others Bunty had packaged up and sent to me, and it—or my answer—would certainly never see print in *A Woman's Place*. Yet in my head, I could not help but reply. My reaction to Worried Wife's plea only proved how I was thinking of late. Not of manners or morals. Not of what was polite or what was proper, or how Miss Hermione might help the countless women who sought her advice in their endless struggle to be better hostesses. My thoughts were on murder. Always on murder.

My head was so entwined in the subject and in the wickedness that caused killers to put their own wants and needs over another's life, I could barely wait to see what Bunty had written to me in her letter, included in the packet. What had she discovered about Lucien Tidwell? Would any of what she'd learned help further my investigation?

The answers to my questions would have to wait. That morning, I was in Burton upon Trent, and I hurried through helping the Children set up their market stall for the day, then excused myself so I could pick up the post that included the aforementioned letter. After that, I had even more pressing business.

It began with a visit to Lucille and Thomas Thuringer, Margaret's parents. They had, as was to be expected, come to aid Margaret the moment they heard of her troubles, and they were now settled at the White Hart Hotel on High Street. It took not a moment in their presence to discern how they had spent their time since arriving from London. Mrs. Thuringer sat in a corner, dabbing her eyes with a handkerchief and weeping. Mr. Thuringer, it seemed, was hardly more practical.

There was a bottle of whisky on the table beside the bed. It was nearly empty.

I did not explain how I happened to be staying with the Children or how I found Margaret there, and neither Thomas nor Lucille had the clearness of mind to ask. I was glad. Even in so serious a business, I was reluctant to reveal that I had been privy to Lucille's letter to Miss Hermione.

Instead, I promised to do all I could to help, and the Thuringers, in turn, informed me that it was a kind gesture, even though they were not confident of its success. It seems they had heard about the murderous affair of the summer before from Margaret who, of course, had the story from Sephora who, I must note, embellished her own importance in the investigation and exaggerated how her courage and intelligence were vital to the solving of the crime.

Could not Sephora come to Burton upon Trent to set things aright?

I regretted to inform them she could not and, in her unfortunate absence, the dejected Thuringers admitted I would have to do.

I gritted my teeth around my aggravation and engaged them in conversation that verified they had little to provide in the way of assistance. Lucille, it turned out, was a skilled liar. She swore she was flabbergasted to hear Margaret had taken up with the Children. Thomas was rather more forthcoming. He swore he would pummel Master if they were ever in the same room together. As Thomas's eyes were as red as his nose, I do believe his courage originated at the bottom of his bottle.

As they were preparing to put their heads together with the barrister they'd brought with them from London to plead Margaret's case in court, I left them to it and continued on my own to the police station where Margaret was being held.

It did not take me long to convince the sergeant behind the front desk to allow me access to the prisoner. But then, I have been told I can be quite persuasive when I put my mind to it.

I had, I admit, expected the worst, but as it turned out, the jail where I was taken was orderly and quiet. Except for the iron door with its small window and the guard who walked the hallway outside it, it was hardly different from our quarters back at the compound.

The Margaret I found inside the cell, though, was.

Margaret's dark eyes were sunken. Her skin was chalky. It had been but three days since she'd been taken into custody and just two days since the inquest, and yet in that time, she had lost weight. Her yellow robe hung from her shoulders like the tattered clothes on a scarecrow. When I stepped inside her cell, she leapt from the bed where she'd been seated and threw herself at me.

"Violet! I knew you'd come." She hugged me so hard, I struggled for air. "You're here to help, aren't you?" She pushed herself far enough away so that she could look up and into my eyes, her expression desperate, her voice balanced (as I suspect she was herself) between utter panic and hard-fought optimism. "Aren't you?"

"I'm going to try," I told her. "But to do that, Margaret, I'm going to need your help."

"Yes. Anything. You know I'll do anything. You've spoken to Mama and Papa?"

"I have. They are worried, of course, and they are trying to be of assistance, but Margaret, their influence and their wherewithal, it may not be enough to untangle this mystery. That is why I'm looking for answers."

Her solemn expression blossomed into a smile. "Thank goodness! You've called on Sephora to help!"

I no more wanted to dash her hopes than I wished to lie, so I avoided the subject and said rather, "We must find our way to the truth." I am not one to make false promises, but she was so pathetic, I hoped to cheer her so I added, "Perhaps then you will see Albion again and return to the Children."

I expected at least a spark of positivity. Instead, Margaret burst into tears. "Return to the Children? Oh, Violet! Don't you see? Don't you understand? I would truly rather hang from the gibbet than go back to that horrible place!"

I will admit to some confusion, and while I tried to sort my way through it, Margaret clutched onto my arm and tugged me to the bed set under the room's only window. It was high up on the wall, and the morning sunlight barely made its way through the bars on it.

I sat next to her. "What are you talking about, Margaret? When I arrived at the compound, you told me you were happy. That your life was complete. That the Children are—"

"Horrible!" she wailed, her voice clogged with tears. "The Children and their compound and the whole idea of living out in the middle of nowhere, it's all horrible. To give up the city? To renounce the theater and the opera and band concerts in the park? To live my life with nothing to wear but one of these awful, scratchy robes?" She plucked at her yellow garment. "They actually expect me to spend my time digging in the dirt! Can you imagine it? Can you, Violet? It is utter madness."

"But I thought you—"

"I was under a spell. Don't you see?" She clutched my arm with both her hands and turned, the better to let me see the spark of conviction in her eyes. "I must have been. I heard Master speak, you see. In London. And something about him . . . it must surely have been witchcraft . . . something about him fascinated me. That's why I went to the Children as a Seeker, and once I was there . . . it all seems like a dream. I was so taken by the place and the people, so happy and content. But now I know, I know for certain, staying with the Children was the most terrible mistake I've ever made. Now that I've had a few days away from them, I've had a chance to think about it and finally see the truth. My head is so much clearer."

I thought back to how I'd staggered to my quarters after the funeral meal. "Yes," I told her. "As is mine. And that makes me wonder."

"About witchcraft?"

"About two teapots." It was not the time to explain, at least not until I had the facts. I made my way to what I thought was the heart of the matter, at least for Margaret. "What of Albion, then? Were you thinking clearly when you said you were in love with him?"

Never did Margaret look more callow than when she wrinkled her nose and pursed her lips. "Can you imagine it? Me, with a fellow like Albion? My parents would be horrified, and I would live a life of utter misery. He actually believes Master's humbug and has no more ambition in life than to live with the Children and search for Aed's advice in the light of the stars and moon." To emphasize the melodrama of it all, she clutched her hands to her heart. "How would a man like that be able to maintain the life I am accustomed to? Why was my brain in such a spin that I thought I might be happy with him?" Margaret screeched. "Really, Violet, you must soon realize exactly what I've come to learn as I've been sitting here. I should have left the Children long ago. You must do the same. You cannot be misled by their silly philosophy."

"I intend to stay only so long as it takes to extricate you from the trouble in which you find yourself," I assured her.

"Yes. Yes." She bobbed her head. "Though without Sephora's help, I'm not sure how you will accomplish it. Nevertheless, finish what you must do, and leave quickly. I should have. I should have left with Sage when he asked me to."

After the significance of what she said made its way to my brain, it took a bit for me to shake away my astonishment and form the words "Lucien asked you to leave? With him?"

Margaret nodded.

"When?"

Thinking had never been one of Margaret's strengths. She squeezed her eyes shut with the effort. "Just that evening. The night he died."

"Did he tell you why he was leaving?"

"He never had the chance." Her eyes clouded with the memory. "We agreed to meet, you see. As we were to be handfasted, Sage said we should get to know each other, and oh . . ." She pounded the bed with her fist. "I was such a fool! My brain was in such a swirl, I was convinced Master knew what was best for me. I thought the handfasting with Sage was what I needed to do to grow closer to Aed. I agreed to meet with Sage, but when I got there—"

"Where?"

"To the old church. When I got there, that's when Sage told me he had no intention of being handfasted to me or to anyone else. He said he finally had everything he needed and it was time for him to go."

"Everything he needed? What did he mean by that?"

She shook her head in confusion. "I asked. Of course I did. But he did not give me an answer. Instead, he said something about how his future was now assured and he'd had enough of the Children and their nonsense. He said as I seemed a good enough sort, he'd take me along and that it would be wise for me to go with him."

"And you said . . . ?"

"I told him I wouldn't dream of it. That was before my eyes were opened. Before I came to my senses." Her tears started up again. "I should have run away with him that very night."

"But he could not run, could he?"

"No." Her voice contained the horror of the memory. "I'd just told him I would never leave Master and that's when . . ." She swallowed hard. "Oh, Violet! He clutched at his belly and made such awful sounds. Like animal cries. And I didn't know what was happening, and I was so afraid, and I thought to call out for help, but the words wedged in my throat and . . ."

The more she talked, the more agitated Margaret became, and I knew I had to calm her or I'd never learn more.

"Margaret." I put my hands on both her shoulders and looked her in the eye. "The next day at the repentance ceremony you said you were sorry for what you did. You said you took Sage's life."

"Oh, I was so stupid! I said it because . . ." She hiccupped around her tears. "I didn't want to be taken away from Master's presence. I would say anything, do anything, to make sure that didn't happen, even if it meant admitting to a murder I did not commit. I thought that would be the end of it, you see. That he would forgive me and I would be allowed to stay with the Children. And now . . ." Her shoulders drooped. "I know what an idiot I was to admit to something I didn't do. I did not kill Sage, and I do not know who did." A single tear slipped from her left eye and glided down her cheek. "And now you know the truth, and not even Sephora for all her wit and all her cleverness and all the courage she showed when she discovered a murderer last summer, not even Sephora can help me now."

I did not address this fiction. There was no purpose in it. Instead, I kept my voice level and my mind on the problem at hand. "You must think, Margaret. In the days before his death, did you see Lucien talking to anyone? Enoch Pullman, perhaps?"

"Not Enoch." She shook her head and I could see she was weighing the wisdom of saying more. "He and Master had words, of course. That night we waited for them at dinner."

I hadn't forgotten. Like Margaret, I remembered the angry voices that had split the quiet of the evening.

". . . will not abide . . ." Though I could not distinguish the voices at the time, it must have been Master who said that.

". . . cannot stop me . . ." And that was surely Lucien's reply.

"Do you know what they might have argued about?" I asked Margaret.

She shrugged. "Sage could be lazy. We'd all seen it. No doubt Master reminded him that he had obligations."

"Yet it makes little sense in light of Lucien's answer. He said Master could not stop him. Stop him from leaving, do you think? Or was there something else Lucien thought to do, something Master could not tolerate?"

"We have no way of knowing," Margaret said. "Perhaps if Sephora was here to guide us—"

"Tell me . . ." I forced a smile designed to divert my mind from the annoyance that bubbled in me. "In the days before his death, did you notice anything unusual about Lucien?"

"As I have said, I hardly knew the man."

"And yet you were to live the rest of your life with him."

She made a dismissive motion with one hand. "Yes, but that is not what I'm thinking. I'm thinking about how I saw him in the garden the day before he died. He was . . ." To demonstrate, Margaret brushed the side of her robe with one hand. "He was fussing with something in the pocket of his robe, and time and again, he pulled out his watch and snapped it open as if it were the most important thing on the face of the earth. I was still convinced there was nothing to the Children but love and light, and I wondered why he would worry about so insignificant a thing as a watch that he had to keep checking on it. And I thought no further of it, but that night, at the church . . ." Margaret shivered. "He kept plucking at his pocket, taking out his watch. His fingers shook so badly. He was frantic, Violet. He could not walk a straight line, the poor man . . . he stumbled toward the altar, mumbling all the while. About his watch. About how important it was. But, how could it be? He spoke of it as if his very life depended on it."

Indeed.

It was a tantalizing thread, one I was sure to follow, and yet I was hardly encouraged. After all, I knew what Margaret did not know since she'd been in police custody at the time of the funeral—Lucien's pocket watch had gone into the fire with him.

Chapter 12

I will admit to some discouragement, and though I thought to find comfort in telling myself there was no shame in it, that the mystery I was faced with was both twisted and devious, I could not help but feel as if there was something I was missing. Who would want to kill Lucien? And why?

I had eliminated Margaret from my list of suspects immediately, and Albion, too, could not have been involved. Aside from his account of his whereabouts on the evening of the murder (a report that I had since confirmed with Phoenix), I thought him far too timid to kill, even for love. I should have been cheered to remove two of those who might have committed the murder, yet the ones who remained made so little sense as to confuse me even further.

Master, certainly, had argued with Lucien the night of the murder. Yet from all I knew of him, he believed in peace, and truly seemed to practice it.

Enoch Pullman had been acting suspiciously, but though he was surly and rude, I had yet to draw a clear connection between him and the dead man.

And then there was the matter of the nasty man in armor who had interrupted Lucien's funeral service.

How odd I happened to think of him as I was leaving my meeting with Margaret at the police station just as I spied a familiar face across the way. The man—the son of the armored hooligan—saw me, too, and made his way in my direction. When he tipped his top hat to me, the sun glinted off his golden hair.

"Miss Manville." He bowed from the waist. "I am fortunate to have encountered you. I thought to have to go to Alburn to see you again so that I might offer apologies on behalf of my father."

"You know my name."

His cheeks were so pale that even the hint of color that touched them appeared flamboyant and out of sorts with his elegant, understated appearance—dark trousers, a gray jacket, a cravat tied so perfectly around his slender neck I had no doubt a valet of some skill had a hand in it.

"I do not mean to appear too forward. I asked after your name. After the ugliness there at the abbey."

"You talked to Master. And I have not had the chance to ask after you and learn who it was who appeared at just the right moment to save me from the drunkard who interrupted the ceremony."

He dipped his head. "Tarquin DeClare. If I may be so bold to say it, you were both brave and unyielding there in the church. No one else stepped forward to defend those two girls from my father."

"You did."

"No." A smile touched his lips and transformed his face. At the church, I had noted that he was fine-looking. Now, even though his face was gaunt and his eyes were shadowed, I saw he was unquestionably handsome. "I defended you."

"And I appreciate it. You put yourself in harm's way on my behalf. Or did you think perhaps my attacker was more bluster than he was a danger?"

His smile fled and worry crossed his face. "Do not underestimate him. The Viscount Hinckley is a danger, sure enough, and has been all these many years. Especially when he's in his cups."

"As he was yesterday morning."

Tarquin looked away. "As he is most hours of the day and night."

"He is not pleased to have the Children living there at Alburn. Is the abbey close to his lands?"

"We live at Norcross Castle." He pulled a face. "It's a nasty old pile. Yet Father . . ." I did not think he meant to sigh, yet he could not help himself. "You saw the way he was dressed."

"The armor, yes." I thought of the flash I'd seen near the castle that first day I toured the compound with Master and knew now it was no trick of the light but a glint of sun off metal. "He wears it often?"

"He has somehow convinced himself he's honoring our ancestors by keeping their memories alive in the eyes of the general populace. It's rubbish, of course, but really, that, at least, is harmless. Father thinks himself as cutting a striking figure, like a knight of old. I'm afraid in the surrounding villages and here in town, he's looked on with pity more than anything else. If he heard the laughter behind his back, it would infuriate him."

"As the Children infuriate him."

He shot me a look. "Father does not believe in Master's god."

"Few do. And yet most are not so enraged as I saw your father there at the funeral service."

"Few? Yet you must be one of them. You surely believe as Master does, or you would not be living with the Children. You are a Seeker, am I right?"

"You know something of the Children of Aed."

"I know you do not look the kind who would follow Master."

I couldn't help but smile. "What kind is that?"

The laugh he gave in response reminded me of the sort that was practiced over a lifetime so that it might be casually delivered. I'd heard it in drawing rooms throughout the Empire and at the soirees that always bored me and found me longing to bolt to the door and run for home. It had the ring of amusement, surely, but there was also a hint of cynicism in it that told me Tarquin was skilled at politics, charming when he had to be, noncommittal, at least until he fully understood a matter. But then, as the son of a viscount, his schooling would have reinforced it. His heritage would demand nothing less.

"I am sorry if it insults you, Miss Manville, but you seem far too intelligent to be one of the Children."

"Am I to be insulted by being called intelligent?"

"You are if I am wrong, if you are just another of the lost souls that somehow find their way to Master. He attracts them like bees to honey."

"Perhaps they're waiting for the sacrifices."

His top lip twisted. "Or the orgies. I think, though, you are not waiting for either. That tells me you must be a true believer. Either that, or—" He turned a look on me that betrayed his surprise. "You don't think the girl did it."

"She didn't."

"Who, then?"

"I hoped you might be able to tell me."

"You hoped I'd tell you my philistine of a father might be a candidate," he countered, shrewdly.

"Is he?"

"Perhaps you'd like to ask him yourself."

Naturally, I looked around, dreading I might see the Viscount Hinckley. He was nowhere in sight, and I turned again to Tarquin.

"Come for luncheon," he said. "I've a carriage waiting nearby. You can ask Father yourself if he is guilty of murder."

"I will, indeed," I answered, and left the Honorable Tarquin DeClare wondering if it was luncheon I was talking about. Or interrogating his father.

⚬⚬⚬

Tarquin was right about Norcross Castle. It was a pile. It sat atop a hill surrounded by forest, a hulking monstrosity that had probably been built at the same time as the abbey and obviously for defensive purposes rather than for elegance or comfort. The walls were thick, and there were towers on either end of the castle, the arrow slits in them like narrowed eyes, watching us. Over the years, the stone had weathered to the color of mud and against the background of barren trees, Norcross looked bleak and foreboding.

"It is more habitable on the inside than it looks," Tarquin assured me when our coach stopped in the courtyard and he held out a hand and helped me down. "And you needn't worry about the food. Father is a glutton and has enlisted the services of a chef from London. He pays Swanton a king's ransom. It is the only reason he stays."

"Lord Hinckley might not be pleased to have a guest for luncheon."

"I saw Hugh before I left for town. In the state he was in, I doubt he'll even notice your presence. If we see him at all."

"Or he will see me and remember that I defied him at the funeral. That, I think, will not make for pleasant conversation at table."

Because Tarquin could not deny this, he said nothing at all, but led me through a massive oak door and into a vast room where suits of armor, the metal darkened by time, stood all around, faceless sentinels. Swords hung on the walls. Shields stood propped against the stone and the faded tapestries that depicted scenes of medieval life—feasts, dancing, battles.

"We take our meals in the banqueting hall," he told me, stopping at a door and waiting until the servant there swung it open for us.

It was a dismal room of great size, the corners of it lost in shadow where the light of the candles that guttered on the table from tarnished candelabra did not penetrate. There were shields and swords on the wall there, too, and even more suits of armor standing at attention. The candlelight sparked against them like the fires of all the wars the knights who once wore them must have seen.

As if he feared the walls themselves had ears and would report anything he had the temerity to say, Tarquin lowered his voice. "You must excuse the gloom. I've tried to talk to Father about the new electric lights."

It was a subject I was keen on. "Yes, my aunt Adelia is considering them for our home in St. John's Wood. Electricity is a marvel—think how it might change our lives! Reading late into the night is such a pleasure, and electricity would make it so much easier."

"Father will not hear of it. He refuses even to have gas.

Says it is an insult to all the DeClares who came before us. I think, rather, that all the DeClares who came before us might appreciate the fact that a little more light and a little less dreariness would be a blessing for our eyes, not to mention our dispositions."

"You do, do you?" The question, and the rough voice that delivered it, came from the far corner of the room, where Hugh DeClare stepped from the shadows. "Not your business to question what I do or don't do here at Norcross, boy," he told Tarquin. "P'haps when you're viscount, you can make all the changes you like, eh?"

So, Tarquin was the eldest and would someday inherit the title. Many would think that a blessing, indeed, yet at the reminder, a muscle jumped at the base of Tarquin's jaw. He hid the reaction behind a smile too stiff at its corners. "I have brought a guest to share luncheon with us," he said. "Miss Violet Manville from London."

"Not a guest so much as a meddler." Clearly, he had not been so drunk at our last encounter to forget the woman who had stood up to him and his maltreatment of Joan and Kitty. The viscount's eyes were blue and milky, and when he stepped nearer, he trained them on me.

"You must be careful of men who present themselves as too cocksure." I heard dear Papa's voice in my ear, offering the advice I'd heard from him when we were once presented to a maharajah who had a reputation for a nasty disposition and a quick temper. *They blow and bluster to hide their own insufficiencies. You must never let them think they've gotten the better of you, no matter how frightened you might be. It is what they're hoping for, you see, and Vi, you are far too intelligent and far too valiant to fall into the trap.*

If only Papa knew! I wasn't at all valiant that day in India.

I was so frightened, my knees knocked. Much as they did now.

Lord Hinckley paced closer. He was without his armor breastplate, and with it gone, I was better able to get a measure of the man. Broad-chested. Wide shoulders. Hands like anvils. Not a man to be trifled with, I knew, even when the aura of whisky fumes didn't precede him as it did now. I also could not help but think he was the kind of man who would not hesitate to overpower anyone; he would not need poison to kill.

I could not bring myself to smile at him, but I somehow managed to sound cordial enough. "I am grateful for the invitation to share luncheon with you," I told him. "It is an honor to be able to visit Norcross."

"Is it?" He grunted. "I'd think you'd be too busy up at the abbey with that band of heathens to care about Norcross."

"History has always fascinated me." It was the truth, so I did not back away from it. Even when he pinned me with a look. "If it is not being too forward of me, Lord Hinckley, perhaps you might show me some of the castle?"

I cannot say if I mollified him or not. I only know he grunted and said, "We'll eat first," before he turned to the table, sat down, and rang a silver bell at his right hand. A second later, a phalanx of servants arrived with trays of food. Tarquin showed me to the chair at Lord Hinckley's right hand and took the seat opposite mine.

He had been right about the food. It was excellent. Or perhaps the simple meals served by the Children and consisting mostly of grains and vegetables had left me longing more than I realized for the kinds of foods easily available in London. The staff at our elbows served roasted chicken, cold ham, potted fish. They set bread, butter, and cheese on the table and sweets on the sideboard along with tea and coffee. To me, it seemed a lavish array, indeed, for luncheon, but in light of what Tarquin had said, that his father was a glutton, I was surprised neither by the selection of foods nor the fact that Hugh dug into it all so heartily. He paid no mind at all to either Tarquin or myself, but finished off half a chicken, a plate of ham, and an entire loaf of bread before I was done with the serving of chicken on my plate. Tarquin, I noticed, asked for ham and chicken. He ate neither, simply sipped a cup of tea and looked across the table at me, clearly embarrassed by his father's grunts and lip smacking.

"What's that you said about seeing the castle?" Without prelude, Lord Hinckley scraped back his chair and stood, a certain sign the meal had ended. He grabbed the bottle of whisky that had been left next to his plate and stalked to the door. "Come on then, girl," he called. "If you want to see it, this is your opportunity."

I wasted no time in catching up with him, and when I joined Lord Hinckley outside the door of the banqueting room, Tarquin hung back and followed us at a discreet distance.

"You one of them bluestockings?" Hugh asked, chugging up a stairway like a straining railroad engine.

"If by bluestocking you mean a woman of education with a wide taste in reading matter, then yes, I am, sir."

"You read that idiot Count Orlando?"

"I have read his stories. I do not put much credence in them."

He was at the landing, and he paused there to take stock of me, and for a moment, I thought he might actually say something polite. Instead, he grunted again and continued on, pointing out a number of tapestries, a room in which it was claimed King Henry VIII had once slept, and the chamber where he, himself, had been born. He gave me little time to ask questions and was always a dozen steps ahead of me, pointing and grumbling and sipping from his bottle, and in just a little while, leading me again down the stone steps, through the main hall, and farther into the bowels of the castle.

It wasn't until we stood in front of a closed wooden door with heavy iron fittings that he bothered to look over his shoulder at me. "You won't dare go down in the dungeon."

I might not have been so brave if Tarquin wasn't twenty paces behind us, quiet and watchful. I would not fancy being alone with Hugh DeClare. "Why not?" I asked, and stepped ahead.

The noise that escaped Lord Hinckley reminded me of a kettle at the boil. He opened the door and the foul smell of mold slammed into us. We were at the top of a stone stairway and without waiting further, he started down into the darkness.

The room below was the stuff of nightmares: bare floors, bare walls, only a trickle of light and that from one window butted against the ceiling.

"Here is where we DeClares put the rogues," he said, no small amount of pride warming his voice. "Brigands and bandits and, yes, murderers."

"Do you believe that is what should happen to the person who murdered Lucien at the compound?"

He barked a laugh. "Lucien at the compound. Another one of the lunatics. The world will hardly miss him."

"And yet if his murderer is not brought to justice, another will be found guilty of the crime. A man such as you, a man who believes in justice, can hardly abide that."

He threw me a look. "You think so?"

"I know you wish the Children to leave the abbey. That

you thought they would once Lucien was dead, that the stain of murder would drive them away."

"And so you think I murdered the man myself?" When he chortled, it struck me that it might have been the only laughter the miserable room had ever heard. "That is a poor reason to kill a man. No." He took a long drink from his bottle. "There are better reasons for killing man . . . and woman."

"Are there? Some would say a man who is arrogant enough might justify his every whim. Even murder."

"And you think I am that man?" He spat on the floor. "Don't get the wrong idea, girl. Don't think that I am a coward and would ever back down from a thing that needed doing. Even if that thing meant spilling blood. It is what happened to Tarquin's mother, isn't it?"

It took me a moment to catch his meaning, and when I did, I sucked in a breath.

He was pleased with my show of surprise. A smile glinted in Lord Hinckley's eyes. "Oh yes, she was a wicked thing. Turning my boys against me was one thing. But then . . ." I knew Tarquin was still somewhere behind us in the dark; I sensed him there, but when Lord Hinckley looked that way and I did, too, there was nothing to see behind us but shadows. "Then she took to consorting with the gamekeeper and really, what is a man to do? I could not risk having a bastard in the line."

"You didn't kill her?"

"Nah!" He laughed and took a long drink from his bottle. "The baggage fell off her horse. Broke her neck. But I would have been justified, wouldn't I? A man cannot abide that sort of disrespect. Not from anyone."

My stomach sickened, but I dared not let him know.

"Where were you," I asked him, "the evening Lucien Tidwell was poisoned?"

"Where was I?" He was a large man, and when he stepped even closer and threw back his shoulders I had no choice but to retreat a step. "How dare you come here, girl, and accuse me? Do you know who I am? Do you know what I could do to you?"

I swallowed down my fear, for I knew it was a show of bravery, and only that, which would extricate me from the situation. "Lock me in your dungeon?" I tossed my head and, as blithely as I could, stepped around him and back to the stairway. "Whatever your ancestors were, sir, whoever they kept here in this miserable hole, we are a country of laws now, and I will not be intimidated in my quest for the truth." I hurried up the stairs before he could notice my hands were shaking.

At the doorway, Tarquin rushed me outside to the courtyard. "That was foolish."

"He left me little choice."

"He is not a man to trifle with. And you . . . Miss Manville, you are quite remarkable in your wit and your courage."

"Hardly. In fact, I should like nothing better than to leave here and return to Burton upon Trent."

He bowed and led me back to the coach that brought us to Norcross, and it wasn't until we clattered out of the courtyard that I dared to let go the breath that strangled my lungs.

"Did he . . . ? The way he said it . . . Did he arrange your mother's death?" My voice was crushed beneath the weight of the words. "Did you know?"

He nodded. "There were rumors, but nothing was ever proved."

"But the authorities—"

"Have been bought and paid for by my father and his father and his father before him. They suspected. They hardly cared."

"I'm sorry." It felt inadequate, but it was all I could say. "A man who is capable of such depravity might surely be willing to kill again if it meant the stain of murder might drive the Children from the abbey."

Tarquin turned from me to look out the window. "You may be right. My father may very well have killed that poor man, but not for the reason you think."

He turned again to me. "Miss Manville, I have diabetes. I am dying."

It was nothing I expected, and my heart clutched and my words faltered.

"Do not feel embarrassed that I've shared the news with you, and do not feel as if you need to offer some comfort. I have known for some time, and every day, I feel the illness claim more of my health, more of my life's purpose. When the time comes, I will be ready."

"When the time . . ." My words wavered.

"Surely it will happen before spring."

I thought about the viscount's words to Tarquin, about how he said Tarquin might change Norcross once he inherited the title, about how Hugh knew that would never happen, and my heart squeezed in sympathy. "And yet your father treats you so. It is shameful."

"It is Father, and long ago . . . Well, I will never forgive him, but I think I better understand him now than I did when I was younger. He's a savage. He will never change. That is the reason, you see, that I, too, wonder if Father might have had anything to do with Lucien Tidwell's death. I have a brother, you see. Monteford. And when I pass, Monty will be my father's heir. You have seen how Father values the lineage. If Monty does not step into my place, if he refuses his inheritance, the title will go to a distant cousin who now resides in America. Father will do anything to make sure that does not happen, that Monty is here at Norcross and will take the reins of the family in hand when the time comes."

"I don't . . ." I passed a hand over my eyes. "I don't understand."

Tarquin explained quite simply. "You see, that is why Father will do anything to bring an end to the Children of Aed. Monty is Master, and when I die, he will be my father's heir."

Chapter 13

I had thought to remain in Burton upon Trent in the event the Thuringers needed my assistance. I did not. I was eager to put distance between myself and my unsettling encounter with the Viscount Hinckley, surely, but I had an even more shameful motive for returning to Alburn. I told myself that if they required help, the Thuringers could simply contact the wise and wonderful Sephora. The less cynical part of me, I am happy to say, silenced the ridiculous notion soon enough. Of course my sister overstated her role in the solving of last summer's murder. Sephora liked nothing better than sensational fiction. I, however, knew the truth of the thing: Sephora had little to do with the unraveling of the mystery and in fact, her impulsive behavior made things worse. Let her pretend courage. Let her spread word of her exploits. Let her live with the dream that she was capable of displaying even a modicum of common sense.

I had an investigation to conduct and really, the pettiness of Sephora's stories mattered little in light of it. At the close of market day, I returned to the compound with the Children, ate dinner with them quietly, and retired to my room on the pretense of being weary.

Upon arriving there, though, the first thing I did was turn

up the flame in my lamp and tear into the packet of letters I'd received from Bunty. Much of what was enclosed there were letters addressed to Miss Hermione, and I set them aside to be answered another day and concentrated instead on the single envelope where *Miss Violet* was written in Bunty's strong, precise hand.

"'Dearest Violet.'" I held the single page closer to the light and under my breath, I read the words. "'I am sorry to tell you—'"

My hopes dissolved and I dropped my hands and the letter in them to my lap. "She is sorry to tell me," I grumbled. "She hasn't found out anything useful about Lucien."

This was surely a setback, and for a few minutes I allowed myself to wallow in the misery of it. That is, until I reminded myself that dear Papa had raised me with a clear sense of duty, a strong commitment to loyalty, and certainly more good sense than the good Lord gave a rabbit. Or my sister, come to think of it. Yes, I admit to being petty, but I was still stinging from the Thuringers' comments. I was the one who asked Bunty for her assistance. I owed it to her to not only read her letter in its entirety, but to maintain my faith in her. She said she would help, and Bunty was a woman of her word.

I squared my shoulders, lifted my chin, and continued reading.

"'. . . there is little to relay regarding Lucien Tidwell. I can report that his landlady, the good Mrs. Nibling, knows practically nothing of the man. In fact, she was never allowed in his rooms to tidy them and even now is in search of a key so that she might get inside and ready them for the next tenant. The publican who owns the establishment where Mr. Tidwell spent a good deal of his time was hardly more helpful. He claims Tidwell was sometimes in dire straits, yet at other times had enough means to drink himself to oblivion. You will surely see what this means, Violet.'"

I nodded and spoke aloud to myself. "He sometimes had money and sometimes was in sore need of it. A gambler, perhaps? A thief? But what has any of that to do with the time he spent with the Children? Or why he was leaving? Or where he might have been going?"

My sigh rippled the paper in my hands. "'I have spoken to someone else as well,'" Bunty went on. "'A man by the name of Daggart who is notorious for having a finger in all the goings-on in Vauxhall. He was acquainted with your Mr. Tidwell, right enough, but swears he knew only that Tidwell was, in Daggart's own words, an odd one. I cannot tell you what any of this means, Violet. I do not know how it might help you. I can only assure you that I am not yet done looking into the matter. I have a plan. Expect another letter from me soon regarding this Mr. Tidwell.

"'As to the other matters you inquired about— Yes, I have, indeed, seen some recent news about the precipitous announcement of the engagement of a certain Elizabeth Victoria Alberta Fitzgibbons, the eldest daughter of the Duke of Avonton. She will be sailing for the Continent at week's end and marrying Wilhelm Heinrich von Bausch, the only son of the Grand Duke of Kranichfeld, as soon as she arrives. I cannot imagine what this has to do with your investigation, Violet, I only know it must be important if you inquired about it.'"

Important, indeed, though I could not then (or now) say how I felt about this piece of news. It was clear the girl known here as Luna had been safely transported to London, and just as obvious she was being sent off hastily before she could take flight again. That told me Eli had accomplished his mission.

For the sake of the diplomatic dilemma he said would result should Luna not marry the man her family had chosen for her, I was happy for his success. Yet, knowing the girl was nothing more than a bit of goods, that niggled at me nearly as much as the fact that I knew there was nothing I could do to remedy the situation for her or the countless other women who found themselves in the same situation. Naturally, I could not then help but wonder how Eli might be keeping himself busy now that his duty to the Crown was finished.

I shook the thought from my head. There was no use in losing my focus and, as had been proven time and again, Eli Marsh was a distraction of the first order, one in which I could not allow myself to indulge. Thus bolstered, I continued reading.

"'As you might imagine, Sephora is rightly upset about Margaret,'" Bunty went on. "'She has spent her time here at home, sulking and crying and, as usual, not caring who she incommodes with her misery. I am sorry to be so plain-spoken in my assessment of her, but that is the truth of the thing. What I wouldn't give to see some spark of resourcefulness in the girl! And yet I must eradicate the very notion. Miss Sephora is certainly not you, nor do I expect her to be. As for you, Miss Violet, I do expect you to be ever mindful of your own safety.'"

There was nothing else for me to learn from Bunty, yet I read over the letter again, just to be sure I hadn't missed anything and to feel the warm glow of her regard, comforted even by the news of Sephora's sulking. As I did, I realized that in spite of Bunty claiming she had learned little, she really had been quite busy and gathered a good deal of information. Lucien's landlady, his publican, even this Daggart fellow . . .

A shiver skittered over my shoulders. Daggart has his

hand in all things going on in Vauxhall? And Bunty knew him? Or at least knew where to find him? I wondered what it meant, told myself I would find out when next I spoke to Bunty, and concentrated instead on what the mysterious Mr. Daggart said about Lucien.

"An odd one, eh? Lucien must, indeed, have been odd to come here when he cared little for the Children. And to try to leave so abruptly, and to tell Margaret his future was assured." The thought weighed so heavily on me I spoke it aloud. "If only he had known all his future held was a funeral pyre."

My own dismal words were all the reminder I needed that there might yet be some positive outcome to the day. But only if I got to work. With the thought in mind, I turned down my light so that it would appear I'd retired for the night. Then I waited.

Yes, I was in England, and a cool autumn wind heavy with the scent of dried leaves and woodsmoke rippled the air, yet I could not help but think of a steaming night I'd spent in India some ten years before. Then, like now, a tingle of anticipation fizzed through my bloodstream as I sat in the dark. I had been in the Sunderbans with Papa and a courageous guide at the time, and we kept silent and watchful. I had been tempted to doze and was kept awake only by the sound of Papa's voice close to my ear.

"It will happen quickly, and you don't want to miss it, Vi."

He was right. Papa usually was. That night, we were rewarded by seeing a tiger swimming through the mangroves, its prey, a chital deer, in its jaws.

I only hoped this night would bring me as much success.

Thus encouraged by my memories, I waited until it was as dark as pitch and the compound was quiet, then put on a cloak and gloves. Only then did I light my dark lantern and slide the cover over the lens to contain its light. Arrangements complete, I slipped from my room. It took me little time to get to the church. As usual, a candle was lit in the center of the prayer circle, and in its dim glow, I peered through the shadows gathered around the pillars and nestled in corners where crumbled stones and vegetation formed dark, misshapen silhouettes, like crouching animals.

If anyone was about, I had already prepared a fiction to explain my late-night foray. I was there to pray. To think carefully on my vocation. Did I wish to stay and declare myself a Novice?

Fortunately, I did not need the lie. There was no one about and, moving quickly and quietly, I stepped into the church. Above me, clouds skittered by on the brisk wind, unveiling stars that glittered like ice crystals then, just as quickly, swathing them again. A barn owl floated over my head, as silent as a ghost. From the nooks and crannies, I heard the grunting of a hedgehog, and not far from where I stood a fox dashed by, searching for its dinner. He did not mind my passing and I did not impede his. I skirted the prayer circle and closed in on the mound of ash on the far end of the church, all that was left of Lucien's pyre and his earthly remains.

There had been talk at dinner of gathering those ashes the very next morning so they could be scattered in the nearest river, and I was grateful to have this one last chance to examine the scene. To that end, I tried to picture it as I had seen it on the day of the funeral ceremony before Master touched torch to wood. I am loath to admit, it was not easy. What had been solid then was nothing now. What had been real then now seemed no more substantial than the memories of a nightmare.

I stepped nearer to where the pyre had been and uncovered my lantern's light, letting it glide over soot and cinders. Yes! There! I crouched for a closer look at the remnants of one of Lucien's boots, a sole blackened and warped by the heat. Encouraged, I searched to my left, the place where I thought his shirt had been neatly folded. But a shirt, of course, would have caught and burned easily, and though I stood and prodded the ash pile with the toe of my boot, nothing remained that might give me a better idea of where, exactly, Lucien's grave goods were set out, or how I might find his watch among the devastation.

Yet I was determined. There must be some significance to the watch. Otherwise, Lucien wouldn't have fussed with it the way Margaret saw him do. A family heirloom? He did not seem the sentimental type. A gift from a lover? I remembered Lucien's sole devotion to himself and his passion for biscotti and thought he was not a man who would easily attract a mate. Perhaps, then . . , just perhaps . . . the watch might reveal some secret that would explain why Lucien had come to join the Children, and yet remain apart from them. Why he planned to slip away in the middle of the night. Why someone wanted him dead.

I found nothing more than dirt and ash and grumbled my displeasure. But I did not give up. I left all that remained of the pyre long enough to kick through the tall vegetation that grew around the nearest pillar, and just as I'd hoped, I found there a length of tree limb, bare of leaves and so dry it easily cracked over my knee to a more manageable length. In the silence, the snap of it breaking was as loud as gunfire.

I cringed, then froze, expecting the Children heard and would come running. But no one did, and I released a suspended breath and got to work. Back at the pyre, I moved from left to right, marking off squares in the ash with the tip of my stick so I would know what portion of the pile I had examined and what I had not, then dug through each section one at a time.

It was slow work, and dirtier than I anticipated. Not to mention gruesome. Within minutes, my gloves were the same charcoal color as the ash and the strong smell of smoke tinged with the odor of roasted meat clung to my hair and clothing. I rubbed a finger under my nose and was sorry I did. Soot gritted along my top lip and I feared I had a grimy mustache. Still, I continued on, poking the stick into the pile, jubilant when it hit something solid, disappointed when I saw that it was no more than a bit of bone or one of the rocks that had been piled at the pyre's base to hold the wooden platform in place.

I kept on and when again my stick knocked into some unseen, hard object beneath a stone, I was tempted simply to ignore it. Tempted, but too curious not to check further, I pulled the stick forward and the light of my lantern hit the remains of a pocket watch. The watch itself looked charred but undamaged, but the metal chain attached to it had not fared so well; it was melted into a ball.

At this point, I neither knew nor cared if the watch might lead to some further revelation about Lucien, I was so happy to have found it, my hands shook. I had just tucked the watch safely into the chatelaine that hung at my waist when a gust blew through the church and teased sounds from the shadowy corners, like the moans of lost souls. The wind whipped through the pile and sent up a billowing cloud of ash that erupted all around me, and I covered my mouth with my hands and turned away.

If I hadn't, I might not have seen a movement near the old altar. A shimmer. Stronger than starlight. It reminded me of the effervescence I'd once seen near Hong Kong, where the sea was red during the day and glowed blue at night. This light, though, was green and as I watched, it grew taller and its light more intense, until I could finally make out its shape.

A phantom in a robe.

I was too astounded to move. It could not have been more than a moment or two, yet it felt a lifetime. Long enough for the specter to float in my direction. I could not scream for my mouth was suddenly dry. I could not escape for the only access to the outside was between two pillars and even as I watched, the glowing shape moved ever nearer them, blocking my route. My only option, then, seemed simple enough.

With a cry I'm afraid made me sound like a foxhound on the trail of a scent, I raced toward the figure.

It turned and fled, and in that one moment, all fear deserted me. This was no ghost, for a ghost, I was sure, would not be concerned about something as insignificant as a living being chasing after it. This phantom was as much flesh and blood as I was, and I was damned if I wasn't going to find out who it was, and why it chose to haunt me.

I had left my lantern near the pyre and now I sprinted through the dark with only the eerie green glow of my quarry to guide me, my feet smacking into stones, my skirts caught and tugged at by the prickly branches of blackthorn. Near the prayer circle, the toe of my boot caught a tangled tree root, and I fell forward. My knees slammed into the ground. My nose followed. My breath left me, and my head spun. I lay insensible, fighting to steady myself and again get my bearings before finally hoisting myself on my elbows. The phantom was there near the altar. Then gone.

I lay there, stunned. It wasn't possible for a living person to disappear so quickly, yet I refused to believe I had been visited by something from beyond the veil. My knees quaking and drops of blood leaking from my nose and mixing with the soot under it, I pulled myself to my feet and limped into the apse for a closer look. There was no one there, no glimmer of green light from the deep shadows in the corners, no sound of anything but my own rough breathing and the curse I grumbled.

That grumble transformed into a whoop when I caught a glimpse of a green glow outside. I hobbled from the church just in time to see the robed figure disappear among the ruins of the buildings near the farmyard, and I followed. Here the stones of crumbled walls were difficult to avoid. My progress impeded, I dodged them and tripped over them. Yet the figure glided through it all. Keeping my eye on it, I sidestepped between a rotted barrow and a tumbled pile of wood that might have once been a fence, gratified when I realized I closed in on the creature inch by inch.

I realized too late why I was allowed to get so close to the phantom. I should have recognized its treachery. It led me to a spot outside a low-slung stone building, its ceiling long gone, its walls in a tumble, and I realized that suddenly, just where I stepped, there was no longer soil beneath my feet, but wood, an old floor that creaked and sagged with my weight. *Damn.*

My mouth fell open and I gasped just as the ghostly figure lifted an arm and pointed at me.

It was the last thing I saw before the wood beneath my boots gave way and I tumbled into darkness.

Sephora

Daggart.

Every time I thought of the brute of a fellow James and I had caught sight of at the Royal Belfort, my knees trembled and my insides quivered. But then, as a proper lady, it was only natural I would have such a reaction to the man, not to mention the dreadful place and the unseemliness of the way he not only greeted Bunty with a hug, but called her by that ridiculous name, Red Maggie.

It was only right that I should be appalled. I was appalled.

And so eaten up with curiosity that I could not stop running the entire scenario again and again through my mind.

How was it Bunty came to know a man with such a tarnished reputation? And why had he first mistaken her for this Red Maggie, and then sat down and put his head together with her? Had she learned anything from him when it came to Lucien Tidwell? How much had she relayed to Violet?

I was not used to thinking so much or so hard, and it made my head spin at the same time it caused me to wonder how Violet did it so often and with so little effort. Perhaps it was the dissimilarity of our forebears that accounted for our differing personalities. Or perhaps Violet, being a spinster, had so much room in her empty life, she needed to fill it and for reasons I could not fathom, she chose to accomplish that by cogitating. Either way, I hoped to never follow in her footsteps. And yet . . .

In my bedroom, I brushed aside my curtains so that I might keep an eye on the front stoop. Oh yes, I'd seen Bunty downstairs gathering her hat and her gloves and her umbrella, too, for it looked as if it might rain that evening. She was going out, and as she had not mentioned anything to me about calling on a friend, I surmised (is that what Violet did when she made discoveries?) that she was off again in search of information about Lucien Tidwell.

I was not about to let her go alone.

The moment Bunty stepped outside, I followed. Once she was in a hansom, I, too, called for one. And if my heart squeezed the slightest bit at the thought that James could not accompany me this evening? I set the disappointment aside. As much as I hated to sound like my sister, I knew there were times when intrepidness must eclipse even tender emotions.

Just as the last time I followed Bunty, her hansom led us through the heart of London and over Vauxhall Bridge. I prayed we were not returning to the Royal Belfort and was relieved when instead, our cabs made their way down what were now familiar streets to the former residence of the unfortunate Lucien Tidwell.

"And yet Mrs. Nibling, his landlady, told Bunty she was never at home on Friday evening," I reminded myself, my index finger tapping my chin. The next second, I caught my breath. "Bunty!" I looked to where she alighted in front of the boardinghouse. "You're not going to . . . !"

I waited not one moment longer to see if she would or if she wouldn't, but hopped out of my own cab just as Bunty knocked on Mrs. Nibling's front door.

"She isn't at home," I said.

Her jaw slack and her face ashen, Bunty spun to face me. "Miss Sephora! You cannot—"

"Be here? Of course I can be. For here I am." I stepped up to her side.

She clutched her hands at her waist. "You must leave. Now."

"You wouldn't tell Violet to leave," I shot back at her.

Bunty's lips pursed. "Violet would be here before me," she admitted.

"And I am here because I followed you. Just as I did the other day. Here. To the pub. And yes, even to the Royal Belfort."

"Miss Sephora, you should not have—"

"But I did. And as I suspect I know what you're going to do here, Bunty, I suggest we do it quickly before Mrs. Nibling arrives back home from her weekly church meeting and finds us inside."

She shook her head. "I will not allow it. If I am to find myself in a predicament, that is one thing. But having you caught up in it!" A muscle jumped at the base of her jaw. "No. That would be unacceptable. Your reputation would be ruined. Not to mention that your dear aunt Adelia would have my head on a platter. But only if I still had a head once Miss Violet was done with me."

This was an impasse, certainly, and I handled it as I had handled such difficulties all my life. I pursed my lips and stomped my foot.

Bunty was not as moved by said show of pluck as I would have liked. In fact, her hands clutched at her waist, she merely waited for my fit of pique to pass, and when she was satisfied it had, she did nothing more than turn from me to Mrs. Nibling's door.

"Very well," I said, and when I did, she thought she had won; the tension went out of her shoulders. "You may venture inside by yourself, Bunty. I will merely stay right where I am and scream to one and all that there is a burglar in Mrs. Nibling's residence."

She whirled. "You would not!"

My smile, I have been told, can be as sweet as birdsong, and I employed it with devastating precision. Would I actually do so ill-mannered a thing as raise my voice in public? Bunty wasn't sure. Nor was she taking any chances. She scooped up my hand in hers and opened the door and together, we stepped into Mrs. Nibling's boardinghouse.

"How do we know what we're looking for?" There was no one about, but I kept my voice to a whisper that kept rhythm to the tattoo of nervousness beating in my chest. I glanced up the stairs in front of us. "You're not actually going to go in search of Tidwell's rooms, are you?"

Instead of answering, Bunty hurried up the stairway directly opposite the door, and because I did not wish to be found standing there, did not know what I would say if I was, and refused to miss out on any of the excitement, I followed along.

At the top of the stairs, we found ourselves in a long, rather drab passageway. The carpet was worn, the pictures on the walls were poorly rendered and badly framed. There was an urn nearby that contained a large aspidistra that had been dead for some time. Along the hallway on our right were three doors.

"How do we know which rooms are Tidwell's?" I asked Bunty.

"When I spoke to her . . ." She proceeded down the hallway to the last door. "When we talked of Tidwell, the landlady pointed to the back of the house."

We stopped in front of the door and I tried the doorknob. My shoulders sagged. "Locked."

Bunty nodded. "Just as Mrs. Nibling said it has been all the time Tidwell's lived here."

"Then how can we possibly—" My question—one so logical it would surely have impressed even Violet—dissolved in a gasp of surprise when Bunty removed two thin metal instruments from her pocket.

"Picklocks!" In fiction that involved coldhearted burglars and intrepid constables, I had certainly read of such things, but I never thought to see our housekeeper using them. And with some skill that suggested familiarity. "You're not going to try to—"

She inserted the instrument in her left hand into the lock on Tidwell's door.

"Bunty," I whispered, "you cannot possibly know how to—"

She inserted the instrument in her right hand into the lock.

"But how can you possibly think you might be able to—"

Ignoring me completely, she wiggled and jiggled the tools, and a minute later, we heard a satisfying click.

When she turned it on me, Bunty's smile was radiant. "Like eating pie when you know what you're doing." A finger to her lips to remind me to keep quiet, she glanced up and down the hallway, then opened the door. As soon as it was closed behind us, she turned up the gas. When the flame leapt and illuminated Lucien Tidwell's sitting room, we both gasped and fell back against the door, our hands clasped again, our mouths open. We stared—Bunty and I—at the closed black curtains, the writing desk where a preserved and mounted raven sat atop a bundle of papers. We gaped at the cabinet that stood along the far wall, one shelf of it filled with jars where eyeballs and entrails floated in clear liquid and the other shelf lined with bottles of thick red fluid—blood! Our eyes wide, our heartbeats thumping out of control, we stood frozen and watched a fat black rat with red eyes skitter around his cage on the floor near the window, then, as one, turned our gazes on the skeleton seated at Tidwell's dining table, its bones the color of cream and its mouth agape as if he were just as surprised to see us as we were to encounter him.

Chapter 14

"It cannot be real." I was grateful, indeed, there was no one around to hear me, for, like an ill-bred scullery maid, I croaked the words.

"The skeleton?" Bunty inched her way to the table, her head bent forward for a better look. "I do think it very much is."

"But . . ." While she may have been daring enough to venture farther into the room, I kept my back planted firmly against the door. "Where would a person get such a thing?"

"From a resurrectionist, I suppose. Those who plunder graves so they might sell the bodies within." With one finger, Bunty poked the skeleton, then nodded, satisfied. "Not to worry, Miss Sephora. I'd wager this one's been dead a good, long time. But it's real, right enough. Though I doubt those are." She cast a look in the direction of the jars on the shelf.

My nose wrinkled, my insides aquiver, I looked that way, too. "How can you tell?"

"Severed eyeballs wouldn't be so perfect as that, would they?" she said, and I didn't ask how she could possibly know. Instead, I looked over the room. There were bats—dead and stuffed, thank goodness—hanging from the chandelier, and in the center of the table, what looked for all the world like the cauldron on the cover of Count Orlando's latest. "What about the rest of it?" I asked.

She looked back at me long enough to smile. "Well, the rat certainly is real enough. And Tidwell dead all these days. See if you can find something for the poor creature to eat."

"Find something . . ." My words died on a gurgle of dismay, but I did as I was told and whispered a prayer that my friends would never know I had been a party to the affair. Oh, what the Society pages would make of the incident! Or would it, rather, be mentioned in a letter to Miss Hermione?

Dear Miss Hermione,

As I have just discovered an acquaintance I have always assumed to be of good family and good character has been feeding rats, I do need to find a way (it does not need to be either polite or kind) to make sure her name is stricken from the social calendar permanently.

I shivered at the very thought at the same time I uncovered a dried biscuit on the writing desk. Careful to keep as far away as I possibly could, I tossed it into the creature's cage, and I may have been feeling a bit light-headed and thus, too inclined to a fit of imagination, but I swore the rat squeaked its thanks.

I turned from it, the better to watch Bunty where she stood with her hands on her hips, glancing all around and trying, no doubt, to determine what to do next. While she concentrated so, I thought I might catch her off guard.

"Who is Red Maggie?" I asked her.

If she was surprised by the question, she didn't show it. She never even glanced my way when she said, "You heard him."

"And saw the way that horrible man welcomed you as if you were an old friend."

Her shrug was barely perceptible.

"You knew him," I said when she said nothing.

"It was a long time ago."

"And was he a blackguard even then?"

"Is he one now?"

A revelation struck me. "He is the one who taught you to use picklocks!"

Bunty's sigh rippled the air. She turned to face me. "The truth of it is, Miss Sephora, I taught him."

"Does that mean—"

She raised a hand, a clear signal she considered the conversation over.

I, however, did not. There are rules, after all. Rules of behavior which those in service must respect. "Did you even have references when you came to work for Adelia? For I am sorry to say it, Bunty, but surely a woman of such high standing as my aunt would never tolerate a housekeeper with criminal connections. Does Adelia know?"

I did not expect her to laugh. "Adelia," she said, "is the one who taught me to use the picklocks."

"But—"

"At the moment, we have more important things to worry about and not much time to find some bit of information that might prove useful to Miss Violet." Bunty closed in on the writing desk. "These papers might tell us something." And yet, she did not start with the stack of papers, but rather with a much smaller pile of newspaper clippings that sat nearby.

"They all concern the Children, which makes perfect sense since he was living as one of them. Still, they may prove valuable." And with that, she tucked the clippings into her pocket.

As anxious as I had been to join in the investigation, I

could not help but be shocked. "You're going to . . . you're not going to . . . Bunty, do you intend to steal them?"

She patted her pocket. "Tidwell no longer needs them, and we do." She looked through more of the papers. "You needn't worry about these," she said, and showed me copies of Count Orlando's dreadfuls. "I won't steal them. We have all the numbers, do we not?"

We did. Still, I could not help but take the dreadfuls from her hands and page through them. I remembered every story well, and wondered that a man like Tidwell—he did, after all, keep a rat in his rooms—and I had the same taste in reading.

I finished with the dreadfuls to find Bunty glancing through the largest stack of papers on the table.

"Dunning notices," she said. "From his tailor, from his stationer, from a place called Alonza's where he apparently ate many of his meals. Look, here, too, is a letter from a man named Fortescue who says, 'You promised to pay, but the money has yet to arrive.'"

"It is just as the publican told you," I reminded Bunty. "Tidwell was sometimes in desperate straits."

"And not only when it came to finances." Bunty had just picked up another letter and, lips pursed, she read it over quietly to herself before she explained. "This is a communication from a woman who pleads with him for, as she puts it, 'the sake of all we once had.' She goes on to demand he return something to her."

"Was he a thief, then?"

"It sounds to me as if there was some relationship between them. She does say the item—whatever it is—is valuable and that it is hers and he had no right to keep it."

"Do you think he complied?"

"Not if this next letter here is to be believed, for it is dated a week later than the first and makes the same demands. This one, though, is signed." Bunty tipped the letter closer to the light. "The woman who entreats Tidwell so is called Eunice Pullman."

Violet

November 14

It was a crow's caw, rough and shrill, that finally roused me. I groaned, blinked to focus my eyes, and found myself looking up through a hole framed with broken wooden planks. Beyond their jagged edges, the sky was just touched with first light.

"Morning?" My throat was parched, my voice scratched over the word. I hoisted myself on my elbows, and when pain shot through my arms and back, I remembered, too late, that I'd taken a tumble in the church in pursuit of the specter and again, another fall here to . . . wherever I was.

In search of answers, I sought to examine my surroundings, but in the gloom, it was difficult to see much of anything. With a groan, I sat up further. I was in a cavern of some sort, and by the looks of things, it was not natural, but manmade. The walls were fashioned of stone blocks, as was the floor. I was fortunate, indeed, that when I fell, I landed not on that surface, but on a mound of dirt soft and moist enough to cushion my fall and only leave my clothing bespeckled with mud and bits of rotted wood. In the distance, I could make out a deeper shadow among those that sat close around me. A doorway into another chamber.

Storage, I decided. Long ago used by the monks. Long since forgotten.

I pulled myself to my feet with a grunt and wiped my hands along my cloak, checking under it as I did to be sure my chatelaine was still pinned at my waist and the pocket watch I had risked my life for was still inside it. Satisfied, I'd just looked up to examine the hole above me so that I might find a way out of it when it was blocked by a silhouette.

"Violet, is that you? Are you down there?" Celestia leaned over to peer into the pit. "Thank goodness." She slapped a hand to her heart. "When you did not appear at first-light prayer, we went to your quarters and found you gone. We've been searching for you."

"I . . ." By way of demonstration, I gestured all around. "I fell."

"And no wonder. We advise Children and Seekers alike to avoid this portion of our land, as it is pocked with structures once used by the monks and then by the Gypsies who trespassed on the land for years after the monks fled. The ground is unstable."

I somehow managed a laugh.

"Are you hurt?" Celestia wanted to know.

I stretched and winced. "Aching."

"Your face is black and sooty. And your nose. It has been bleeding."

I touched a finger to the crusty patch on my upper lip and lied when I said, "It must have happened when I fell," because I was not ready to explain about the phantom and my pursuit of it. Not until I had more time to fully understand what had happened.

"Well, you are certainly in need of a washing and a cup of tea," she said. She knelt and reached out a hand, but though we were both tall and we both stretched, her arm was not long enough to reach down to me, nor was my hand able to grasp hers. It hardly mattered. If we had been able to take hold of each other, there was no way she would have been able to pull me from the hole.

Celestia knew it. "I will go for assistance," she said. "Wait here."

I laughed again because it was clear I had no choice but to wait, and while I did, I chanced a closer look at my prison. Near where I'd fallen was a flat, toppled stone. On examining it, I saw it was once an altar.

"Not storage then, but a chapel," I whispered. "But, underground? And with a doorway beyond, leading farther into the bowels of the earth?"

I knew then exactly where I was. Not a storeroom at all, but the anteroom to a crypt. Beyond the inner doorway, I had no doubt I'd find the bones of countless monks who had once inhabited Alburn Abbey. I knew if I dared to follow the shadowy passageway, it would lead me under the church.

"And in the church, there might be a place to enter the crypt," I told myself, "and outside the church, more than one place to exit and come again to the surface."

Exactly as the phantom had done.

It was all the time I had to think about the specter who'd led me on my merry chase, for just then, Master and Phoenix arrived with a ladder, and while they steadied it, I climbed from the hole. My head finally above the surface, I took in a lungful of fresh air and with a smile, greeted the leaden morning as if it were, instead, the finest of days.

"We are grateful to see you!" Phoenix, too, smiled. "We have been worried."

Carefully, I steadied myself, a hand against the wooden planks in front of me, and when my fingers met with a soft, waxy substance, I wiped my glove against the skirt of my gown and climbed the last of the rungs.

"Careful. Step here." At the top of the ladder, Master took my hand and led me to solid ground. "We must mark off these places with ropes," he told Celestia. "We cannot risk this happening to anyone else. It is fortunate Violet was not hurt seriously."

"I am fine now," I assured him. "Though I sorely need a bath and clean clothing."

"And you will be even better once you are warmed." When she'd gone for help, Celestia had retrieved a mug of tea, and she handed it to me.

I cupped it. Even through my gloves, the warm mug felt heavenly in my hands. But I did not drink.

One pot or two?

Until I understood the significance of the two pots that were always brewed at meals and teatime, I did not dare sip. Instead, I professed that I was bone-tired and anxious to get back to my room.

Master and Phoenix left with the ladder, and I watched them walk away, thinking as I did about my last look at the glowing green figure, of the distance between us and how tall it appeared. Phoenix? He was far too short to pass for the apparition. But Master . . .

Celestia put a hand on my shoulder and startled me from the thought. "You must be shaken from your experience. Let me accompany you back to your room. I have been here many times before and know my way through this maze."

It was good she did, for we wound our way through the crumbled buildings and around other places where a misstep might result in disaster, and when we were finally back at the church, she paused.

"What were you doing out here last night?" she asked me.

I remembered the lie I'd prepared. "Praying. I must determine if I should become a Novice."

She gave me a level look. "Praying at the circle in the church, perhaps, but I doubt that is why you were among the ruins."

"I thought I heard—"

"What?"

My mind spun to concoct a plausible story. "It was dark and I was weary from the day. No doubt that is why I wasn't thinking clearly. I thought I heard a person crying for help and so I searched, but I saw no one. That's when I fell. I realize now what I must have heard was the shriek of a fox."

"First you say you were here to pray, then to search for a fox." The smile Celestia offered me was not as friendly as it was poised between forbearance and disbelief. "Are you sure you weren't searching for something else out here in the dark?"

"Why? Have others seen things here?"

"I am sure you've heard reports of the ghost."

"And yet I do not believe them. No more than you do, I think."

Celestia had a peculiar smile, warmth and ice wrapped in an air of authority. She was not so much arrogant as she seemed detached from the physical world. A part of it, and yet not. She reinforced my opinion when she said, "We are all one with the universe."

"People and spirits alike?"

She bowed her head. "Aed teaches us this is so."

I continued walking. "I saw no spirits here yesterday."

She fell into step beside me. "But you did see Hestia yesterday. You went to the market, but you did not stay to assist the Children there."

"Finding the truth is assistance in its own way. Margaret needs our support."

"And you hoped that by talking to her, you'd learn more about Sage. What did she tell you?"

"He planned to leave, and he asked Hestia to accompany him."

This was surely news; her dark brows rose.

"At the time he died, his robe was discarded, his belongings were packed," I added.

She cocked her head. "Enoch did not mention—"

"You sent Enoch Pullman to Sage's quarters to retrieve his grave goods?"

"Enoch is not comfortable here. Perhaps you've noticed. He was kind enough to offer his help, and I thought by accepting his assistance, I might help him feel more a part of our community."

"Might he have had other reasons?" I wondered.

"For wishing to help?"

"For looking through Sage's belongings."

The thought had not occurred to her and even now, being less suspicious than I, Celestia had a hard time understanding what I meant. "Did he take something he shouldn't have?"

I, being far more mistrustful, knew I had no choice but to say, "I would have no way of knowing, since I know nothing of what Sage owned and I have never been in his quarters."

"Of course." There was her smile again. Fire and ice. "Sage and Hestia were not particularly close. Why do you suppose he wanted her to leave with him?"

"He knew she didn't belong here any more than he did."

"Hestia is devoted to Aed."

"She certainly was when she arrived here. Now, she confesses she was deluded."

Celestia's shoulders shot back. "She told you as much?"

"Margaret regrets decisions she made."

"Such as her decision to murder Sage."

"Such as her decision to ask forgiveness for a sin she did not commit."

"Yet she did confess. Why?" The truth dawned on Celestia. "She wanted to stay here with us and she would have admitted anything in order to do that. She wanted to remain with Master."

I bowed my head in acknowledgment before I said, "Time away has made Margaret see things in a more practical light. Before then, yes, she did not want to leave Master. He is a powerful presence." We arrived at the courtyard, but I was not ready to end the conversation. "They quarreled," I said quite simply. "The night Sage was killed."

"Hestia and Sage?"

She knew it was not who I was talking about, but since she refused to say it, I had to. "Master and Sage. You heard them. Just as we all did that evening before dinner. Master was angry. And whatever they disagreed about, Sage said Master could not stop him."

She set her lips in a hard line. "It means nothing."

"Coming just hours before Sage was killed, it might."

She flinched as if I'd slapped her. "You don't think . . ." She ruffled her purple robe with both hands. "What you imply is ridiculous."

"What was Master angry about?"

"I could not possibly know."

"And yet, I think you know all the secrets of the Children of Aed."

"There are no secrets here. Only Aed's light and blessings."

"And Master does Aed's bidding. And you have Master's ear. Surely he must have told you. Why was he angry with Sage?"

She took her lower lip in her teeth. "It does not mean what you think it means. It cannot."

"Then you should have no reluctance sharing."

To be sure we were alone, Celestia glanced around. "We had been busy that Saturday, the day before you arrived with the other Seekers. No one was able to go to town to pick up the post until late that afternoon when Albion collected it. As always, the letters were given to Master. He, then, gives them to their proper recipients. Of course you understand Master would never pry into the business of any of the Children."

"But this time, he did."

A look very much like remorse crossed her face. "I do not know why. Something about the letter addressed not to Sage, but to Lucien Tidwell, aroused Master's suspicions. He chanced to read it and when he did—"

"He was upset."

She let out a long, slow breath. "He is a good man. He has been blessed by Aed."

"And you love him."

She clutched her hands at her waist. "We are joined for eternity."

"Then it is only natural you do not want anything to happen to him."

"Not for a crime he didn't commit."

"Yet someone did."

She barked a laugh. "Hestia. It must be."

"And if it's not?"

"Perhaps Enoch Pullman, then. You said he had other reasons for being in Sage's quarters."

"Or the man in the armor?" I suggested.

It took a second for her to remember the scene at the funeral, but when she did, a smile blossomed on her face. It was not a happy smile. Neither was it amused. This smile reminded me more of a predator who'd just clapped eyes on a bit of juicy prey. "Yes. Him, certainly, for he'd like nothing better than to see us discredited."

"Who else?"

"I do not know." A tremor quivered over Celestia's shoulders. "But it is not Master," she said, and she turned and walked away. "I assure you, it is not Master."

I could not say if she was right or wrong, only that she was biased in her opinion and that I must be open to every possibility.

After I had a washup.

The thought propelling every step, I returned to my room, tossed my gloves on the table, and took off my clothing so that I might hang my cloak and dress on a hook near the door. It would take more than a good brushing to remove all traces of my night's adventure. If only Bunty were here! In her stead, I would take some paraffin from the lamp on my table later and dab it on the dirt, but the truth of it was, I was not sure if the dress was salvageable.

As the thought occurred, I looked over to where my clothing hung and caught my breath.

The fingertips of one glove shimmered, as did a spot on my cloak just there near the waistline. Even as I watched, the flicker intensified until it glowed green, a twin to the light which illuminated the specter that had tried to lure me to my doom.

Chapter 15

My surprise lasted no more time than it took for a chill to crawl up my spine. After all, I knew from the moment I first encountered it that the phantom could not be real. Now I had proof, and I closed in on my cloak to take a careful look at the spot I'd rubbed after my hand met the waxy substance there at the edge of the hole. Phosphorus. It surely must be. Though my knowledge of chemistry was rudimentary at best, even I knew the substance could be left in the light and thus, absorb it. In the dark, then, that light was released. I was fortunate, indeed, that I had been wearing gloves, for phosphorus can cause burning. Even so, I thoroughly washed my hands and kept a wet cloth on them while I sat to consider this peculiar development.

Someone smeared a robe with phosphorus so as to give the appearance of a phantasm. That much I knew for certain. Whoever might have done it, that person was determined to frighten the Children and keep them away from the church at night and so heartless as to watch me fall, then no doubt look into the pit as I lay insensible to see if I'd been injured. Or killed.

What wasn't clear was what the person hoped to gain

from this charade. Or if this phantom had anything to do with Lucien's death.

As determined as I was to get to the heart of the mystery, I needed time to recover from the accident, and I slept long enough to be woken by the sound of the gong that told me it was time for tea. I put on clean clothing and left my room, not joining the Children, but going, instead, to the church. While the rest of our company was gathered in the courtyard, I would have time to continue my investigation unimpeded.

I began at the back of the church, and there I found my dark lantern where I'd left it when I'd gone in pursuit of the phantom. As it had been a gift from Papa when we visited Sittanavasal, I was happy to have it back, and happier still that because of the afternoon light, I did not need to use it. I looked over the scene and saw that just as they'd said they would, the Children had gathered Lucien's ashes. The pyre was gone, the ground swept clean. I had just determined there was nothing new to be learned at the site when a breeze scattered the clouds and a shaft of sunlight flowed into the church, illuminating the ruin so that I could not help but gasp in awe at the outline of golden light against the framework of the clerestory windows and the pillars that had stood like sentinels for so many years, testament to the enduring faith of the monks.

It was there, in a tall tangle of hawthorn and holly that choked a pillar, that the light sparked and winked at me. There was something metal in the vegetation, surely, for nothing else would flash so. I followed the glint, eager to find the glittering object before the clouds gathered again and cloaked the metallic spark, and when I reached the spot, I stooped to sweep a hand through the undergrowth. When my fingers met metal, I plucked the object from the ground and held it in front of my eyes—a golden stickpin topped by a poorly fashioned lion.

What had been simple curiosity as I searched metamorphosed into suspicion. I knew who owned the bobble, but what had Enoch Pullman been doing here where undergrowth made walking next to impossible and the prickly vegetation caught clothing and scratched skin?

As I stood there wondering, I couldn't help but think of a stage act I'd once attended with Adelia and Sephora in London. There, a man who claimed to have mediumistic abilities demonstrated what he called token-object reading, in which he took belongings from their owners in the audience and purported to read the pasts and futures of the people from those objects. I needed no such purported talents to make use of the same technique. Silence pressing my ears, I folded the stickpin into my palm and imagined the scene as it must have appeared to Enoch Pullman. From where I stood—where he, too, must have stood—the place the pyre had been was on my left, and I could not imagine that he would need to conceal himself if he wished to observe it. But to my right . . . I looked that way . . . From here, Enoch had a perfect view of the prayer circle. A place he could see. But not be seen.

The spot was isolated, and so thorny and hidden, I was certain Enoch could not have come upon it by accident. He had searched out the place, chosen it, and he stood here so long, waiting and quietly shifting, he had lost his stickpin.

The very thought sent prickles of anticipation through me, and I wiped away the dribble of blood on my hand that marked a spot where my skin had scraped the leaves of a holly, and pocketed the stickpin. No sooner did I extricate myself from the thorny patch than I went to the courtyard.

As I expected, the Children were gathered around the tea

table, and I wasted no time in approaching Enoch. He was
standing to the side, alone, and he'd just taken a bite of watercress sandwich when I closed in on him.

"I must speak with you," I told him.

He grunted around the mouthful. "I have nothing to say
to you."

"And yet I think you might." I removed the stickpin from
my pocket and showed it to him, and when he made a move
to snatch it out of my hand, I closed my fingers over the pin.
"Shall we talk here? Or in private?" I asked.

His top lip curled. "Do you imagine I care what these others think of me?"

"You might when I tell you all I have discovered."

Grumbling, he finished off the sandwich and followed me
to a spot very near where Eli and I had concealed ourselves in
the overgrown rhododendron.

His feet slightly apart, his fists on his hips, Enoch stationed
himself between me and the courtyard. He meant the stance
to look fierce and himself, confident, and he might have suc-
ceeded except for the bit of butter on his chin. "I will tell
them you stole the pin from me," he growled. "Knowing you
are a thief, Master and his Children will be loath to have you
join their company."

"I have no more intention of joining their company than
you ever did."

"That is no concern of yours."

"Yet the reason may be. You are not here as a true Seeker.
You are here because Lucien Tidwell was here. You followed
him."

"I never did!"

"You were in Finsbury Park the day Master spoke there.
Do not deny it. I saw you there. And I am sure you did not

attend simply to hear what Master had to say about hazels and oaks. You had your eye on the acolytes the entire time. In fact, you were so intent on watching them, you nearly knocked me down. All the while, you tried to get near them. To get near Lucien, I would wager. You never had the chance while Master was speaking, and afterward, all was chaos and you lost him in the crowd. After all, one blue robe looks much like another. That is why you came here. And the moment you were out of the cart that brought us here, you caught sight of Lucien and went after him. I suspect he avoided you. He had no wish to speak with you. Tell me, how did you know him?"

"Tell me how you happen to have my stickpin."

I weighed the bauble in one hand. "I found what you lost."

He grumbled. "Yes, obviously. I suppose . . ." He grunted. "I should be grateful you retrieved it and now will return it."

He held out a hand.

I ignored it.

"And where did I find this pin, do you think?" I asked instead.

"Bah!" He sliced that hand through the air. "You might have found it anywhere. I had it with me when I arrived and now, I no longer have it. I realize a woman is not so logical a creature as a man, so I will explain as clearly as I may. This means I misplaced the pin at some time while I was here, and as I have been all over the property, it might have dropped in the dining hall, or the courtyard, or the garden even, as these infernal Children have had me pulling up carrots."

"It might have been in one of those places. But it wasn't. I found your pin, rather, in the church."

Another grumble. "Where we are meant to pray, yes. That makes perfect sense. I am sure it was at that ridiculous circle."

"Not at the circle."

He sniffed. "Then . . . then the stickpin must have slipped from my lapel during the funeral service. When the Children cleared the ashes, no doubt they found—"

"Not near the pyre," I told him.

When he shifted from foot to foot, I congratulated myself. I'd hoped that by goading him, I might make Enoch lose his composure and blurt out the truth. I was not quite there yet. But I was close. "It is a preposterous game you play, Miss Manville. As I was walking into the church. As I was coming out of the church. What difference does it make where I lost the pin?"

"It would not. Except when you lost it, you were concealed behind a pillar."

When he swallowed hard, his Adam's apple bobbed. "That is not possible. Why would I—"

"There is no other way the pin could have been where I found it. Such a tangle of vegetation. Such a private, isolated place."

"There is a simple explanation. I . . ." He stumbled over that explanation. "That is, I—"

"You certainly weren't behind the pillar during the funeral. Or even at the sham that was Margaret's forgiveness ceremony. Those times, you stood with the rest of us. But you were concealed behind that pillar at one time, exactly at a place where you could see the prayer circle clearly. The very place where Lucien breathed his last."

Color shot into his face. "I did not kill the man, if that's what you're implying." His words tore through the afternoon air and Pullman himself must have recognized the vehemence of them, because he pulled in a deep, trembling breath. "No," he mumbled, "I surely did not."

"Yet you know something about what happened to Lucien. Something you saw, perhaps? Why hide behind the pillar if it was not to keep your eye on him?"

His nose twitched and the dam within him seemed finally to break. "I had thought to talk to him. All that day. When we arrived, as you said, he avoided me. And later, after that ridiculous promise ceremony, he slipped away again. When I saw him leave his room that night—"

"The night he died? You were watching him?"

Enoch nodded. "My own room has a view of his and I turned off my light and opened my door but a bit so that I might observe his."

"You anticipated him going out, then?"

His shrug was nearly imperceptible. But then, Enoch struck me as a man who did not like to admit he must sometimes trust things to chance.

"Where did he go?"

"To the church. You know as much. I . . ." He flicked his tongue over his lips. "I followed, and I would have spoken to him then and there, but on arriving, I could see he was in some distress. He fussed and fidgeted."

"And you did not think to assist him?"

"I might have, but then that girl—"

"Hestia?"

"Yes, she entered the church and, not wanting to be discovered, I slipped into the shadows."

"So that you might spy on them."

"Really, I thought more that I would wait until whatever business they had together was completed, then I would have the opportunity to talk to Lucien myself. I never had the chance."

"Because as Hestia said—"

"It was an awful sight." He squeezed his eyes shut. "Lucien

began moaning and pacing, and the girl, she was frightened, and I thought I really should come forward, but then, how might that have looked?"

"It would have looked as if you stepped out of the shadows to help a fellow human being in distress."

"No, it would have revealed that I'd been concealed in the shadows in the first place." It was a weak excuse at best, yet to Enoch, it was sufficient. He scraped a hand along his chin. "The next thing I knew, he was on the ground, and the girl was screaming as if the devil himself was on her heels."

"And still, you did not reveal yourself."

"How could I then, for the rest of you came running, and how would it look if I happened to be there? No. I waited until you were all assembled and then I crept to the entrance and came up behind the crowd and joined you."

"But you never stepped forward to admit you knew Lucien. And you certainly must have. Even I, a *lowly woman . . .*" I instilled the words with enough acid to let him know I hadn't forgotten his insult. "Even I know you would not have followed him here otherwise. Your reluctance to reveal all only serves to make you look more guilty."

He opened his mouth to offer a protest, then snapped it shut again and was quiet for so long, I thought he might never answer. That is until his chest rose and fell on a faltering breath.

"I wished it," he said, and he lifted his chin. "Yes, I confess it. I wished Tidwell dead. Yet if you know that much, you may as well know the whole truth of the thing." His pluckiness dissolved, his shoulders slumped. "I had made the plan in my head. A hundred times I thought how I might waylay him, how I might attack and kill him. But even had I the opportunity, I did not have the nerve."

"What was Tidwell to you?"

"At one time, I thought he would become my sister's husband." The chuckle he added to the end of the statement contained no amusement. "He courted Eunice, you see. My twin."

"And treated her poorly."

"Not at first, no. But Lucien, he was an odd fellow." It was exactly what Bunty had learned from the man Daggart. "He could be happy, friendly. Charming, you might say. It was how he caught Eunice's eye. His merrymaking. His generosity. He was clever with words and could make her laugh with his stories. Yet as time went on . . ." His lips puckered. "Lucien would fall into black moods. As if his thoughts were a million miles away. As if he cared not a whit for anything but whatever it was that was swirling inside his brain. He'd promise Eunice a visit to the park, then she would not see him for weeks on end. He'd tell her he envisioned a future where they would have a home and a family together, then she'd hear rumors there were creditors at his doorstep. So many, we were told, he might never be out of debt. I never revealed it to Eunice, but I heard he even begged for drinks over at the Button. Then he completely disappeared from her life. Little did I imagine he would be here. I heard the news from a mutual acquaintance and so I went to Finsbury Park to see if it was true."

"Impolite, surely. Inconsiderate. Lucien was unreliable. Yet your sister loved him."

He shook his head. "Oh yes, Eunice was taken by the man, heart and soul."

"And you are surely a noble brother to defend her honor so. She was compromised by the relationship?"

Color shot into his cheeks. "Are you asking . . . ? Do you

mean . . . ? You are presumptuous for a woman, that is for certain. Especially since Eunice's role in the affair is really none of your business."

"Agreed. But yours is. And once your fondest wish was achieved and Lucien was dead, you did not leave the Children. There is a reason you stayed. Just as there is a reason you rooted through Lucien's room the morning of his funeral."

He let go a long breath. "When she was so much under Lucien's spell, Eunice gave him a token of her affection."

"And now she wishes it returned."

His shrug hardly explained. "It was a family heirloom. And valuable. Lucien had no right to it. I needed to recover it before he had the opportunity to sell it, for I was sure he would. The hounds were at his heels. He was in desperate need of money."

"This token, what was it?"

"A ring. Been in our family for four generations."

"And you really thought you could convince Lucien to give it to you?"

Enoch's shoulders rose and fell. "I suppose I wasn't thinking clearly at all. I meant to approach him, to reason with him in the name of what he and Eunice once felt for each other. And I will admit, if that did not work, I imagined myself using some show of force. I even carried . . ." He reached into his pocket and pulled out a knife of the kind that I had seen tradesmen use, one with a wooden handle with an unlocking mechanism in it, a folded blade hidden inside. "I did not have the courage to use it. You must believe me."

"Cutting a man and watching the agony on his face, yes, that would take courage, indeed. But poison is subtle. A murderer might administer it, then simply walk away."

"Which I did not. I was at the church. You discovered as much when you found my pin. I watched Lucien die."

"And took some pleasure in it, I think."

He did not deny it. "Lucien dishonored Eunice. And our family. Word has gone around about them. Everyone knows. Eunice is disgraced. She will never find another suitor, much less a husband."

"It seems to me, then, that Eunice should be the one who is angry at Lucien."

"Ha!" The sound burst from him and echoed back from the stone buildings that surrounded us. "She is not angry at all. She is pathetically miserable, as only a woman can be. She locks herself away in her room for days at a time and finds no pleasure in anything at all. She refuses even to leave the house. Do you see what this means? Can you possibly understand or are you as senseless as my sister? If Eunice can find no husband, then she will be forever a burden on me, on my finances. At least if I had been able to retrieve the trinket, I would relieve some of my losses."

It was not surprise that choked me so much as it was anger, and it was some moments before I could hiss, "That is why you came here? Not to help alleviate the hurt in your sister's heart, but to add a credit line to your ledger? That is unconscionable."

He stepped away. "You wanted the truth and there it is. I have not left because I hoped to find the ring. And now Lucien is dead, I suppose I never will. I have given up all hope of locating the ring, just as I've given up hope that Eunice will ever live anywhere but under my roof. Stupid girl!" He nodded in my direction. "I have heard Celestia say there is a cart coming tomorrow to return those ridiculous girls, Joan and Kitty, to London, and I will be leaving with them."

"Without the ring."

"Perhaps one of the Children will find it, eh? And send it on to me."

Or send it to Eunice so that she might sell it and buy herself a life away from her selfish and mean-spirited brother.

Of course, I could not put that particular thought into words, so instead I told him, "I will search for it when I have the chance. Tell me, what does this ring look like?"

He took my offer as earnest. "It is gold," he said. "There is a diamond in the middle of it and it is flanked by two smaller diamonds."

His words struck a chord that nudged a memory.

"Wait." When he turned to walk away, I dared to put a hand on his sleeve. "You have not told me, why do you suppose Lucien came to live with the Children?"

He shook off my hand. "The last time I spoke to him, he said he was involved in an investigation. Such balderdash! He was a hack, nothing more. A man of some little talent who sold a story or two to the newspapers—"

"And so had money."

"Then spent it like a drunken sailor and went for months without writing another word and thus, had none."

"You know what he wrote?"

"I never cared enough to ask and really, Miss Manville . . ." He sniffed and turned to walk away. "I cannot see why you do, either."

I waited until he was gone to begin to piece together the ideas that flooded through me. I thought of the penny dreadful Phoenix had shown me on the train. Of the photograph of Count Orlando's hand holding a quill. Of the ring he wore. One larger diamond surrounded by two smaller.

I knew then exactly why Lucien had come to live with the

Children. He was investigating, right enough, so that in his persona of Count Orlando, he might make up his titillating stories of the Children of Ud.

And I knew another thing, as well. I had uncovered another motive for Lucien's murder.

Dear Miss Hermione,

What has become of our world? There was a time a lady of means and status, a lady such as myself, could trust to the ease of finding reliable help. Girls coming to town from the country (some of whom were actually of better character than one might expect of those born in lowly circumstances) streamed into London in search of work, and work they did. Competently for the most part. Relentlessly if they wished to maintain their positions. They kept their minds on their work, their hands to the task, and did not clamor as these modern girls do, to have more than one half day a week off from their duties and to work fewer than eighteen hours a day.

I do not need to remind you, Miss Hermione, for I am sure you also remember the days when servants did not demand a fortune in exchange for their services. They knew their place and, in the right order of things, they kept to that place. As it should be.

Now, the girls who come to me seeking employment are demanding as much as thirteen pounds a year in payment! It is appalling, indeed, and though I know you cannot change an entire generation of young women who are lazy and somehow feel entitled to rob us of our wealth with higher wages and of our comfort with a lesser quality of work, I do believe your influence can bear upon some of them.

Talk some sense into them, Miss Hermione. They sorely need it. The continuance of the Empire demands it.

An Aggrieved Employer

Dear Aggrieved Employer,

You are correct. Everything you have communicated to me in your recent letter is truly appalling.

But oh, Aggrieved Employer, not in the way you mean it.

One half day away from work each week?

Eighteen hours of work every day?

All of this for thirteen pounds a year?

It is no wonder to me, and it shouldn't be to you, either, Aggrieved Employer, that women are leaving service to work in the factories that have sprung up around our country. That they are learning skills such as typewriting that they can use in our burgeoning businesses. That they are becoming telegraphers, and hostesses at A.B.C. tea shops.

Certainly in these cases, the hours demanded by their employment are fewer and the wages are higher than those you mention, though Miss Hermione must point out that if a woman is not remunerated exactly as a man is for comparable work, we are not as civilized a society as we pretend to be.

It seems then that I do not need to talk sense into a generation of women who are determined to make their way in the world. It is you, Aggrieved Employer, and those like you, who must learn the value of the work the serving class provides for us. And to compensate them appropriately. If we do not, then our common sense has deserted us, indeed.

Miss Hermione

Chapter 16

November 15

I wrote to Bunty forthwith, eager to tell her the details of all I'd discovered, but as the day after I learned the shocking news about Count Orlando's true identity was a Sunday, I would have to wait until the next day to return to Burton upon Trent to post my letter. Thanks to the efficiency of Her Majesty's postal service, that letter would arrive in London on Tuesday, and perhaps the information in it might allow Bunty to further her inquiries in the great metropolis. Until then, I knew I had best use the resources at hand and the knowledge I had gleaned to advance the course of my investigation and home in on the most likely suspects. After everything I'd learned, I felt I must turn a good portion of my attention to the DeClare family.

I was surprised to realize I was sorry for it. Not because of Hugh DeClare. He was a vulgar, horrible man, yet I knew I could not look at him through the lens of what I thought of his character, not when it came to the investigation. I must remain objective, logical. I must consider the facts, not the way he made my flesh creep. One fact, it was clear, was that he cared for no one but himself. Not for the poor, dead wife he had spoken of so callously. Not for Master, for Hugh was concerned only that his younger son take up the reins of the title. He certainly did not care for Tarquin, either. Tarquin, who was considerate and charming, even in light of his father's cruelty. Dear Tarquin, who was doomed.

In my room that Sunday morning, dressing so that I might go outside and assist the Children with their chores, I wiped a tear from my eye and retrieved my buttonhook to fasten my boots, forcing myself as I did to concentrate on the problem at hand. Yes, Hugh DeClare seemed a likely murderer. No, Master did not, at least not on the surface. But I could not look away from him. If Master knew Lucien and Count Orlando were one and the same—if that was what they had words about the night I arrived at Alburn—I must consider him as much a suspect as his father.

Yet more disturbing even than the idea of Lucien's murder was the realization that either Master or Hugh had stood back and done nothing as Margaret was accused of the crime, taken before the magistrate, and committed to trial. That was not only horrifying, but completely unacceptable, and I renewed my vow of bringing justice to Lucien, and freedom to Margaret.

I had but a few minutes before I needed to help with breakfast in the refectory so I started in the simplest, and the most logical place: Lucien's watch. Though it looked to be silver, it was, in fact, gimcrack, thin silver plate over cheap nickel. After all I'd deduced from my conversation with Enoch, this did not surprise me. Lucien himself was all artifice, posing as a Seeker, becoming a Novice and an Adept all in the name of spying on the Children, then turning the truth about them topsy-turvy with salacious fictional details.

As it had the night before when I learned of Eunice's love token and Enoch's search for it, Lucien's deception took my breath away, but I refused to let either my outrage or my astonishment distract me from the task at hand.

The watch. It was coated with soot and grime from the funeral fire, and the silver plate had melted then solidified into tiny beads upon its surface. I scraped them away with the blade of a knife and was relieved, indeed, that being nickel and thus able to withstand high temperatures, the watch case beneath had not sustained any substantial damage. When I pushed the button at the top of the timepiece, the case popped open.

There, nestled inside the case, was a sprinkling of dried vegetation. I pinched some of it between thumb and forefinger and sniffed. The odor was not unpleasant and vaguely familiar and I sat back, satisfied with my mission to retrieve the watch yet still confused as to why it—and the bits of herbs inside it—mattered so much to Lucien. Why was so trivial a thing so important to him? It must have been, for as Margaret told me, he'd fussed with the watch at the church, and even as he writhed in agony, the poison eating away at him, he fiddled with his watch. Could the bits of herbs have had anything to do with what he told Margaret, that his future was assured?

This was the riddle I must solve if I was going to get to the bottom of the mystery, and like those token-object readers in London, I wished I could learn more from simply holding the watch. As that was assuredly not going to happen, I snapped the case closed and tucked away the watch. It had no further secrets to reveal.

November 16

It was maddening, truly, to have so little to lead me, and the next day, I still turned the conundrum over in my head as I joined Enoch, Joan, and Kitty where they stood with Celestia in the courtyard. Those three would leave forever; I would go along as far as Burton upon Trent merely for the sake of posting my letter to Bunty.

"You are certain?" Just as I arrived, Celestia looked from one girl to the other. They had never earned their yellow robes, they never would, and they stood in the chill morning air in the clothes they'd arrived in, threadbare dresses of drab cloth, shawls so thin they did little to keep out the cold morning air, boots with soles nearly worn through. "You desire to return to London?"

Joan swallowed down the last of a piece of dark brown bread and nodded. "Ain't what we thought it might be here," she admitted. "Not the ghost or—"

"Or the orgies?" Celestia offered her a gentle smile.

For the first time since she'd arrived at Alburn, Joan did not smile back. She plucked a bread crumb from her bosom and popped it in her mouth, and I noticed there were two more pieces of bread twisted and tied into one corner of her shawl.

"Where will you go?" I asked Joan when I stepped up to her side.

The girl's shoulders rose and fell. "Ain't got no references. And Mrs. Beechum—"

"She won't have us back," Kitty chimed in. A tear slipped down her cheek. "She is altogether too dreadful to do us such a kindness."

Celestia and I exchanged looks. We both knew that without references or prospects, there would be no place for the girls other than sleeping rough.

Unless . . .

"They might stay here," I suggested to Celestia. "Without becoming Novices. There is always work to be done and I have seen the girls contribute as much as they are able."

"I think not." Celestia's smile was stiff, and feeling the full chill of it, it struck me that my words had been right on the mark. I meant contribute in regards to work. Celestia thought of it as financial. In that regard, Joan and Kitty had nothing to contribute, no dowry to offer to Aed. It was time for them to go.

I knew better than to think I could change a society, to wish away the injustices that visited girls like Joan and Kitty more cruelly and more often than they touched those of us who were protected by our positions and our wealth. Yet I could not stand by and watch them fade into the faceless mass, those poor creatures who roamed the streets of our cities and learned, firsthand, the horrors of our poorhouses.

An idea struck, and if I took the time to consider it, I feared I would convince myself it was a mistake at best and a disaster at its worst. I looked from one girl to the other. "I have seen you work here. You are helpful in the kitchen and good with the chickens and with harvesting the garden. But do you think . . . ? Do you suppose you might be able to learn new skills? Are you conscientious enough?"

Kitty wrinkled her nose. Joan poked her in the ribs. "She means do we do our work as we should." She swung her gaze to me. "We do, miss. Or we would if we had references and could find a place that would employ us."

"It would take a good deal of hard work to learn a skill

that does not involve cleaning or cooking or laundry. Do you understand that?"

Joan's cheeks shot through with color. "If you're meaning, miss, that you wish to turn us into strumpets—"

"Not at all!" I did not laugh, because for girls like Joan and Kitty, there was nothing funny about the situation. Too many girls like these were left on the streets with no other option. It was either submit to employers such as the aggrieved woman who had so recently written to Miss Hermione or eke out a life of degradation. "I was thinking rather of typewriting," I said, and added, "At least for Joan, for you can read and would be capable. I know of a place that will give you lessons."

Her bottom lip puckered. "As if I could afford such a thing!"

"It will, in fact, be free thanks to the fact that I have recently purchased a typewriting machine. And Kitty . . ." I turned her way. "You could learn as well, but you must first know your letters."

The girl's face lit. "Joan can help."

"Yes, I believe she will, but we will also arrange for a tutor. For both of you, in fact. The more educated you are, the more likely you are of being able to take care of yourselves. If this idea appeals to you—" I removed a calling card from the silver case in my chatelaine and handed it to Joan. "As soon as you arrive in London, you will go to Parson's Lodge. The address is there on the card. You will take a . . ." Again I reached into my chatelaine and this time, removed a coin and handed it to Joan. "You will take a cab there, and when you arrive, you will speak to Bunty, the housekeeper."

"And what shall we tell her, miss?" Joan turned the card in her hand.

"Show Bunty my card and tell her I sent you and that she is to arrange for accommodations for you and some new clothing as well. When I arrive back in London, I will take care of the rest."

The girls squealed with pleasure and, hanging on to each other, boarded the cart. Enoch Pullman sat opposite them. I was next in, and Phoenix, who would accompany us, offered a hand to assist me.

Celestia seemed nothing if not relieved to be rid of three Seekers who had no place with the Children, but, done studying them, she looked my way, a V of worry between her eyes.

"You'll be back, won't you?" she asked. I wondered if she wanted me to say I'd return. Or if she rather hoped she'd never see me again.

"I still have questions and I can find the answers only here."

She shook her head, and her plait of hair moved like a thick black snake against her right shoulder. "You are looking for the answers in the wrong place. You would be wise to remember it."

Was it a warning? Or a threat?

As Phoenix urged the cart horse forward and we started our journey, I did not have the opportunity to find out, but when we rumbled past the church, I chanced a look back and saw Celestia watching me. So calm. So serene. It sent chills up my spine.

☙

At the train station in Burton upon Trent, I bid my fellow travelers farewell, hoping as I did that Joan and Kitty had the sense to do as I'd instructed and go directly to Parson's Lodge. As for Enoch, I assured him I would search for his sister's ring. It was no false promise. The person who possessed the ring might well be Lucien's killer. After, Phoenix was kind enough to take me to the post office on High Street to post my letter and collect any post for the Children.

"You don't mind keeping yourself busy for a bit, do you?" he called down to me when I descended from the cart. "Celestia has given me a list of supplies to purchase."

We set a time and place to once again meet, and I entered the post office to the clatter and hum of men working to sort the mail. The fellow at the desk was young and rail thin. He had a shock of flaxen hair and spotty skin. When I handed him my letter, he gave me a smile. It did not last when I asked if there was anything waiting for Alburn.

"That lot, eh?" His gaze darted to my left then to my right as if he expected to find one of Count Orlando's gruesome fiends at my shoulder. "You don't look the sort."

"I am not any sort," I assured him. "Other than the sort who is trying to collect the post."

"You're not wearing a robe."

"I do not have a robe."

"Then how do I know you're one of them? You ain't got that look about you, menacing like."

I was sorely tempted to point out that I could be quite menacing in my own way when my patience was tried, but knew that stratagem would do me no good. Instead, I smiled at the same time I backed away from the desk behind which he stood. "Very well. If you will not give me the post to take to the Children, you will simply have to bring it up to the abbey yourself."

He went as pale as bread dough. "You don't really expect me to . . ." He swallowed hard and leaned forward, lowering his voice to share what he thought to be sinister information. "There be depravities there."

"Yes, there most certainly are." My smile was bright. "And when you bring the post, you can get a firsthand look at them. There is a sacrifice scheduled for this afternoon." I looked him up and down. "You are thin, but you'll do. We make a soup, you see, of those we cook over an open fire. You're lucky, indeed, to be chosen. All for the glory of Aed!"

His eyes were as pale as a fish's. They popped. "You wouldn't!"

"I wouldn't have to if you would give me any letters that might be waiting for those at the abbey."

"Y-yes, miss. Cer-certainly, miss." Without taking his eyes off me, he backed away. "I'll check and see what might be here, miss."

He was back in but a few minutes, no less flustered than when he pictured himself roasting on a spit. He held three letters and passed two to me. One was addressed to me from Bunty, and I eagerly accepted it. The second, also for me, was from Tarquin DeClare, and I knew instantly there must be information in it that would help my investigation; otherwise, Tarquin would not have bothered to write. The third letter the young man clutched in one trembling hand while he ran a finger of the other hand along the inside of his stiff collar.

"I had no knowledge of this here letter being here, miss. I swear. Last time one of them fellows in a robe came around to collect the mail, I gave it over to him as I always do. But this here letter . . ." He looked at the envelope in his hand as if he was afraid it might erupt into flames. "I never clapped eyes on this here letter, so you see I could not have given it to him. But I found it, I did, just on Saturday. It was beneath a bin, where it must have fallen. And it went unnoticed I don't know how many days. You're not going to . . ." He darted his tongue over his lips. "There aren't magic words you can say, are there? To punish me, like, for losing the letter? I mean, I wouldn't want to be changed into a toad or nothing."

"Toads are so unimaginative!" I gave him a spirited laugh. "I should think you'd make a far better scarecrow, propped up in some farmer's field for years on end. Oh yes." I narrowed my eyes, hoping to look mysterious and thinking he must surely know I was teasing. "In all weather. Wind and rain and snow. And you, hung there with all your intellect intact but unable to move. Frozen, as it were, in time. Watching the world move around you, but unable to save yourself. Enchanted. Cursed."

He shoved the letter at me and as soon as I took it out of his hand, he chafed his palms against the legs of his trousers. "Like I told you, I'm sorry it's coming to you so late and I hope you don't hold that against me and the like, but—"

"All that matters is I have the post now." I turned away, but my conscience pricked. It was unwarranted, surely, to leave the young man in fear. "I will not forget your kindness. You can be sure of that."

"And you will not curse me?"

It was a simple enough promise to make.

Still smiling about the incident, I made my way outside. There was a park across the road, and I found a bench and first opened the letter from Tarquin.

"Father was in Nottingham with his mistress on the day in question," it said quite simply. "He could not have administered the poison."

I did my best to take the news in stride, but the truth of it was that I was sorely disappointed. Though it betrayed my sense of logic and all I held dear in the name of finding the truth, I had wanted Hugh DeClare to be guilty. Now, he was eliminated from my list of suspects.

Next, I opened the letter from Bunty. I will admit to feeling something of a jolt when I read that Sephora had not only followed her on her recent visit to Lucien's rooms but insisted on investigating alongside her.

Sephora?

I set the letter in my lap, the better to turn over the thought in my head, but no matter how many times I considered it, I could not align it with all I knew of my half sister's habits and inclinations. Could it be . . . ? Was it even possible . . . ? Were there depths to Sephora's character I had yet to plumb? Could there be intelligence working behind that frothy exterior of hers? Boldness, even?

I was not only surprised, but pleased. I had always hoped there might be some backbone to my half sister and now, it seemed, that wish had come true. My only question—at least for myself, at least for now—was how I might cultivate and encourage her, and I vowed I would think on it more closely when I had a quiet moment. For now, I turned my attention to the rest of the letter, and found encouragement in what Bunty and Sephora had discovered in Lucien's rooms.

Not only did Bunty validate the story Enoch told me about his sister, Eunice, but her report of Lucien's macabre furnishings reinforced my belief as to Lucien and Count Orlando being one and the same. Logical and orderly myself, I found it difficult to understand the more artistic bent of a writer's brain, but I had heard often enough that they were mercurial creatures with odd habits. I had no doubt that Lucien's attention to all that was ghastly and horrific fueled his imagination.

Satisfied I had uncovered useful information and pleased that Bunty (and yes, Sephora) had corroborated it, I turned my attention to the third missive, the letter that had been lost and just recently recovered. It was postmarked from London on November 5, three days before the man it was addressed to had been murdered.

A shiver of anticipation cascaded through me, and I wasted no time in tearing open the letter. It was signed by a man, I was sure, for the handwriting was thick and blockish. He was called Speedwell and the fact that he identified himself no further told me he must be someone Lucien knew well. I read the letter quickly then read it again to align the information in it with what I'd already discovered, this time mumbling the words below my breath as I read.

"'I am anxious, indeed, to see the full proof of what you've hinted at in your recent communication,'" Speedwell wrote. "'If you are correct, Tidwell, this matter will solidify your claim to journalistic renown, eclipsing even your fame as CO. No other has been able to unravel the tentacles of the scandal. No other has been able to uncover the truth and thus expose the guilty party. I eagerly await your return so that we can put our heads together on this. Oh, how the revelation of the killer's true identity will make the sales of our publication soar!'"

Scandal? Killer? I could not help but burn with curiosity. Could the proof Speedwell hinted at have anything to do with the scrap of brightly colored paper Lucien valued so? I barely had time to think on it, for the rest of the letter was equally astonishing.

"'As to the other matter,'" Speedwell went on. "'I will be anxious to hear the full tale of how you obtained the sample of the herbs you sent.'"

Herbs?

The word slammed into me, as did its meaning. Lucien, it seemed clear, had discovered more of the herb than what he kept inside his watchcase. Those bits were insurance, I would wager, in the event what he sent to London was lost or damaged. Speedwell had the bulk of the herb and as I, myself, had thought to send what I'd found to Hayward and Son, a druggist I was acquainted with back in the metropolis, I was grateful Lucien had done my work for me. Eager to hear what conclusion Speedwell had arrived at, I read on.

"'Just as you suspected, it is a drug of the sort that addles the mind, and the chemist I spoke to said that when ingested, it might cause euphoria and even delusions.'"

My stomach sickened and I gasped. Like Lucien apparently had, I, too, had suspected all along.

One pot or two?

The one pot brewed and served only to Celestia and to Master. The other tea was meant to keep the others happy and smiling, compliant, so that they might do their work and pledge their lives and their fortunes to the Children. This tea was from a different pot, a special brew that turned the light of day into fierce and flaming proof of Aed's love.

I shook my head, disappointed in my own abilities to reason. I had been experiencing proof of the drug all along and yet had not seen—or allowed myself to see—the truth sooner because it was impossible to believe in such duplicity. Now, all seemed clear. A drug in the tea explained why Margaret had come to her senses about the Children once she was imprisoned and out of their sphere, and why on that first day I arrived at Alburn and shared in afternoon tea, I had seen the watercolor illusion in the abbey.

Yellow. Red. Blue.

Like the colors of the scrap of paper I'd found in Lucien's room.

Chapter 19

I hurried to the place where I had arranged to meet Phoenix, and when he arrived, I hopped onto the seat next to him even before he brought the horse to a complete halt. On reaching Alburn, I was out of the cart just as quickly. My heart beating a furious pace, my breaths coming fast, I bypassed tea (though Phoenix told me I looked overexcited and would benefit from a toasted crumpet or two) and hurried into the church.

At the entrance, I paused, scanning the empty space, casting my mind back to that first day I arrived, to my tour of the grounds with Master. I had seen the flash of light outside the castle, the light I now knew was the Viscount Hinckley in his armor, but at the time, I was as baffled by it as I was by the way my head spun and the ground felt uneven beneath my feet. Then, I wondered if that confusion accounted for my experience in the church. Now I knew better. My mind had been numbed and my senses duped by the drug contained in the cup of tea I'd consumed that made the light sharper and blurred my vision, and though I remembered the scene clearly, the image in my mind was as diffused as a watercolor and as hazy as the memory of a dream.

I remembered standing at the prayer circle with Master, so

now, that is where I started my re-creation of the event. I re-called how he told me of Aed's love for his Children and their obedience to his will, all the while keeping his back turned to the apse. It is no wonder, then, that he did not see what I had seen.

At the time, my ears rang and my head spun. Now, I felt the silence press close around me, my senses on the alert. As I did then, I closed my eyes, and when I opened them again, I looked across the transept just as I had done that day, toward the place where I'd seen a figure appear as if out of nowhere in a blur of color, sun, and shadow.

"It was there," I told myself. Keeping an eye on the spot where I'd first seen the figure, I went and stood where it had been. "Not a figment of my imagination. But a person. A man by the size of him."

Lucien?

"He was here and then in the blink of an eye, vanished. Much as the phantom did the night I came to investigate at the funeral pyre."

I had determined that the glowing green phantom might have disappeared into the crypt below the church and now, I wondered the same about the figure I'd seen in daylight. Could he have come up from the crypt? Is that why it seemed he'd materialized out of thin air? There was no sign that person had been there, and no way I could see that led into the crypt below the church, not there near the altar or in the choir where I saw the figure again when it reappeared. No flash of red, no glimmer of yellow, no splash of blue like the colors on the scrap of paper I'd found under Lucien's bed. Nothing.

I had been so filled with hope by what I'd read in Speed-well's letter, so sure that if I walked through what had happened that day when my brain was too addled by the drug to see the truth, I would discover something that would help me straighten out the tangled web of my investigation. Now, I felt myself at an impasse, much as I had felt since the night Lucien died here as Enoch Pullman watched from the shadows and Margaret stood frozen with panic. Disheartened, I dropped onto the trunk of a topped tree. The better to think. The better to rest and clear my troubled mind.

And that is when I saw it. A smear of color not visible to anyone who might be standing nearby. A smudge of yellow. A dash of red. The very slightest bit of blue.

It was there below the toppled remains of what might once had been the marble steps that led to the ambo, tucked between a tangle of vegetation and a mound of twigs and small stones, a place where it might have been quickly hidden when the person who held it realized he was not alone in the church, that Master and I stood not far away.

It was a single piece of paper. Carefully, so as not to damage it, I plucked it from its hiding place.

I am not sure what I expected to see, but it certainly wasn't this, a broadside perhaps twenty inches wide and thirty long. It was printed, as these advertisements so often are, in colors so garish as to be sure to attract attention, and when I saw that the bottom left-hand corner of it was torn away, my breath caught and my heartbeat quickened. I had no doubt if I fitted the bit of paper I'd found in Lucien's room to the torn corner, I would have a perfect match. So, this was his treasure, the proof Lucien promised to Speedwell. I studied it, wondering as I did how the advertisement might, as Speedwell had said, lay bare a scandal and shine light on a murder.

The Great Alastor, Man of Many Mysteries!
Royal Theatre of Magic

The words were emblazoned across the yellow background of the poster in letters that danced over the head of
a golden-haired magician in evening dress and a tall top hat.
His arms were out at his sides and playing cards flew from
his left sleeve; flowers sprouted from his right. The beautiful
flaxen-haired woman at his side wore a flowing blue gown
and held out a tray to Alastor. The instruments on it—a sword
and a goblet and a glistening crown—floated above the tray's
surface, levitated by a magic apparently so astonishing, even
she seemed bewitched.

Tiny red devils cavorted around Alastor's feet, their pitch-
forks raised, yet he seemed not to notice their frolic. His intense, fiery gaze was focused instead ahead of him, looking
into the eyes of all who dared to look upon him. Smoke rose
from his fingertips.

I did not understand how Lucien could speak of this
odd advertisement as assuring his future. Or how Speedwell
thought of it as proof. But I knew one thing. I had seen the
magic before my very eyes. Smoke arising from Master's fingers when Margaret begged forgiveness and admitted she had
killed Lucien, the signal that Aed was not pleased, that the
authorities must be called, that a young girl must stand accused so that there was no need to search for a killer. The real
killer.

I lost not a moment, but raced to my room to conceal the
advertisement, then hurried to the stable. With any luck, Phoenix would not have unharnessed horse from cart and he could
take me again to Burton upon Trent. I needed to let Bunty

know what had happened immediately and had no time to write and post a letter. I must send a telegram.

Sephora

November 20

"Two sovereigns?" The woman in a horror of a white dress awash in lace, ruffles, and ribbons gave me a squint-eyed look. She clearly thought I was mad, yet that did not keep her from flicking her tongue over her lips when she glanced at the coins in my hand. The face of our Queen looked up at her from the gold sovereigns. Regal. Tempting. "You want to give me two sovereigns just so you can—"

"Have your dress. Yes." The very thought was nearly as appalling as the idea of actually wearing the dressmaking disaster, but I choked down my disgust and managed one of my usual dazzling smiles. "I will give you two gold sovereigns if, just for this evening, you allow me to wear your costume and take your place onstage."

"You?" She laughed. One of her front teeth was missing. The others, I am sorry to report, were a rather noxious shade of green. I was hardly surprised. Thora—for that is what the broadside posted at the front of the Royal Theatre of Magic called her, even though I'd learned from her that her given name was Bess Plunket—was no paragon. Her chin was pointed and far too weak to be at all attractive. Her eyes were set so close together, I imagined she could see little beyond the bridge of her own nose. Her skin was blotchy, and her hair was sponged with so much bandoline I thought it would be frozen just as it was—a riot of wisps and fat sausage curls—from now until the end of time. "You want this here dress? To go out there onstage? A lady like you? And do what, darlin'?"

"Assist the Marvelous Maxwell, of course. Just as you do onstage each and every evening."

"You want to assist . . ." When she laughed, she held on to her sides as if they might burst. "Do you know the Marvelous Maxwell? He's really called Reggie Nunkin, and Reggie, he's a right son of a bitch. Nasty as a pigsty and usually drunk. Why'd you want to put on my clothes and go prancin' around onstage after the likes of 'im? You ain't thinkin' . . ." Her lips puckered. "You don't think that he can, like, really do magic, do you? That you can get close so as to learn his mysterious secrets?" She hooted. "That's just what the posters say to sell tickets! That he can make rabbits and flowers and fire appear like they come from thin air. That he can saw me in half like it's real and them in the audience get flustered and then relieved when I am safe and sound at the end. You don't think I'm barmy, do you? You don't think I'd really let some bloke what smells like fish and gin take a saw to me?"

"I am sure you are far too sensible for that," I told her, though of course, I did not know Thora well enough to be sure that was true. From what I'd seen of her, I highly doubted it. "Nor do I think the Marvelous Maxwell has any real magical powers." I felt this was important to establish from the start so she knew I was not easily hoodwinked, not as poor Margaret had been by the Children of Aed with their talk of enchantment and miracles. "I merely wish to talk to this Maxwell fellow. And I have tried. I have been here at the theater all day, yet he eludes me. I thought perhaps if I was onstage with him—"

"That he'd pay you the least bit of mind?" She slapped her knee. "You are a dainty thing, but a puddin' head nonetheless. Reggie thinks of nothin' and no one but himself. Himself and where he'll get his next bottle."

"Yet I was hoping he might be able to provide me with the information I am seeking."

"Information, eh?" Thora looked again at the coins in my hand and the message was clear; she, too, might have information. For the right price, it could be purchased.

I took another sovereign from my purse, thinking as I did that at this rate, I would pay Thora more in one night than she made in a month from appearing as the Marvelous Maxwell's assistant. I remembered the name in Violet's telegram, the man she said it was vital for her to learn more about. We had tried. Bunty and I had scoured London for countless hours over the past days searching for information about the man whose picture Violet had seen on an advertising poster. Violet being Violet, of course she did not say why this Alastor was so important to her, but she hinted, and oh, those hints were tantalizing. Secrets. Scandals. Murder. I was intrigued, surely, but even more importantly, I was as committed as Violet was to assuring Margaret's freedom. I would do anything to make that a reality. Even if it meant appearing in public in a hideous gown.

"He is called Alastor the Great," I told Thora. "Or perhaps it is Alastor the Wonderous. Something of that ilk. I need to learn all I can about him."

Thora waved away my words as if they were no more than annoying gnats. "Never heard of him."

"But you must have. He performs here at the Royal Theatre of Magic."

She wrinkled her nose. "Not since I been here, and I been here going on three years this coming spring. But then . . ." She raised a bony shoulder. "Magicians is odd folks. They change their names like they change the tricks in their acts. So as to attract more attention, don't you know. To start over, so to speak. Maybe this Alastor fellow, maybe he's someone else by now."

"Someone like the Marvelous Maxwell?"

"Not bloody likely! I've known Reg since back before I came here, you see. He used to work the fairs and the festivals, going 'round the country, performin' his tricks. At some of them, I was there, too." She gave me a broad wink. "There's workingmen what come from all over to them fairs and a girl has to look after herself, if you get my meaning." I was afraid I very much did, but thankfully, Thora gave me no time to think about it. "He was Magical Alexander back then, was Reg. Never Alastor."

"But this Alastor was here. At the Royal Theatre of Magic. That is what the poster Violet found says." Thora, of course, cared for none of this. She didn't know who Violet was and had no concern whatsoever for what Violet had found. "Someone must know him."

"P'haps." Thora shrugged. "What I've been told is that magic, it's a small world, as they say. One magician knows another and another and so on. If you spoke to Reg . . ."

Her eyes were aglow when she looked again at the coins in my hand, and I knew Thora was reminding me we might have an agreement and I might have a chance to finally speak with Reggie Nunkin, known onstage as the Marvelous Maxwell. If I was willing to pay for the privilege.

"Yes. Yes. Here you are." I dropped three coins into her outstretched hand. "Now remove your dress and tell me exactly what I am supposed to do."

❧

What I was supposed to do, according to Thora, was very little, indeed.

First of all, I was to walk out in front of the audience looking pert and pretty.

It goes without saying, pert and pretty are second nature to me. In spite of the hideous costume I borrowed from her that was too big in the waist and too wide in the shoulders for someone as delicate as myself, I could assuredly accomplish this part of the job with far more panache than Thora ever dreamed of possessing.

After that, she told me, when Maxwell stepped onstage, my job was to look impressed by his presence, enthralled with his talents, overwhelmed to be there with one of the truly great magicians of our time.

Once Maxwell started into his act, my role in the magical charade somehow became even simpler; I was to give the magician whatever the propman working from the wings handed to me.

This, obviously, would be easily accomplished.

There was more. For instance, I would need to do whatever Maxwell instructed as far as sitting here or standing there, and when he completed each of his magic tricks, I was to look amazed so as to elicit applause from the audience.

Looking amazed even when I did not feel the least bit impressed seemed the easiest task of all. After all, every young woman who had been brought up to be a proper lady knew the art of deceit. A compliment to a rival about how her dress flattered her coloring when she really looked ghastly in green. A smile at a suitor with crossed eyes simply because he was the youngest son of an earl. A laugh when there was actually nothing funny. Applause at the opera when . . . Well, my goodness, no one really enjoyed all that yowling and shrieking, did they? I mean, no one other than Violet.

Yes, I was prepared and would make my first appearance onstage in just a few minutes' time, as soon as the act that went on before Maxwell's (there was talk of a magic lantern show and I was disappointed not to see it) was finished. Until then . . .

The mirror in the backstage dressing room was cloudy and the lighting dreadful. I turned to my left and my right, doing my best to arrange my hair and add some color to my cheeks by pinching them. Perhaps if people in the audience were looking at my face, they would not pay so much attention to my gown.

"It is madness, I tell you."

The voice came from behind me, but I did not need to turn around to catch sight of the speaker. I knew Bunty had entered the dressing room. I could see her reflection in the mirror. She looked like a thundercloud.

"I won't allow it," she grumbled.

"Won't allow it? You?" I will admit, I did not like the thought of admonishing Bunty for being so forward. As impossible as it would have been for me to believe when Violet and I first came to live in England, over the past weeks, investigating side by side, Bunty and I had formed a relationship of sorts. Dare I call it a friendship? I did not wish to hurt her feelings. But she was, after all, still a servant, and as a servant, she could hardly say what I was or was not allowed to do.

I spun to face her, the better for her to see my moue of disapproval. "You wouldn't speak so to Violet," I told her.

"There would be no use speaking so to Violet. Miss Violet will do what Miss Violet will do, whether I approve of it or not."

"Then why shouldn't I do the same?" To show her how little I cared for her opinion, I spun back toward the mirror and fussed with my hair. "I can be every bit as strong and as independent as Violet. I can be bold, just as Violet is. And I am as intelligent as she is, too."

Was that a smile I saw shoot across Bunty's face? It was gone by the time I turned around. "There is no other way for me to talk to Maxwell," I told her in an attempt to make her see my reasoning. "And besides, what harm can it do? I will walk out on the stage, do what I've been told to do, and while I'm at it, charm this Reggie fellow so much that after he concludes his act, he'll talk to us about Alastor. It should be easy enough. Even in this dress, I look far better than Thora ever did. He will be completely smitten by me. Men always are. Then he'll be willing to talk. It is the only way, Bunty. All other avenues of our inquiries have led us to dead ends."

Her shoulders drooped. "You're right enough about that. Yet I cannot think . . ." She wrung her hands. "Oh, if someone you know is in the audience, if your aunt Adelia catches wind of what you're about, if there are any journalists lurking in the theater—"

I gasped. I had not thought of journalists. "No. No," I told Bunty and myself. "None of that is possible. Aunt Adelia won't know because neither of us will tell her. And really, Bunty, how can we expect anyone of my acquaintance to be at such a shabby place as this? As for journalists . . ." As if one of their number might actually be lurking in the corners of the tiny dressing room, I glanced around. "There is no news here, no sensation. Nothing for a journalist to write about."

"Yet Lucien Tidwell may have been here and you know what Violet learned about him."

"That he was Orlando! Yes!" I pressed a hand to my heart, as thrilled to know the secret as I was bereft at what it meant. "What will happen to his wonderful stories of Ud now that he is dead? And what was he doing here? There must be some connection between Tidwell and this place. Otherwise, he would not have valued the advertisement Violet discovered. In a church, did she say? Under a dirty old rock?" The very thought caused me to shiver. "Violet does get herself into the most ridiculous predicaments."

"It seems she is not the only one." Bunty's voice was crisp.

She was right, and I hardly cared. Ridiculous dress or not, I had to do all I was able to help Margaret. I gave myself one final look in the mirror and hauled the sagging shoulder of my dress up as I did. "By the time the evening is over, I will have Reggie eating out of my hand. Charming men is, after all, one thing I'm very good at."

"Oh, aye."

A stagehand pounded on the door and told me it was time to get moving and Bunty stepped aside. "You will be careful, won't you, Miss Sephora?"

I fluffed my gown and tossed my head. "I won't need to be careful, Bunty. I am going to be fabulous!"

I stepped confidently into the hallway, through the wings, to the very edge of the stage, waiting there for the master of ceremonies, a man in a threadbare red velvet jacket and orange-and-brown plaid trousers, to complete his introduction. He did so with a flourish, stepping back with a little bow and sweeping his arms in my direction. "Thora!" he called.

The name did not register in my mind. I did not move.

He cast a slant-eyed look into the wings and motioned again. "Thora!"

"That's you." One of the stagehands pushed me, and to hoots and catcalls, I stumbled onto the stage.

It was smaller than I expected. The audience was closer than I thought they might be. The limelight that glowed there at the center of the stage was a brilliant white and brighter than I imagined. It made me squint. Fortunately, I did not have to endure it for long. To a smattering of applause, the Marvelous Maxwell took the stage and wasted no time bumping me aside so he could be in the full glow of the limelight when he took a bow.

The musicians in the pit began a cheery (and rather off-key) rendition of "The Boy in the Gallery" and Maxwell turned his back on the audience. "Who the bloody hell are you?" he rasped.

Thora was correct about the gin and fish. Remembering my mission, I managed a smile nonetheless. "Bess is unwell. I'm here to—"

"Hat and eggs!" He snapped his fingers, turned to the audience, and shot me a look when I did not move fast enough to fetch what he wanted. Those things, a very tall top hat and five eggs, were provided to me by a stagehand and I gave the hat to Maxwell, smiled at the audience, and froze.

James Barnstable sat in the front row next to Bunty.

I can only imagine how my cheeks reddened, for they felt like fire. How could James possibly smile the way he was smiling when he gazed at me and I wore a dress that looked as if it came from a church jumble? I might have melted right into the pitted wooden floor of the stage if Maxwell's voice didn't ring out.

"I will now cook an omelet for you over a candle and in this very hat," he said. He held out a hand and hissed, "Egg."

I handed him the first egg. Then the second, the third, and the fourth. Each time, he held the hat up high over his head where everyone was sure to see it and cracked one egg after another into it. Finished, Maxwell put one hand to his ear.

"What's that?" he asked, though no one from the audience had said anything at all. "You don't believe the eggs are real? Thora!" He snapped his fingers, and this time when he held out a hand, I put the last egg into it. I had no time to move away, for he set down the hat, snatched up my hand and held it palm up, and before I could even imagine what he was going to do, he cracked the egg into my hand.

It was real, right enough. As embarrassed as I was by the dress I wore, I was more embarrassed still to have egg running down my hand. Maxwell roared with laughter, grabbed his hat again, and lit a candle that stood at the ready nearby. He held the hat over the candle and recited what I only could imagine were supposed to be magic words.

"I have cooked an omelet over a candle," he announced. I hardly cared, for I was looking for something on which I might wipe my hand. "Thora, do you think I've cooked an omelet?"

I remembered my job. And my mission. "I don't see how that could be possible," I said, scraping my eggy hand along the skirt of the dress. "It would take real magic to make that happen."

Maxwell gave me a wink. He tipped the hat and an omelet dropped out.

I did not have to pretend amazement, and I suppose that was a good thing. The audience applauded, and when Maxwell told me to, I took the omelet and the hat and the candle to the wings and disposed of them.

After wiping my hands on a cloth provided by a stagehand there, I returned to center stage with a deck of cards. "I need to talk to you," I told Maxwell, barely moving my mouth. "I need information about Alastor, the magician."

"Haven't heard that name in years!" he whispered back.

"But you know him?"

Whether he did or didn't, I had no time to learn, for Maxwell began his next trick. He held the deck of cards above his head so that the cards faced his audience, then dropped them away one by one, telling them as he did which card they were looking at.

I might have been impressed as they appeared to be if I wasn't looking out from the stage and at the man in the otherwise empty balcony who held a mirror aloft so that Maxwell could easily see the cards' reflections.

When he was done with the entire deck, the audience applauded, and pretending to be amazed, I jumped up and down. At least until I realized the shoulders of my dress were sagging. I hauled them back in place and spoke to Maxwell out of the corner of my mouth. "What happened to him?"

Maxwell bowed, smiled, shrugged. "Disappeared from the scene," he said, gliding to the rear of the stage to retrieve a large wooden box on wheels. "Had no choice, I suppose." He made a flourishing gesture at the box, another at me. "After what happened to Maude."

"And Maude was—"

"My assistant!" Maxwell ignored what I was saying and swung out an arm to me and, taking my hand, he led me to the box. Hanging on to me, he loosened a latch that dropped

the front of the box and the audience saw that there was nothing inside it except for a thin cushion at the bottom. "Maude
worked for Alastor for years." He took my hand and paraded
me around the box. "A pretty thing, the way I remember it.
That is until the night she was attacked by a deranged devotee."

I might have gasped if I had the chance. But Maxwell
lifted the hinged top on the box and walked me to a set of
steps. "Up and in," he said.

I peered into the box. "But it's so small, and—"

"And now, ladies and gentlemen," he announced, though
as far as I could tell, there were neither ladies nor gentlemen
in attendance. In fact, the audience—with the exception of
Bunty and James, of course—were a ragtag bunch. A drunk
fast asleep in the second row. A woman in a dress that was far
too revealing paying attention to the men around her rather
than to the show. "I give you that most challenging and inscrutable of all magic tricks. The most puzzling of illusions.
Thora—" I had not moved, and he poked me to get me going.
"Thora will recline here in this box."

"I will?" I gulped, and evidently the audience thought my
trepidation was part of the act. They hooted and applauded.
At least those who were awake did. I swallowed hard. "I
will," I said again, more forcefully, then added in an undertone to Maxwell, "If you tell me what happened to Maude."
I climbed into the box and sat on the cushion. Maxwell put a
hand to my shoulder to get me to lie down. I thought about
what Violet said in her letter. Scandal, and secrets, and murder. "Was she killed?"

"Oh, no. Nothing that simple!" With a flurry of nonsense
words I suppose were meant to sound mystical, Maxwell
closed the front of the box so that no one could see my body.

Then he closed the top of it, too, so that only my head stuck out. He leaned down, his face so close to mine the odor of fish nearly made me swoon. "Cut to ribbons, that one was. Could never be out on stage again or folks would'a run screamin' from the horror of it."

I gulped and glanced over at Bunty, who dabbed a handkerchief to her tearstained cheeks, and to James, who looked outraged on my behalf.

"There was no scandal? No tawdry secrets?"

Grinning, Maxwell reached behind the box and came up holding a sword that glinted in the glow of the limelight.

"Plenty of scandal, little miss," he hissed. "And a good many secrets, too."

I squeaked. "And murder?"

"Ah, murder!" He brandished the sword above his head and announced, "I will now cut Thora in half!"

"What?" James exclaimed, jumping out of his chair.

"What?" Bunty fell back against her seat in tears.

"Have no fear." His eyes gleaming with what looked more like madness than magic, Maxwell grinned down at me. "It's all a part of the act."

"The act, yes." I swallowed hard. "What happened to Alastor's act after Maude was attacked?"

"Changed his name to Dante." Maxwell sliced the air with the sword. "Changed his act. Did well for himself." He stood behind the box where I was trapped, a wicked smile flashing in his eyes. "Until one night when he took a seat in a magical cabinet and closed the door behind himself. His new, pretty assistant, she was supposed to open the door and find him gone, then open it again, and he was to reappear. It was trickery, of course, all done with false walls." He raised the sword and jammed it into the box just at the level of my waist and, with another bit of trickery, caused a latch inside the box to snap. The lower half of the platform where I reposed gave way and the sword met nothing but air before it punched through the front of the box.

I screamed. The audience gasped and I, calling upon a store of dramatic talent even I did not know I possessed until that very moment, looked their way and gave them my most dazzling smile. Thus assured I had magically survived the slashing blade, they shouted their approval and Maxwell took a bow, looking my way as he did. "He went into the magical cabinet that night, right enough. But he never came out again. Alastor really had disappeared."

Chapter 18

Violet

November 27

I had no word from Bunty, and this worried me. Was my request for her to learn all she could about the magician, Alastor, proving too problematic? Did she not wish to disappoint me by admitting she'd found nothing? Or were there other, more sinister reasons for her silence?

This was a possibility I did not wish to consider, yet I could not turn away from it. If Bunty was in some danger in London while I was in the countryside, I would never forgive myself. Yet I could not let that worry eat away at me and distract me from my mission. On the Monday after I sent a telegram to Bunty telling her about the advertisement for the magic show, I returned to Burton upon Trent, and when I found no post waiting there from her, I assuaged my worries on that front with a visit to Margaret.

She was drawn, and thinner than she had been when last I saw her. There were smudges of sleeplessness beneath her eyes. When I mentioned I was working assiduously to secure her freedom, Margaret burst into tears.

"You cannot! It is impossible." She threw herself on the cot in her jail cell and buried her face in the thin blanket. "I am doomed, Violet. Even the barrister Mama and Papa have engaged to help me says there is little hope."

"Then the man is an idiot."

"Really?" Margaret sat up and sniffled. "Do you really think so? Perhaps Sephora has discovered something that will help?"

"I cannot speak for Sephora," I said from between gritted teeth. "I can only tell you what I have accomplished. From what I have been able to ascertain, I believed there were two possibilities when it came to the guilty party. One of them was Hugh DeClare, Master's father. He has reason to want the Children to disband and Master to return home. He has recently been eliminated from my list of suspects, and that leaves only one other." The cell was small, yet I inched closer to Margaret so I could lower my voice. "I believe Master himself may be involved."

She wrinkled her nose. "I don't think so. He's . . ." Thinking it through, Margaret shook her head. "The Children of Aed are as barmy as badgers, and in spite of the predicament in which I find myself, I am grateful to be away from them. Yet Master . . ." Considering what she was about to say, she pressed her lips together. "He always seemed a good sort of chap, don't you think?"

"That is exactly what I'm trying to determine. Yet we cannot ignore the fact that he and Lucien exchanged harsh words."

She nodded. "That night before dinner. I remember it well, as it was so out of Master's character to raise his voice."

I weighed the wisdom of revealing Lucien's secret identity to Margaret. It was the kind of thing, after all, that a young girl like Margaret would revel in, and I could imagine her breathlessly conveying the news far and wide. Then again, the fact that Lucien was dead was more significant than the news of either his abysmal writing skills or how he made his living. And securing Margaret's freedom was surely more important even than that.

Even so, I thought it best to ease into my explanation. "There is evidence that proves," I said, "that Lucien might have been something of a humbug."

Her head tilted to one side, her top teeth working over her bottom lip, Margaret thought about this for a long while before she said, "Does it have anything to do with a fellow called Speedwell?"

I seldom find myself at a loss for words, yet on this particular occasion I could hardly help it. Anything I might say lodged behind a ball of stupefaction that blocked my throat. Instead of speaking, I stared at Margaret.

She, for reasons I cannot fathom since I am customarily the most even-tempered and understanding of creatures, tolerant even of girls like Sephora and Margaret who do not always use their brains as they should, winced and shrank back as if she expected I might start into a woefully long lecture.

I did not, asking instead, "What do you know of Speedwell?"

"Nothing." She sounded much more like the Margaret of old when she admitted it, featherbrained and insensible to all but those things that directly affected her. Yet there was something in her eyes, some awareness that made me take a seat on the bed next to her and wait to hear more.

She shrugged. "There was a letter," she said. "One addressed to Sage, only it didn't use that name, but his given name, Lucien Tidwell. And it was signed by someone by the name of—"

"Speedwell." I thought of all I knew about the name and the man associated with it, the one who was anxious for

Lucien to return to London and bring proof of what he'd uncovered with him. The letter from Speedwell I'd intercepted
had been misplaced at the Burton upon Trent post office and
did not come to the light of day until I collected it. The one
Margaret spoke of must surely have been delivered sooner.
"When did the letter arrive?"

"It was brought to Alburn the night before you arrived,
and had I been paying more attention to my duties as a Seeker
and less to the desires of my own heart . . ." She turned away,
the better to be sure of not having to look me in the eye. "Perhaps I should not have been doing what I was doing. Then
things might have turned out differently."

"What you were doing was certainly not murdering Lucien Tidwell."

"Or anyone else," Margaret pointed out.

"The letter?"

"Yes." She smoothed a hand over the dress her parents
had provided for her in order to rid Margaret of her yellow
robe and themselves of the memory of how wayward their
daughter had been. "As I said, it all started the day before
you arrived. I remember it well because that evening, Albion
had been sent here to town to retrieve the day's post. At the
time . . ." She swung around and lifted her chin. "I foolishly
thought I was in love with him. Which surely excuses the fact
that once Albion returned, he did not immediately deposit the
post with Master as is usually done."

"Because Albion was with you."

"And we were . . ." Color raced into Margaret's cheeks.
"We had a tryst. Where no one could see us. There is little
privacy with the Children. Surely you have noticed. Celestia was always looking over our shoulders. And Albion and

I . . ." She gave me a sidelong, pleading look. "You won't tell Mama and Papa?"

"I have nothing to tell them. Not until you tell me."

"And when I do—"

"Your secret will remain between us," I assured her, as kindly as I could through my impatience.

Margaret picked at the skirt of her gown. It was slate blue, and not nearly as au courant as the dresses she usually wore. There was no lace on it, no bows or ruffles. The dress had a tightly fitted bodice, narrow sleeves, and a high neckline. I wondered when they chose it, if her parents thought it might be the last dress they would ever procure for her and, my heart clutching, I resolved once again to untangle her from this mess.

"It is awkward to explain," she said. "Especially to a spinster like you. You are always lost in your thoughts and in your books and do not live a life of social pleasures and passions. Not like Sephora and I do. We—Sephora and I, that is—we have talked about it, and we believe it is impossible for you to understand matters of the heart."

I'm not sure how I managed a smile. "Let me be the judge of that."

Her hands on her lap, her fingers twined, she divulged what to her was clearly a guilty secret. "There is a place, you see, and it may not seem like a very good place, but as it happens, it is the best of all possible spots simply because it is right in the middle of things. In the open, so to speak, so that no one ever bothers to look at it and no one ever bothers to see it."

"And you and Albion would meet there."

She nodded. "This place—you must not ever divulge it

to anyone—is right outside the room where the girl Luna stayed. There is a very large rhododendron bush there, you see, and—"

My cheeks flushed. Thinking of what had happened between Eli and myself in the shelter of the rhododendron, I could not control the reaction. Margaret was so embarrassed to admit her secret, I doubt she noticed and for that, I was grateful.

"You and Albion, you would hide there so that you might talk," I said.

"Talk. Yes. That, and . . . well, other things." Her gaze shot to mine. "You won't tell Mama and Papa? They would be sorely unhappy if they knew. And I would die of embarrassment, simply die, if I was obliged to tell them. But you see, at the time, I thought what we did was proof of our love for each other and our commitment to the life Aed wanted for us."

Discomfited, she closed her eyes, and I knew I must help her along or she'd never tell me the rest of the story, or how it related to Lucien and Speedwell. That was easy enough. It was a simple inference to know what had happened there behind the rhododendron. "That Saturday evening," I said, "when Albion arrived at Alburn with the post, he did not give it immediately to Master because the two of you found time to . . . er . . . meet." I could picture it in my mind, the hushed quiet of the evening, the way the darkness wrapped around Alburn and made it seem a place of another time. I imagined the chill night air, so like the last time I saw Eli. I remembered his scent, and his touch, and the taste of his lips, and I heard my own voice, wistful with longing. "The rhododendron is large. Its foliage is dense and provides camouflage as well as privacy. In the dark, the stars twinkle through the leaves of the shrub like diamonds, pinpricks of light, like the crystal prickles of anticipation that touched your skin when your lips met."

"Violet!" Margaret's exclamation shook me from the memory, and I found her staring at me, her eyes wide with disbelief. "You speak like a heroine from one of Count Orlando's stories."

I had, and I banished the note of dreaminess I was afraid had crept into my voice. "I have a very good imagination," I assured Margaret. "Now tell me, when did Master finally receive the letters? And was one of them from this Speedwell fellow?"

"Albion was called to help Phoenix in the stable on Saturday evening and never had time to give Master the post. He did not deposit it with Master until the next morning. That Sunday. The day you arrived."

"And what happened then?"

"We had our breakfasts and Albion told me he had left the post with Master first thing in the morning. Then we thought . . . that is, we were sure we were going to be promised to each other later that day, you see, and we thought we might get together again behind the rhododendron to celebrate our commitment to each other. There is a spot deep at its heart, you see, where two people might sit side by side. If, that is, they sit very close together. And we did, and I can barely make myself admit it, Violet, but we kissed."

I held up a hand. "What does this have to do with the letter from Speedwell?"

She cleared her throat. "When we were finished there in the rhododendron and ready to slip out from behind it, that's when we saw Master walk by. His face was dark. His expression was ugly and very unlike his usual. He had a letter in his hands."

"One of the letters Albion brought to Alburn the night before?"

"At the time, I did not know for certain. I only knew that Master looked as angry as any man I'd ever seen. We waited until he'd gone by, then Albion stole out from the cover of the rhododendron to begin his day's chores and once he was gone, I, too, left our hiding place. Master's quarters are close by, just on the other side of the path that leads to the far end of the courtyard. And that's when I heard him. Roaring like a lion."

"At someone?"

"I wondered the same thing, as it did not seem in Master's character at all. That's why I . . . I am ashamed to admit it, but I crept closer and peeped in the window. And there was Master, all alone, that letter gripped in his hand. He pounded his fist on the table. He cursed . . . oh, the words he used . . . and he grumbled and he paced the room so that I was obliged to crouch and hide or he might have seen me. A few minutes later, he came marching out of the room and over to the church where I knew Celestia would be that time of the day."

"You followed him?"

"I thought to," Margaret admitted. "I wanted very much to hear whatever Master might have told Celestia about the letter. But as I passed his door I saw that he had left in so much of a hurry, he had not closed it. Once he was gone, I dared to glance inside and just as I did, the letter he'd left on his desk fluttered to the floor in an errant breeze. Oh, Violet! I cannot tell you how my knees shook and my hands trembled and I could not catch my breath. But I was consumed with curiosity. I was reminded of Eve, tempted by the snake and thrown out of paradise when she gave in to her baser instincts. Yet I could not stop myself. I darted into the room and read the letter."

"It was from Speedwell."

She nodded. "And addressed to Lucien, and that surprised me because I could not imagine Master intercepting any of the post that came to the Children. And yet for whatever reason, he did. He confiscated the letter. He opened it and read it. It was about . . ." Here, as if she was still confused by what she'd read, she had to pause and think. "It was all about Count Orlando and the stories about the Children of Ud. The letter thanked Lucien for the last story, though I can only think that meant Lucien had purchased a copy of the latest adventure and sent it to this Speedwell fellow. Whatever else could that possibly mean?"

I sucked in a breath and mumbled, "Then Master did know!"

She hung her head. "What he knew for certain was that I had sinned grievously. You see, he came back to his room. He found me there holding the letter."

My heart skipped a beat. "He was angry?"

"He did not appear to be. At least not at me. He asked me if I'd read the letter and I admit it, I lied. I told him no. I told him I was walking by and saw the paper there on the floor and thought to pick it up before it got dirty or trampled."

"And he believed you?"

"He must have, Violet, for if he knew the truth, I am sure he would have said something to admonish me."

"Yet he did not. Not even when you uncovered the truth, that Lucien was in actuality Count Orlando."

She took a moment to ponder what I'd said, then burst into laughter. "Don't be ridiculous, Violet. Lucien cared only for his own stomach and his own comforts. He could not have been the man who wrote such fantastical stories."

"I am more sure of it than ever. That is precisely what Master and Lucien had words about the night I arrived at Alburn."

"But the letter did not precisely say—"

"No. Not precisely. But it said enough. If Master knew Lucien was the one disparaging the Children, not only spreading lies and rumors with his outrageous stories but profiting from them as well, it would explain Master's anger. But there is more, I think. You see, I, too, have been privy to a correspondence between Lucien and Speedwell. And I do believe that while Master learned Lucien's secret, Lucien had learned Master's, too. The miracles and signs from Aed are nothing more than stage magic, and Master is as much of a humbug as was Lucien. Lucien found the proof and hid it and he needed to retrieve it. That is why he was in the church when he died. Once he had the proof, he was planning on taking it and showing it to Speedwell. As he told you, he was leaving Alburn once and for all."

"But why didn't Master send him away the moment he found out what Lucien was doing?"

It was a surprisingly logical question coming from Margaret, one I had asked myself as well. "For one thing, Master may have had difficulty locating Lucien that day. Except for the ceremony where Seekers and Adepts were promised to each other—and that was far too public a place to make a scene—Lucien spent the day keeping well out of sight. As it turns out, he was avoiding Enoch Pullman, but it seems he avoided Master, too. I am thinking they did not see each other until before dinner."

It was a great deal for Margaret to take in, and I let her

ponder it, before I added, "Lucien's betrayal of the Children and the possibility that he knew Master was nothing more than a charlatan provides Master with a very good motive to want Lucien dead. And in the event you really had read the letter from Speedwell and worked your way through the puzzle, Master knew you might uncover that motive. He found a way to dispose of you as well."

"But Violet, I am hardly disposed of."

"Not yet," I said, and her face paled at the reminder. "But you are here, are you not? And you are an accused murderer. No matter what you say in defense of yourself, no one is going to believe it. Master cleverly arranged that, too, by leaving that bottle of potassium nitrate in your room, exactly where it was sure to be found."

I could not spare another moment but returned to Alburn immediately, intent on finding whatever proof I could to tie Master to the heinous murder of Lucien Tidwell and so, free Margaret from prison and the fate that awaited her there. I knew precisely where to start.

I arrived just as the gong announced tea, and as it was a cool and windy day, I knew the meal would be served in the refectory. With the Children busy there, I had the rest of the compound to myself. I waited until they had time to gather then hurried to Master's quarters.

I knocked and when, as I hoped, there was no answer, I pushed open the door. Master's room was not different from mine, or Margaret's, or Lucien's for that matter, no better appointed, no more luxurious. It would not have surprised me if I still believed him to be the loyal follower of Aed he purported himself to be. Yet knowing what I knew now, suspecting as

I did, I thought there might be a sign of his hubris, a hint of the stage magic that kept his acolytes enthralled, blindly following.

His bed was no bigger than mine, the mattress was no thicker, and there was a woman's linen shift folded and left atop it that told me Celestia was a frequent visitor. There were books on a nearby table, a few personal items such as brushes and combs on a shelf. In fact, the only other furniture here that was not in any of the other rooms was a field desk, folded and set against the far wall.

Papa had one much like it and his—though not made of mahogany and without the brass fittings of Master's—had been our constant companion from one end of the Empire to the other. As Papa was often busy with his duties as soon as we arrived at a new posting, I, at a young age, took over the unofficial responsibility of arranging his rooms, making sure his trunks were unpacked properly, and having all, including his field desk, ready and waiting when he needed it. The desk was now one of my most cherished possessions. It was an old friend, and I was intimately familiar with its workings. I closed in on this desk and found an escutcheon on the top of it, just as it was with Papa's. I pushed it then reached under the desk and pulled up. That engaged the latches that held the legs in place and opened the desk to reveal a flat writing surface and opposite, a raised area that held multiple boxes for ink and pens and a leather sheath that housed a silver letter opener with an elaborate handle, a *D* and a *C* entwined.

The interior of Papa's desk was wood, scored and pitted by years of service in the name of the Crown. Master's was lined with green leather, accented by yet more brass. I had hoped there would be documents inside it, namely the letter from Speedwell, but there was no sign of it.

I was not done searching, for I knew the half of the desk that housed the pen and ink holders opened, too, tilting up to expose storage space. It was the place Papa always kept his personal correspondence. My breath poised with anticipation, I snapped it open and looked inside. There was a single letter there, one addressed to Lucien Tidwell, and I scooped it up. I had just prepared to close the desk again and leave with the purloined missive when Master's door swung open.

"I hope you are not doing what I think you are doing." Celestia stood in the doorway, a slim black silhouette against the outside afternoon light. "We have had quite enough criminal activity here of late, don't you think?"

"I wasn't—" But of course, I was, and as I still clutched the letter in one hand, it was impossible to deny. "That is, I was just walking by when—"

She knew better than to listen to what sounded even to me like a feeble explanation. She swept into the room. Her expression, usually so serene, was frozen in fury, and more than ever, the thick plait of hair that hung over her right shoulder reminded me of a fat snake. "How dare you violate Master's privacy?"

There was no use trying to make excuses, not any longer. I raised my chin. "I told you I am here searching for answers."

"These things do not concern you. And I have had enough of your meddling." She glared at me. "It is just as well we have new Seekers arriving today. One came alone already. The others will soon arrive, and when they do, I will send the cart back to town immediately. You will be on it. And you will not return."

"What, no forgiveness ceremony for me?" The cynicism of my words was impossible to miss, but it made little difference. Celestia stood before me, majestic and terrifying, and I had no apologies or options left.

"Yes. Of course. I will leave." I set the letter on the desktop. "I will return to my room immediately and pack my belongings. I understand how disappointed you must be in my behavior. Yet, I did ask for your help with my inquiries. I might not have needed to resort to so drastic a measure if—"

"You are in no position to make accusations."

"Just as you are in no position to align yourself with a charlatan."

In other circumstances, I would have said the expression that dashed across her countenance was almost a smile. Now, there was more of an edge to it. Her nostrils flaring, Celestia closed in on me. "How dare you—"

"He is really Alastor the magician, isn't he? He keeps deluded Seekers in his thrall by performing stage tricks like the one he performed at Margaret's forgiveness ceremony. Smoke rising from his fingers, indeed! He is as much of a humbug as Lucien was, and Lucien found out."

"You know about that, too, do you?" She moved like quicksilver, seizing the letter opener from the desk, and when she stepped nearer still, the blade winked and flashed in front of my eyes.

I stepped farther from her. Or at least I tried. My back was to the wall and I had no further path of retreat. When she slashed the letter opener through the air, I held my breath and planned my escape. With the wall behind me, the open field desk to my right, and Celestia in front of me, I had no choice but to race for the door and bowl her over in the process. I braced myself for the moment.

"You will keep your lies to yourself," she hissed, swinging out her arm in an arc that aligned the letter opener with my throat. "I will make sure of that."

"Well, there you are! I've been looking all around this

place for you. Miss Manville, am I correct? And you must be Celestia. I was told you might be here as well."

The voice that came from the doorway startled both of us. Celestia froze, her hand still in the air, and while I had the second's advantage, I pushed my way away around her and darted for the door. I might have made it there if I didn't take one look at the man who stood there and stop, immobilized.

A smile on his face, Eli Marsh looked from one of us to the other and said, "Good afternoon, ladies. I hope I haven't interrupted anything important."

Chapter 19

It was impossible to talk to Eli. Not until he escorted both Celestia and myself to the refectory. She, still as pale and as cold as ice and with a look in her eye that told me she would surely have attacked me if not for Eli's timely intervention, took up her position behind the teapots and poured. I stepped into line behind Phoenix, but my hands shook so, I could not take any of the food set out on the table. Eli piled his plate with boiled eggs and watercress sandwiches, and when Celestia poured from the green pot, he gladly accepted a cup of tea.

"This is Mr. Marsh, who has come to us as a Seeker," Phoenix told me when the three of us sat in a snug corner farthest from the serving table. "I collected him from the station in Burton upon Trent only a short while ago, so he's newly arrived."

"And just in time, it seems." Eli swallowed down a sandwich and offered one to me, and it was the first I realized that with my visit to town and my talk with Margaret, I had not had time for luncheon. Swallowing around the lump of uneasiness in my throat, I nibbled the sandwich, and catching sight of me eating from Eli's plate, Phoenix, ever thoughtful, jumped from his seat.

"You haven't got a dish," he said. "I will fetch you one."

I waited until he was three steps from our table before I turned to Eli. I was just in time to find him blowing on the hot tea before he tasted it.

"You don't want to drink that," I told him quietly. Taking the cup from his hand, I deposited it on the table.

He reached for it. "No, I don't want to drink it. I would prefer a cup of good, strong coffee, but you English are so hidebound when it comes to afternoon tea, I haven't much choice. I'll make an exception this time. It was a long journey up from London. I'm thirsty."

"Then go right ahead." I gestured toward the cup. "Drink it down." I gave him enough time to lift the cup to his lips before I added, "That is, if you'd like your mind addled by the drug in it."

He looked at me over the rim of the cup. "How do you know?"

"I know."

He darted a look around the room. "Given to all?"

"Just those they want to convince to stay. It appears you are one such Seeker. What are you doing here?"

"I've come as a Seeker, just as you said."

"Yes, but what are you doing here? Certainly you can have no business at Alburn now that your kidnapping has been accomplished. I hear she is already married."

"I hear she's spending her new husband's fortune as if there was no end to it."

"Whatever she spends, I would say she deserves it."

"Word from the Continent is that they are madly in love and have been since they first clapped eyes upon each other. Does that make a difference to you, Miss Manville? Or are you as opposed to love as you are to a man achieving the task he was sent to accomplish?"

"No doubt you earned your fee when you returned young Luna to her family."

"The duke and duchess were most grateful. As were some others. Pity you weren't in London to accompany me. I had a lovely tea at Buckingham Palace."

"Did you request coffee there?"

His smile was sleek. "Believe it or not, I can be civilized when necessary. I drank what was poured and made polite conversation. My illustrious hostess informed me I was quite charming for an American."

"And what is your task now? I cannot think you've come all this way simply to take the country air."

"Well, it seems the first order of business was saving your life. Would you like to explain?"

"Why you saved my life? Or why it needed saving to begin with?"

"I already know why I saved you." It wasn't my imagination, he moved a hair's breadth closer when he said this, and his gaze flickered ever so briefly to my lips. "I will admit I am puzzled as to why the woman in purple was about to lunge at you with a . . . can I possibly be right . . . was that actually a letter opener in her hands?"

"One made of silver, to be exact."

"At least she has good taste when it comes to dangerous weapons."

"She may not actually have murdered me." Of course, that might have been exactly what Celestia was trying to do, and thinking it over, I drummed my fingers against the table.

It was at this point Phoenix returned with a plate of food for me, and I could say little more. In fact, it was not until we had finished our meals and Phoenix left to help clear the tables that I was able to move my chair the slightest bit closer to Eli's so that I could say, "You were about to explain why you are here."

"And you were about to tell me why that woman . . ." He looked over to where Celestia now sat next to Master at the head of the table. "She looked as if she wanted to kill you."

I refused to be upended by the memory. "She might have tried. I am doughtier than I look."

"You look sufficiently doughty to me."

"Do I?" Pleased I might intimidate with a glare as easily as I could disarm with wit and intelligence, I smiled. "I had devised a plan to knock her down and escape over her. Thanks to you, I didn't need it."

"She doesn't look the type to give up easily."

I did not want it to seem that we discussed anything more momentous than the weather and tea so I did not look where he was looking, at Celestia. "She did what she did because she is in love," I said quite simply.

"And that excuses even an attempt at murder?" He whistled low under his breath. "If you truly believe that, there are depths to you I hadn't imagined, Miss Manville. Ones I would very much like to examine more closely."

It was neither the time nor the place to think about the suggestion, and the tingles of anticipation it sent cascading through me when I considered what he might mean by it. It wasn't the place to talk about it, either. We could not risk attracting attention with any appearance of familiarity.

"I will provide you with the details later," I told Eli. "For now, tell me why you're here."

"I have information and thought you'd like to know it."

"Ah, that explains why you are posing as a Seeker."

He nodded. "I thought the information was too important for the post and I didn't want to trust that a telegram would make its way to you. Your murder victim, Lucien Tidwell, was—"

"Count Orlando. Yes, I know."

I will admit to momentary satisfaction when his dark brows rose. "But how do you—"

"What matters is that Master knew. He also knew that Lucien had uncovered his secret past. You see, Master was once—"

"My dear Children." Just as I was speaking about him, Master rose from his chair and stepped to the front of the room. "It is a blessing, indeed, to share this meal with you and to welcome Mr. Eli Marsh, the first of our guests to arrive today. And yes, I know. It is not a Sunday and our Seekers usually come then, but today's Seekers have asked for special permission to begin their residences here at Alburn a bit sooner than is usual. I am pleased to tell you he has agreed . . ." Master looked our way. "You are sure of this, Mr. Marsh?"

Eli rose and smiled so brightly, anyone might have thought he'd been sipping the tea. "As I told you when I arrived, Master, I have studied and thought upon my path. I am sure I was guided here by the light of Aed, and as his disciple, I will obey his word."

"We have prayed on it." Master gestured to Celestia. "It is a most unusual request you've made, that you might arrive as a Seeker and become an Adept immediately, but on talking to you, your wide-ranging knowledge of Aed and the sacredness of all creation . . ."

"You have wide-ranging knowledge?" I asked below my breath.

". . . has proved to us," Master continued, "that you truly belong here with the Children. All that needs to be demonstrated is your willingness to work as do the other Children. Our gardens need tending. Our animals need care."

"Your church could certainly use some repairs," Eli said. "I am a skilled stonemason."

"You're a skilled stonemason?" I hoped my astonished question attracted little more attention than the quick look Eli gave me.

"I am willing to start," he went right on. "Today, if you allow me. I realize there are far too many repairs for any one man to undertake, but might I suggest we work on the lintel above the main entrance first? It looks unsteady as it stands, and a few repairs will guarantee the safety of the Children as we process in prayer to Aed."

"Process? Prayer to Aed?" I mumbled so low below my breath, I am not even sure Eli heard.

"An excellent suggestion." Master raised his teacup in Eli's direction. "But not today. You can begin work in the morning."

"Yet I have another suggestion that could be accomplished today." Her purple robe fluttering around her like butterfly wings, Celestia rose. "As Master has mentioned, we have another Seeker joining us today. She has impeccable references. I myself have looked into them. Like Mr. Marsh, she is sure she needs to spend little time as a Seeker and wishes to become a Novice as soon as we are ready to welcome her to that role. As the unfortunate passing of Sage and the disappearance of Luna has negated one handfasting, and the incarceration of Hestia has annulled another, I would offer a suggestion. Another promise ceremony. The instant our new Seeker arrives."

I nearly jumped from my chair in protest and Eli realized it; he thumped my foot with his.

He bowed from the waist. "If it is Aed's will," he said.

"And the handfasting as soon as is possible," Celestia continued. "We had thought to have a ceremony later this week."

"And still may if all works out," Master said. "For now, let us pour cider and wait for our newest Seeker. Then the ceremony will begin."

"Have you gone insane?" I asked Eli after he was seated again. "They want to promise you. To a woman you've never seen before."

"Jealous?"

"Certainly not." It was the only reasonable answer to a suggestion so ludicrous, and far better than admitting that though I knew the promise ceremonies and handfastings of the Children were not legal, there was something about thinking of Eli being so easily committed to another woman—a stranger—that unsettled me. "But—"

"Perhaps I should request that Master change the arrangement a bit, eh? That I should not be promised to this new Seeker, but to one who has been here these few weeks. What say you, Miss Manville? We could be handfasted by the end of the week and live happily on in the glow of Aed's light."

"Don't be an ass. I don't wish to be handfasted to you any more than you wish to be handfasted to me." I paused for a heartbeat to give him time to counter this assertion and when he did not, I went right on. "And it hardly matters. Celestia has told me I must leave."

"Then I will simply have to accept whatever young lady they present to me."

"But—"

"It isn't a binding obligation," he mumbled. "And I cannot object. I must look willing to follow whatever path Master puts in front of me. It's the only way he will believe my sincerity."

"You've delivered your message about Lucien. Why stay? Leave with me. Today."

As if he was actually considering it, he tipped his head. "Last time I was here, I asked you to leave with me. And you—"

"Stayed, and it was a good thing, too, as Lucien lay dead in the church and Margaret was accused. But now—"

"There is something more happening here than just Lucien's duplicity. And I intend to find out what it is."

"I had hoped to find some sincerity here," I admitted. "The Children, they are a trusting lot. They will be sorely saddened when they find out Master is not the mystic they believe him to be and that all he desires is to relieve them of their fortunes. You've promised payment?"

"A rather large sum to prove my devotion."

"Perhaps my lack of dowry is the real reason Celestia wants me gone. Has she looked into my background as she has done with this new Seeker? If so, she would know I have little to offer. And that, you see, is what it is all about. Though for the life of me, I cannot understand who would allow themselves to be so bamboozled as to willingly turn over a fortune. It would take an especially foolish person, don't you think?"

"Ah!" At the front of the room, Celestia signaled for attention. "I hear the carriage delivering our newest Seeker. She is a lady of some substance, you see, and hired her own transport to bring her here. Her dowry will enrich Aed's coffers. How fortunate we are!"

"Just as I said," I grumbled. "Some silly girl looking for romance and adventure. She has no idea what she's getting herself into."

Eli grinned. "Marriage to me, for one thing."

He deserved the sour look I gave him. "That, and having her fortune and what autonomy she may have taken from her. Her husband chosen for her, sight unseen. Her dowry put to others' use. It would take a fool for certain."

"And we will know who that fool is in just a moment," Eli said as the door opened to allow our visitor inside.

And that is when I saw this newest of fools, the woman who in a matter of moments would be promised in marriage to Eli Marsh.

Sephora

Just as they had been at the Royal Theatre of Magic, all eyes were on me, and as I had done then, I played my part. I am happy to report that on this day, I was dressed more appropriately to be the center of attention, in a gown of ochre trimmed in brown and with a fetching hat to match. Pretending to be caught off guard by the attention of those gathered in the refectory, I opened my eyes wide and rounded my lips into an O of surprise.

When I spied the woman in purple at Master's side, the expression froze on my face and my blood ran cold. I had not the time to allow a frisson of fear to stop me and no chance to send Violet a look of warning or to tell her to pretend she did not know me before she jumped from her seat.

"Sephora, what on earth are you doing—"

"Ah, it is my darling . . . cousin!" I hurried forward and wrapped her in a hug, whispering in her ear as I did, "You must pretend my name is Sephora Blunt, for when I wrote to Master about coming, I did not want to use the Manville name and alert him to our relationship. Now you have revealed our acquaintance. No matter. I have something important to give you." I moved from Violet's arms and dared a look at Master and the dark-haired woman. "I must offer my thanks to Violet, for without her, I wouldn't be here at all," I declared. "She is the one who steered me from the darkness and into Aed's light."

"Has everyone lost their minds?" Violet wondered, but as did the others, I ignored her.

"I am here to be accepted as one of the Children," I professed, and oh, how I wished my voice did not waver over the words. Yet under the steady gaze of the woman in purple, it was impossible to keep my heart from pounding. "Here . . ." I swallowed down my misgivings. "Here to become a Novice."

"Celestia . . ." Master gestured to the woman, and I did not know if she was pleased to be singled out; I did not dare meet her eyes. "She believes there is no better way to welcome you into your role here than to promise you to one of our Adepts," he said.

It took me a moment to work through what this meant. "Then that is what the dowry is for," I mumbled, and at my side, I felt Violet go rigid.

"You brought a dowry?" she asked under her breath.

"As I was instructed," I said and then, with all the panache of Maxwell the Magician when he wielded his magic sword above where I lay in that silly box with the false floor, I whisked my offering from my pocket.

"Your mother's pearls?" Perhaps Violet could not help herself when she moved forward and put a hand on the necklace. "Sephora, you cannot think that you can give these people—"

"I do not give this bauble to any person," I said so that all could hear. "I offer it to Aed."

With that, I stepped forward and put the necklace into Master's hands. It stayed there but for a second, for Celestia whisked it from him and held it to the light. As she was busy admiring it, I took an envelope from my pocket and pressed it into Violet's hands.

"You must see this," I whispered to her. "Alastor is—"

"Master, yes I know," she whispered back.

"And Celestia is—"

"Watching us," she whispered. "She is pleased with your offering."

I smiled and pretended to be pleased, too, though I must say, seeing my dear mama's pearls in the hands of this woman, I felt a stab of regret and an urgency rise inside me to reveal all to Violet. Right then. Right there. Yet I knew I could not. I swallowed my trepidation just as Master spoke.

"Now that Sephora has given an offering to Aed, we are free to welcome her to our number," he said. He held out a hand to me. "Step forward, receive your new name, and meet the man with whom you'll spend the rest of your days."

"Man? Spend the rest of my—" A different sort of terror enveloped me and I looked around the room at the faces that were turned to me. A young fellow with shaggy hair and sad eyes. An older one with sagging jowls. A very much older one, as thin as a rail. I looked back at Violet. "Am I really meant to be promised to one of them?"

"For the rest of your days," she told me.

It was the first I spied Eli Marsh standing not far from Violet, but before I had a chance to think what he might be doing there, Master called me to step up to the front of the room. I did, and just as I did, so did Eli.

"You mean, you?" I asked him before I swung my gaze to Violet. "Him?"

"Here on the same mission that occupies me," she told me quietly. "You needn't worry. Once we prove that Master is Alastor—"

I shook my head just as Eli took my hand, breaking away only long enough to do what any cousin might do in such a moment. I gave Violet a hug and spoke in her ear, "Master is not Alastor. Alastor was murdered three years ago."

Chapter 20

Violet

Right there in front of my eyes, my half sister, Sephora Catherine Adelia Manville, who spent all her waking hours thinking of nothing more weighty than fashion, melodramatic novels, and the advantages of the right sorts of friendships with the right sorts of people, was promised in marriage to Eli Marsh, the one man who had somehow managed to shatter the ice castle I had built around myself in the years since I had been forced to end my relationship with Ash, the young man I'd fallen in love with in India.

Like the others there in the refectory, I witnessed the simple ceremony, yet in my head (and perhaps more importantly, deep in my soul) I could not fathom it, so much so that when it was over and the Children gathered around the couple to offer their best wishes, I stood paralyzed in the corner of the room. Sephora and Eli? I knew the ritual was neither legal nor binding, that, in fact, it amounted to no more than a stage play designed to impress the gullible and separate Sephora from her mother's pearls. But no matter how I tried to think through it, no matter how many times I told myself no one in Alburn had the authority to make the pledge official except in the eyes of a long-dead god, I could no more escape the chill that seeped through me than I could ignore the empty spot inside me where I swore my heart used to reside.

Sephora and Eli?

"Sephora and Eli, what a wonderful thing!" Smiling, Phoenix closed in on me and handed me a cup of cider. "After all the sadness here of late, it is a blessing, indeed, to celebrate a joyous occasion."

"Yes, isn't it?" I accepted the cider, then immediately deposited it on the nearest table. I could not swallow when my throat was filled with sand.

"I say"—Phoenix looked me up and down—"you look a bit pallid, Miss Manville. Are you perhaps not feeling well? Or . . ." His eyes grew big. "Did you think you might be the one promised to Mr. Marsh this afternoon?"

Hearing him say the words I never would have dared think much less speak made me realize how foolish I was being. Eli was there at Alburn because of the death of Lucien Tidwell. Sephora was there . . .

It was at this moment I remembered the envelope she had slipped into my hand before the sham ceremony. I had secreted it in my pocket and I touched a finger to it and recalled what Sephora had said. "Alastor was murdered three years ago."

My gaze slid to Master, whom I had been sure was hiding his past and using stage tricks to deceive his followers. If he was not Alastor, why had Lucien considered the magic show poster so precious?

I did not have the answer and, as unbelievable as it seemed, it looked as though Sephora might.

There was more to her visit here than the simple act of playing the soon-to-be bride (which I could not help but notice she did with a great deal of relish, smiling and giggling and throwing in a blush or two for good measure). Sephora had come with news relating to my investigation. There was nothing else that explained her presence. I must turn my attention away from my own preposterously hurt feelings and back to what really mattered.

To that end, I closed in on the newly promised couple. "We must speak," I said to Sephora.

"Oh, we must, indeed!" Like any cousin sharing such a happy occasion, she squeezed my hand and smiled, her gaze sliding from me to Celestia, who hovered nearby. "We must plan what flowers I will carry for the ceremony and how Mr. Marsh . . . er, that is, Eli and I will furnish the rooms in which we'll stay on the night of our nuptials, and what I will wear, of course. What I will wear is of the upmost importance."

"You will wear the yellow robe of a Novice." When she stepped nearer, Celestia's voice contained all the warmth of a burnished sword. "We have one that once belonged to the girl, Luna, who fled our fellowship." She looked Sephora up and down. "You are of the same height. But we may be required to let the seams out to fit it over your hips."

Sephora's fingers tightened against mine, and I knew I must divert her before her devotion to Aed's peace and tranquility was further put to the test. "We will cozy ourselves in my room and discuss all," I said with a smile I hoped reminded Sephora she must hold her tongue. I gave her a tug.

"First, though . . ." Celestia stepped between us and the door. "You cannot enter into so important a relationship until names are bestowed."

"Names. Yes!" Sephora hung back, closer to me, farther from Celestia. "I thought about it on the train traveling here.

I would like to be called Starfire. Isn't it simply the most marvelous name, Starfire?"

"It is not for you to choose," Celestia reminded her. "Master names our Novices."

Hearing his own name spoken, Master left off a conversation with Eli. "I have just had the honor of informing our newest Adept that from this day forward, his name will be Azrael."

"The angel of death in some Abrahamic religions," I said. "A rather interesting choice."

"And not nearly as gruesome as it sounds," Master assured me. "Azrael transports the souls of the dead to other worlds. As such, I would like Azrael here . . ." He nodded toward Eli, "to help the Children in their work, to transport them, so to speak, to new skills such as the masonry he spoke of. As for his sweet intended . . ." Master bestowed a smile on Sephora. "I think we must call her—"

"Delilah," Celestia cut in. When she looked at my sister, there was something in her eyes that made a chill crawl up my spine. "Named for the one who betrayed Samson."

Master winced. "But surely—"

"Delilah." Celestia's voice was as sharp and as true as an arrow sure to hit its mark. "It is perfect."

She would brook no opposition. Master did not even try. He put a hand on Sephora's shoulder. "We will find a vocation for you, as well, Delilah. Perhaps now that Hestia is gone, you might take her place in the gardens. There's a great deal to do this time of year, turning over the soil, preparing for the spring planting by adding manure from the fields and stables."

I do believe Sephora might have swooned if I had not kept

a tight hold on her. "As I said, so much to think about!" I said, and then, because I would be put off no longer, I wound my arm through Sephora's to lead her to the door. "When will the handfasting take place?"

"Tomorrow," Master told me.

I stopped only long enough to turn to Celestia. "I may stay that long? So I might see my cousin happily married?"

Master answered before she could. "Of course! Celestia has told me you have decided to leave us, and I will say, I am sorely disappointed. But . . ." As if I might offer an explanation, he raised a hand. "I understand. If you are not ready to make a commitment to Aed as these two wonderful people are . . ." More smiles, this time for Eli and Sephora. "Perhaps you will change your mind at some time in the future."

"Perhaps," I told him, then before anyone else could keep me from finally taking Sephora aside so we might talk privately, I hauled her from the refectory.

We were barely in my room with the door closed behind us when it opened again and Eli slipped inside. Sephora had taken a seat at one of two chairs at my table, and he took the other. I sat on the bed.

"I don't know how long they'll let us have together so you'd best tell us quickly," I said to Sephora. "What are you doing here?"

She wrinkled her nose. "What is Mr. Marsh doing here?"

"He is helping with the investigation, exactly as Bunty is supposed to be doing. Yet I have not heard a word from Bunty and now here you are."

"Bunty wanted to send a letter," Sephora explained. "But I thought it was simply too important a thing to send through the post. I . . ." She did not pretend well at penitence, she never had. At least for this moment, she made the effort. "I stole into Bunty's quarters very late last night while she was asleep and I took the letter and I left on the first train out of London this morning. Luckily, I had already arranged the groundwork for my visit. Earlier in the week, I wrote to Mas ter to ask if I might come. My thought then was simply to catch you up on all we've learned."

"We?" I stared at my sister. "Then what Bunty told me is true. You've helped with the investigation."

She straightened her shoulders. "Bunty tried to go off on her own and investigate, but I would simply not allow it. I was with her when we entered Lucien Tidwell's lair, bravely stepping up to her side and facing the horrors within."

In the time it took me to roll my eyes, Eli spoke. "And this thing you have brought today for Violet?"

"Yes. Yes." Sephora popped out of her chair and hurried to my side. "I would never have obtained it on my own, of course, but James . . ." Here she had the good sense to blush and for once, I thought it actually authentic. "He is a police constable," she told Eli, then quickly added, "but of course, you know that. You and James were there with us last summer when Violet and I brought an unscrupulous killer to justice."

My question hovered on the edge of impatience. "What does James have to do with this mystery?"

"That is simple enough." Sephora clutched her hands at her waist. "You see, I was performing as Thora with Maxwell at the Royal Theatre of Magic and—"

It was hard to believe my frustration with her convoluted account of events might be eclipsed by any other emotion, yet icy water filled my veins and a sense of danger squeezed my heart. It was intermingled with complete astonishment. "Sephora, you did not—"

"I most certainly did, and you can't blame Bunty for that,

either, as I acted before she could stop me. And it was a good thing I did, Violet, or I would not have found out about Alastor, or about his assistant, a woman named Maude Gancher. You see, she . . ." Sephora had obviously learned a thing or two from reading histrionic literature, for she paused here to heighten the drama. "Maude was golden-haired and very beautiful, you see, and a man who often sat in the audience became obsessed with her. When she spurned his advances, he attacked her with a knife." Sephora shivered. "It is terrible to even consider, is it not?"

"She was killed?" Eli wanted to know.

Sephora shook her head. "Horribly disfigured. So much so that even when she was recovered, Alastor would have nothing to do with her. Though Maude implored him to allow her to perform with him again, he found a new assistant. Maude haunted the theater begging for his help and, eventually, he could stand it no more. Maude was thrown into the street and told to never return."

"She is the assistant pictured on the poster," I said, and to show them, I retrieved the broadside from my trunk where it had been hidden. "It was Maude Lucien was interested in, not Alastor. Because—"

"Because Alastor was murdered by the very weapon he had often used on stage to pretend to cut Maude in two. That is most certainly telling, isn't it? It was a most sensational and scandalous crime and the newspapers were full of stories about it. Bunty and I were able to find and read some of them. It all happened three years ago, and we were in the East then, Violet. We did not know of the sensation."

"But what did James tell you of the incident?" Eli wanted to know. "Was the murderer apprehended?"

"That is what I've brought for you to see." Sephora pointed

to my pocket and I removed the envelope. So that Eli and I might both see what was inside, I went to the table to open it.

It was a photograph of a woman and when I studied it, a shiver ran through me. She was blond, beautiful. Or at least she might have been if not for the hideous scars that scored the right side of her neck.

"This is the photograph the police took when Maude was arrested for Alastor's murder," Sephora said. "She was found guilty, and she was being transported to prison to await her execution when she used some magician's trick to free herself of her handcuffs. She escaped."

I stared at the woman in the photo, at her expression, cool and aloof even though she was in police custody. It was then I knew the truth.

I passed the photo to Eli. "Lucien discovered the truth. Maude was here, one of the Children, hiding where no one would ever think to look for her. Coloring her hair would be an easy enough thing to do, and her telltale scars are concealed beneath the plait of hair she wears over her right shoulder. When Lucien returned to London and revealed all, the police would be sure to apprehend her."

It was at that very moment my door burst open. Thinking to see Celestia, I tensed. Eli leapt to his feet. But it was Master who entered my room, and I breathed a sigh of relief. At least until I realized there were ugly truths he needed to be told. Thinking how it would hurt him to learn Celestia's true identity, I swallowed hard. That is until my throat went dry and my breaths suspended.

Master had a pistol in his hand.

"The photograph," he said, and motioned with one hand. "You, Delilah, bring it to me."

Sephora looked to me for guidance and, seeing no choice,

I nodded. Her hands trembling and her steps unsteady, she presented Master with Maude's photograph. As soon as it was in his hands, he seized her, one arm around her neck, the gun pressed to her head.

"There is surely some mistake here," I somehow managed to say, even though my heart pounded. "We have done nothing but uncover a terrible deception. I am sorry to tell you, the photograph, it is Celestia. She murdered a man. She escaped and has been with the Children since."

As if I'd said nothing at all against the woman he loved, Master simply flicked his wrist, the barrel of his pistol directing us to the door. "You'll come with me. And you . . ." He took stock of Eli at the same time he tightened his hold on Sephora's neck so that she let go a yelp. "You will make no move to overpower me or to escape. I promise you, if you do, I will shoot Delilah forthwith and Miss Manville after. Do not make the mistake of thinking I am not capable. I am, after all, the son of a viscount. A thousand years of wars and politics breeds a certain ruthlessness in us all."

He ordered us outside and down the path that led behind the church and to the wasteland pocked with structures that were once the monks' farm, Eli and I going ahead, Master and Sephora behind us, his pistol pressed to her back. It was in the farthest of the buildings, a tumbledown stone hut with a sagging roof with a gaping hole in it, that he stopped and bid me inside. Just as he stepped over the threshold to join me in the cramped, dark hut, Master swung his pistol, catching Eli on the side of the head, knocking him to the ground.

I had no time even to stoop to examine him before Master warned, "Don't bother to call out. You are far enough away here from the rest of the compound. No one will ever hear you. And if you do, if you attract any attention, Delilah will pay a steep price."

Eli lay insensible at my feet, and in the last of the evening light, Sephora's eyes looked like blue jewels. There were tears on her cheeks. I did not believe in Master's talk of spirits and the guiding hand of Aed. I believed only in what was logical and reasonable, what I could see and know to be the truth. Now, I knew if I could not help Eli, he might never wake up, and if I watched Master walk away with my sister, I might never see her alive again.

Desperate to reason with him, I blurted out, "You need to know, Master, about what really happened in London three years ago. Celestia—"

His words cut through the air and caused my heart to stop. "Celestia has just told me the truth—the whole of it. Aed will forgive her, and who am I to challenge a god? He has shown us signs—"

"Trickery," I said. "Stage magic. Don't you see? Maude is familiar with it all. She used phosphorus, just as magicians use in their acts, to make the phantom in the church glow. And potassium nitrate, I would wager, is also used on stage. Why, even your staff at Margaret's forgiveness ceremony must have been coated with some substance. That is why smoke rose from your fingers. It wasn't Aed telling you he was displeased and that Margaret had to be turned over to the authorities, it was Maude. She needed Margaret gone to remove suspicion from herself. She is not a believer. She is using you and the Children for her own ends. She is—"

Master closed the door in my face, and just after I heard the key turn in the lock, I heard his voice one last time. "I must do what I am doing. It is Aed's command."

Chapter 21

It is important to note, it was not simply good fortune that caused me to have safety matches in my chatelaine. I carried them with me always, prepared for any contingency. I struck a match and in its feeble light, took a quick look around the darkened hut. I was thankful to see a scattering of twigs not far away. Staying out of the way of the mice that scampered from the pile, I gathered the wood and set it alight, then found dried vegetation to add to the flames. My fire offered only a little in the way of illumination and heat, but it was better than nothing, and in its light, I hurried to Eli's side and knelt so I could cradle his head in my lap and examine the bruise on his left temple. I used my handkerchief to dab at the blood that oozed from the gash caused by the butt of Master's pistol.

Eli's breaths were shallow. His skin was cooler than it should be. I took one of his hands in both of mine and chafed it. "Can you hear me?"

He groaned, and for that at least, I was grateful.

I continued to rub. "I have a fire going," I told him, though I could not say if he either heard or understood. "I will draw you closer to it."

It was an excellent plan, but not easily carried out. Though

I pride myself on my physical prowess, Eli was tall and strapping and the only way I could move him was to grab both his feet and drag him. We were nearly to the fire when his head met a protruding rock I had not seen.

"Damn it, woman!" I might have rejoiced that he was conscious if he didn't sound so indignant. His eyes fluttered open. "My head already feels as if it's been struck by an anvil. Are you trying to make it worse?"

As I was standing over him at the time, breathing hard from the exertion of relocating him, it was a simple enough thing to prop my fists on my hips and glare down at him. "I am trying to help you. You might at least show some gratitude."

He groaned. "You're right. Thank you."

Again, I reached into my chatelaine, and this time, brought out a bottle of lavender salts, another item I found infinitely practical. I uncapped the bottle and bent to put it near enough to his nose and was rewarded when Eli cringed, blinked, and sat up.

"Enough," he said, waving me away. "You have ministered to me all I need." He glanced around the hovel. "We are locked in?"

"Yes, and Master has taken Sephora and threatened to harm her if we escape and mount a rescue."

He scraped a hand through his hair. "Then we have few options."

"Exactly why I thought to make you comfortable before I freed myself and liberated my sister."

I suppose I might have excused what looked like a sneer as a trick of the poor lighting. Or it might be that he was in pain from his injury. "There are two windows," he said. "Neither is wide enough for us to climb through. There is a hole in the roof." He tightened a muscle at the base of his jaw against the pain so that he might tilt his head to look up. "Too high for us to make our way out that way."

"That leaves the door."

"It looks too sturdy."

It did. It was, and I knew it, I just hated to surrender to the inevitable. I dropped down to the ground beside Eli and propped my arms on my knees. "Then what are we to do?"

He put his head in his hands. "Let's begin with a few moments of silence."

"But—"

"Please."

I allowed him as much, waiting impatiently until he drew in a deep breath and looked again at the ceiling of our prison. "It is already dark. What will the Children be doing now?"

"Finishing their chores, preparing for tomorrow." As much as I tried to remain calm, I could not contain the anger that shot through me. I brought down my fist on the ground beside me. "I cannot believe Master would protect Celestia when he knows the truth of her past."

"Love is a powerful thing."

It was not something I expected from him, and it brought me up short. "And you think—"

"That it is only natural Master will do whatever he must. If it were me and I had to provide protection for the woman I loved . . ." I was not imagining it—he let his gaze slip briefly to mine. "I would advise her to make her way to the coast, to leave the country."

"With Sephora's mother's pearls," I grumbled.

"Some of what was given in dowries was actually for the continuation of the Children, I imagine. But I would venture to guess a great deal of it went into different coffers so that someday Celestia and Master might escape the country and live comfortably in a place where the authorities were unlikely to find them."

"And now is that time. They have no choice. Celestia and Master will leave."

"That, or they must rid themselves of everyone who knows Celestia's secret."

I had already thought as much. Still, I was not happy to hear him say it. My heart bumped my ribs. My voice clogged with emotion. "Sephora can't possibly defend herself."

"You don't give her enough credit. She was smart enough to find her way here, wasn't she?"

"Yes, but—"

"And she managed to pass the photograph of Maude Gancher to you."

"She did, but—"

"After she'd done enough investigating of her own back in London to put together at least some pieces of the mystery. She could not have known Maude was Celestia, not until she arrived here and met Celestia. Yet she knew the photograph was vitally important. She is actually canny and quite clever. From what I can see, Sephora is a good deal like her older sister."

I thought this over and faced a new reality. "And I am not giving her credit for her talents," I admitted, chagrined. "When we are out of this predicament, I will change my ways."

He flashed a brief smile. "Will you?"

"I will try," I said, and I meant it. "What will you do?"

"After we're out of here and safe again?" His sigh was as soft as the darkness that surrounded our halo of flickering light. "I had thought to spend Christmas in Venice. I hear it is lovely during the holiday season. Fireworks, concerts, fish on

Christmas Eve, panettone after lunch on Christmas. It sounds idyllic. I suppose now I must say I'll enjoy all that if we make it out of here alive."

It sounded idyllic, indeed, but I dashed all thoughts of Venice from my head. We had more pressing concerns, and considering them, I rose and dusted off my gown. "We must think how to get out of here. You will be little help." As Eli did not dispute this, I knew he truly felt quite poorly. "I would suggest you stay right where you are. That way, if . . . when . . . Master or Celestia come through the door to fetch us, if they come to . . ." I swallowed around the tightness in my throat. "If they come to dispose of us, they will see you and only you, and that may take them aback long enough for me to attack from my position behind the door." I put a hand to my chatelaine. "I have my pistol."

"As do I. With my head spinning so, I am not convinced I could discharge it with any accuracy, but at least the noise might startle them. I will take care of that. You will be behind the door. I do agree that is a good plan. But whoever comes through that door, when he steps inside and comes at me, you will take the opportunity to run. Then and only then will I take my shot. You, in the meantime, will get away fast and far."

"And leave you behind?" I folded my arms across my chest. "I won't."

"You must. I can't run, and if I tried, I'd slow you down. Our only hope is for you to—"

I knew what he was going to say. Our only hope was for me to evade capture, to find help, to bring the authorities. He was right, but I did not like the thought that it would leave him there, alone and vulnerable, and Sephora still in Master's clutches. I might have mounted a further protest if at that moment, the inside of our hut didn't light up as if with a flash of lightning. I looked up at the hole in the ceiling just in time to see a light streak by. And another. And again another.

The display was as puzzling as it was dazzling, and I was awestruck. Eli, too, was caught by the wonder of it. Swaying, he pulled himself to his feet and stood at my side.

"What's happening?" I asked.

He slipped an arm around my shoulders and side by side, we watched the sky flash.

"Meteors," he said. "Not a shower of them, a veritable storm. There are dozens."

"Hundreds." So that we might have a better look, I carefully piloted him nearer the hole and we found the entire sky—at least what we could see of it—afire with the glittering streaks. Some left brilliant trails, like the phantom's phosphorescence, that continued to glow for several seconds after the meteors themselves had vanished.

It was fearsome and splendid, and we were so caught in the magic of it, we did not realize anyone had approached the hut until we heard the key turn in the lock. The door swung open. Master stood outside.

If I had been less distracted by the sight of the meteors and the feel of Eli's arm around me, I might have been better prepared, and I cursed myself and gauged the distance between myself and the door. Could I get out my pistol in time? Could I run as Eli had suggested?

I did not have to do either.

Master did not enter the hut, but stood in the doorway and looked over his shoulder at the night sky. "You've seen it?" he asked.

In the dark, I could not see if he had his pistol in his hands, but I was not about to take the chance. I retrieved mine from my chatelaine and put an arm around Eli's waist to support him, and we stepped outside. Hundreds of meteors streaked across the sky with dazzling light that illuminated Master's face.

"I was wrong," he said. He passed a hand over his eyes. "Surely this is Aed's way of telling me. I was wrong to think to protect her and wrong to attack you so, Mr. Marsh." He hung his head.

Could a meteor shower really be what saved us? Was he sincere? The tears on Master's cheeks told me he was, and while I contemplated this surprising turn of events, quite literally thanking our lucky stars, Eli spoke. "Where is Celestia?" he asked. "Gone?"

"She . . ." His hand trembling, Master gestured into the night. "When I saw Aed's fire in the night, when I realized what it meant, I told her we must repent our ways. That she must confess her sins, not only to Aed, but to the authorities."

"And what did Celestia say?" I asked.

He sobbed. "She admitted that her devotion to Aed was never more than a ruse. She knew my love for her and thought I would protect her at all costs." His shoulders heaved. "Her dedication to the Children. Her devotion to me. It was all a lie."

I was not feeling kindly enough to care. "Where is she?" I snapped. "And where is Sephora?"

"After I told Celestia Aed had spoken about her guilt, after she laughed and called me a simpleton, she ran into the night. I am afraid . . ." He swallowed hard. "I am very much afraid she took your sister with her."

I could not waste another moment. I handed Eli my bottle of lavender salts so he could wake further and raced toward the compound, each of my steps so fueled by my concern for my sister, I paid little mind to the pits I could fall into or the scattered stones that might trip me up. I got as far as the church when I heard a commotion, a chorus of voices calling out. Inside, I found the Children gathered. Near where the altar once stood there was a flat stone that had been forced aside—damn, I never thought to move it when I searched for the phantom's lair—to reveal the stone steps that led into the original crypt. Celestia stood near the top of them, a mis-shapen sack on the step at her side. She had one arm around Sephora's waist. In her other hand, she had Master's silver letter opener. She held it to my sister's throat.

In the glow of the candle that burned in the center of the prayer circle and the dizzying meteor display that sparked over our heads, I saw that Sephora's face was pale. Her eyes were wide with fear and panic. When she saw me, she jerked for-ward, but Celestia would have none of it.

Panic bubbled through my insides, yet I forced it from my voice and tucked my pistol to my side where Celestia could not see it. "You must not move," I told Sephora. "We will have this settled soon enough and all will be well."

"Is that what you think?" The show of lights above us streaked Celestia's face, adding shadows and sparks. "All might have been well if you had minded your own business."

"Or paid more attention when I was searching for the place where the ghost rose out of nothingness," I said. "Then we might have ended this sooner. Now . . ." I looked at the bulg-ing bag next to her. "Eli was right, you took a portion of the dowries and kept them for yourself so that you might someday escape. You couldn't take the chance that anyone would find your treasure, so you created the phantom to frighten them away."

"All except Lucien Tidwell," Celestia spat.

"In his search for the ghost, he found the advertisement for the magic show where you'd hidden it in the crypt and knew it was somehow important. He asked questions of his friends in London and learned much. You had to stop him before he left here and the story was revealed."

It was at that moment that Master and Eli entered the church and came to stand near me. Eli swayed on his feet. The tears on Master's cheeks looked like trails of fire thanks to the meteors that flew over our heads. Seeing him, a man in love and so sorely betrayed, I sucked in a breath and looked at Celestia in wonder. "You didn't care who hanged for Lucien's murder as long as it wasn't you. You hid the potassium nitrate in Margaret's room and thought that was the end of it. But when I refused to believe Margaret's guilt, you were more than willing to lay the blame on someone else. You even pointed a finger at Master."

"And now it no longer matters." Celestia dragged Sephora to the top of the steps. "You there." Phoenix and Albion stood nearby, and she shot them a look. "Ready a cart for me.

"And you." She swung her icy gaze to me. "You are not to move. Not one inch. I am leaving here with the Delilah who betrayed me. When I know I am safe from your meddling, I will leave your precious cousin along the road."

I dared a step forward. "She is not my cousin. She is my sister. And precious to me, yes." No more so than right at that moment. The truth engulfed my heart, forcing its way past my fear. I could not let Celestia leave with Sephora, for I knew if I did, I would not see her alive again. And I would face any danger to make sure that didn't happen. "She is an innocent in this. She has no knowledge of your history or your crime. I do, and the first chance I have, I swear, I will tell all. If I am with you, though, you can compel my silence until you are safely away."

"Or I can compel your silence another way. I will take your sister with me and she can return to you once I have safely reached Argentina. If you send a cable ahead, if you speak a word of this to anyone . . . if any of you speaks a word . . ." Her gaze landed on each of the Children in turn. "I will gladly push her overboard."

"No!" Sephora found her voice and it echoed against the ancient stones. The light of the meteors flashed; fire and shadow and a meteor bigger and brighter than the others burst directly above us and left a trail of glowing sparks.

Sobbing, Master held out his arms to Celestia, imploring her. It was just then we heard the jingle of horses' harness from outside. Assuming it was Phoenix returned, I paid it little mind.

A second later, Bunty raced into the church, an umbrella raised in one hand like a sword.

"You take your hands off Miss Sephora!" Bunty yelled.

"Aed is not pleased," Master howled.

In that moment of distraction and chaos, I had one chance to set things right. I raised my pistol, my aim at Celestia true, but as I squeezed the trigger, Master leapt at me, hitting my hand. My shot missed its mark, slamming into Celestia's shoulder, knocking her back.

Celestia screamed, dropped her knife, and made a grab for her bag of treasures. Her foot slipped. Sephora sprang up the stairs and out of the crypt just as Celestia tumbled into it, a blur of purple illumined by the spark of Aed's fire over our heads.

Chapter 22

Just as I always carried matches, it seemed Eli went nowhere without handcuffs. I was grateful, for after the sturdiest of the Children hauled a moaning, cursing Celestia from the crypt, he restrained her. We had not forgotten she once used a magician's trick to escape another such confinement, so she was tightly bound, too, and tethered inside the very cart she thought would be the means of her escape.

Bunty, who had woken back in London, realized what Sephora must have been up to, and followed, tended to my sister. The Children gathered around Master. Eli took me aside. Streaks of light accented the purple bruise on his forehead, and when he put his hands on my shoulders, I wasn't sure if it was to comfort me or to steady himself.

"I must take her to the authorities," he said.

"I had expected no less. I am coming with you."

"You have your sister to care for."

"Bunty will manage. You've been injured."

He dared a smile. "Ah, you're worried about me."

"I'm not worried." I had no choice but to insist because, of course, I was gravely worried, so much so that thinking of his injury, I feared I might burst into tears, and that would not do. That would not do at all. "I am being commonsensical. If you need help along the way—"

"Three of the big fellows in blue robes are coming with me. We will deposit Celestia with the police in Burton upon Trent."

"And as you seem to have something of a reputation when it comes to these sorts of things, they will ask you to accompany them to Nottingham with her and from there, to London, no doubt."

He backed away and gave me a bow that was the slightest bit shaky. "Then I will see you in London."

"That's what you said last time."

"You remember."

"It is hard for a woman to forget when she is so sorely used."

"Sorely used?" He had the temerity to laugh. "Hardly. And even if it was true, I would say when you bashed me with your umbrella, you got your revenge."

I could not argue. Or kiss him goodbye the way I wanted to, seeing as we were surrounded by the Children and Master, Sephora and Bunty. Instead, I watched the way the glistening streaks of the meteors' trails added planes and angles to his face, and vowed I would remember him that way, with the sparkle of Aed's light upon him.

I told myself not to forget it when he climbed into the cart and left with his charge. It wasn't until he was gone that Master approached.

"I am sorry," he said, seemingly with true penitence.

"As am I," I admitted. Whatever else Master had done, he had truly loved Celestia.

"But knowing the truth . . ." His shoulders rose and fell.

"I have made up my mind. I will return to my room now and write to my father renouncing all rights to his title. If you would be so kind, would you see it is delivered to him?"

"It may be better for you to give it to him yourself."

He shook his head and raised his voice, looking around at the Children. "Tomorrow, we will leave Alburn and this sorrow behind us. We'll take ourselves to a place that is remote and wild, where we will start anew." The Children nodded their agreement and left to tend to their packing. "And you, Miss Manville." Master turned back to me. "I know you will not join us, though we would be lucky to have you as part of our company. What will you do?"

"Me?" I wrapped one arm around Sephora's shoulders. "The very first thing I'm going to do is tell my sister how grateful I am for all her help in this matter." I gave Sephora a squeeze. "I am proud of you," I told her, "and Papa would be, too." I slipped my other arm around Bunty's waist. "The next thing I will do is remind Bunty that she is irreplaceable. And then . . ." I sighed with satisfaction. "I will take my family back to London so that we might start afresh, too."

December 5

I finished my Miss Hermione duties for the day and stepped from my library and into the hallway, my head tipped, listening.

"They are not talking and giggling," I commented to Bunty, who was just coming by, her arms laden with freshly pressed linens. "Aren't they in the parlor?"

Bunty's silvery eyebrows rose. "They are, indeed."

"But I hear no talk of fashion. No plans for the latest balls and parties. If Sephora and Margaret aren't talking about that, what are they talking about?"

"No doubt the conversation is about James Barnstable." Bunty started up the stairs. "For he was here and left, just a few minutes ago, and now I have no doubt in between Miss Margaret and Miss Sephora discussing how grateful they are that Miss Margaret is no longer in custody, they are dissecting every one of that nice constable's words and actions."

"James called on Sephora? Here?"

"Came for tea and ate every bit of seedcake I served." Smiling, she headed up to the first floor. "The boy has an appetite, to be sure, and decent manners. She could do worse."

I was far too broad-minded to object to Sephora being courted by a policeman, yet knowing James was bold enough to call on her without asking my permission rankled, as did the fact that Sephora did not inform me of his arrival.

It was rude, not to mention unacceptable. Annoyed, I hurried to the parlor. The door was closed and I raised my hand to knock.

She could do worse.

Bunty's words vibrated through my brain.

"She could indeed," I told myself, giving the door one last look before I turned and started up the stairs to my room. "And James, he could surely never do better."

December 8

Dear Miss Hermione,

It's a devil of a thing. There is a woman, you see, a fine woman with a keen mind and a cunning wit, who has caught my eye. Damnation, she has more than caught my eye! She has ensnared my heart, besotted me with her confidence and her beauty as surely as she has annoyed me beyond measure with her willfulness.

I fear I may actually be falling in love, and I would like to find the right way to tell her. I thought perhaps you could help.

You see, I will be staying at the Gritti Palace in Venice for Christmas. My travel arrangements have me arriving on December 10, and to have her there with me . . . ah, that would surely make the holiday complete.

But how to ask?

I implore your help, Miss Hermione. I am not a man who is used to begging, but for this woman . . . for this woman, dash it all, I would do anything!

⚬

"Bunty!"

It is not often that Bunty hears such urgency in my voice. She had been in the kitchen and she rushed into the hallway, soapsuds on her hands, a tea towel flung over one shoulder. Sephora, too, heard me call out. She hurried out of her bedchamber and stood on the first-floor landing, looking down on us.

"What is it?" both Bunty and Sephora wanted to know.

"It's . . ." Caught between a frisson of excitement and the

cold reality of being petrified by being so close to abandoning mother wit and every bit of common sense I had, I paced the hallway from the library to the stairs. "Traveling cloaks. A gown or two. Plenty of practical boots for hiking and walking," I mumbled, and hurried up the stairs. "I need to pack and leave. Now!"

"Now?" Bunty followed me upstairs to where Sephora stood looking at me in wonder.

"Leave?" my sister asked. "Violet, where on earth are you going?"

There was a lightness to my step I'd never felt before and a lilt to my laughter when I told them the news. "I'm leaving town for a bit. I hear Venice is lovely at Christmas."

Acknowledgments

Yes, there really was a spectacular meteor storm over England on the night of November 27, 1885. When I read about it and realized how well it played into the story of Aed's fiery presence, I couldn't resist having Violet witness it.

And what a sight it must have been! According to historical reports, the Andromedids Meteor Shower was a "grand display" and "incessant." Six or eight meteors could be seen every second. The night also marked the first time a photograph was ever taken of a meteor, and that by Ladislaus Weinek, an Austro-Hungarian.

Aed would have been pleased.

As always, there are many people I need to thank for the story that's become *Of Hoaxes and Homicide*. My brainstorming group (Shelley, Serena, and Emilie, check out the dedication of this book!); the fabulous editorial, publicity, and marketing team at Minotaur; my agent, Gail Fortune; and my family, who indulge my flights of fancy, accompany me on research trips, and never think it's strange (at least they don't say anything about it) when I read about poisons and magic.